A Taste Of The Nightlife

A Vampire Chef Novel

SARAH ZETTEL

AN OBSIDIAN MYSTERY

OBSIDIAN
Published by New American Library, a division of
Penguin Group (USA) Inc., 375 Hudson Street,
New York, New York 10014, USA
Penguin Group (Canada), 90 Eglinton Avenue East, Suite 700, Toronto,
Ontario M4P 2Y3, Canada (a division of Pearson Penguin Canada Inc.)
Penguin Books Ltd., 80 Strand, London WC2R 0RL, England
Penguin Ireland, 25 St. Stephen's Green, Dublin 2,
Ireland (a division of Penguin Books Ltd.)
Penguin Group (Australia), 250 Camberwell Road, Camberwell, Victoria 3124,
Australia (a division of Pearson Australia Group Pty. Ltd.)
Penguin Books India Pvt. Ltd., 11 Community Centre, Panchsheel Park,
New Delhi - 110 017, India
Penguin Group (NZ), 67 Apollo Drive, Rosedale, Auckland 0632,
New Zealand (a division of Pearson New Zealand Ltd.)
Penguin Books (South Africa) (Pty.) Ltd., 24 Sturdee Avenue,
Rosebank, Johannesburg 2196, South Africa

Penguin Books Ltd., Registered Offices:
80 Strand, London WC2R 0RL, England

First published by Obsidian, an imprint of New American Library,
a division of Penguin Group (USA) Inc.

First Printing, July 2011
10   9   8   7   6   5   4   3   2   1

PUBLISHER'S NOTE
This is a work of fiction. Names, characters, places, and incidents either are the product
of the author's imagination or are used fictitiously, and any resemblance to actual per-
sons, living or dead, business establishments, events, or locales is entirely coincidental.
    The publisher does not have any control over and does not assume any responsi-
bility for author or third-party Web sites or their content.

To Julia Child, Alice Waters, and Bela Lugosi

ACKNOWLEDGMENTS

I very much want to thank Esther M. Friesner and Lisa Leutheuser for their help in making this book happen. I also want to thank Vanessa Sly for taking the time to share her experiences in the world of professional kitchens, and Chef Alex Young and the crew at Zingerman's Roadhouse (especially Javier), who let me into the kitchen to see the Friday night dinner rush firsthand. Additional thanks are due to Joseph Fodera of Worldwide Security Consulting, Inc., who helped me get Charlotte properly arrested in New York.

In addition, and as always, I'd like to thank the Untitled Writers Group and the Excelsior Writers Group for their patient and helpful commentary.

And finally, I'd like to thank Marty Greenberg, the wonderful person who made this book possible.

I

"Charlotte! We got Anatole Sevarin!"

I replied to this news with the most reasonable words in the most reasonable tone I could manage: *"Get out of my kitchen!"*

In case you think I overreacted, let me tell you that my kitchen is in the back of Nightlife, the restaurant I co-own with my brother, Chet. It was Chet who had just charged shouting past the hot line in the middle of the dinner rush.

"Did you hear me?" My brother waved his cell phone over his head excitedly. "Anatole Sevarin!"

I heard him. I also heard:

"Fire two duck!"

"Pick up twelve! Pick up nine!"

"Where's my carpaccio?"

"Nineteen one and two want those specials no 'shrooms."

It was Friday night and the house was packed. Because we cater to vampires, paranormals and their guests, our dinner rush happens later than at most places, even in autumn, but I'd already been on my feet for eight hours. My sous chef, Zoe, was out because her mother was in the hospital (note to self: call, find out diet restrictions, send decent food), so I was doing her job as well as mine. We had way too many order tickets on the "dupe slide" over the cold prep station, and in another hour the vampire theater crowd would be out looking for someplace to eat. We had to get those full tables served, satisfied and cleared.

So I looked up at my brother and said, "Get. Out. Of. My. *Kitchen!*"

"Robert's seating him at table twenty-four." Chet grinned so widely I could see his fangs.

Did I mention my brother's a vampire? Which—aside from the fact that he didn't belong there—was why I really didn't want him in my kitchen; never mind if the city's most prominent undead dining critic had just walked in without a reservation. Chet has a tendency to forget how flammable he is these days. He says I forget how fast he is. I say they're called flash fires for a reason, and I am not going to sweep him off the floor. He can just lie there and be ashy. He says the health inspectors would write me up.

I say then he'd better stay the hell out of my kitchen.

You can see that of the two of us, I am the reasonable one.

Right then, however, he just stood there grinning like an undead idiot, and I knew he wasn't going to move until I acknowledged his news. I didn't want to give him the satisfaction, but I could hear the ticket machine chattering away and on the stove three sauces and two gravies started to bubble ominously.

"I'll talk to you after rush!" I told Chet. "Now, *get!*"

Seemingly chastened, my brother slunk toward the door, but between one eyeblink and the next, he'd whisked back, grabbed me, swung me around and set me down.

"Yes, Chef!" he called, already gone.

The kitchen had gone unnaturally quiet. As soon as my vision cleared, I was greeted by the unprecedented and most unwelcome sight of my staff standing still.

"What?" I demanded. "Have we closed early?"

"No, Chef!" the crew chorused.

"Tonight we are *perfect*—get me?" Anatole Sevarin wrote the dining column for *Circulation*, the number one city paranormal publication, in print or online. There was no point in treating him as less than a VIP just because Chet had ticked me off. "And I see all the plates for twenty-four, before they go out and when they come back!"

"Yes, Chef!"

I stepped back up to my station in the middle of the hot line, ignoring some highly suspicious grins.

The cacophony resumed.

We got Anatole Sevarin. My heart sang as I tasted our special scarlet-eye gravy for seasoning and added a grind of pepper. *We got Anatole Sevarin!*

Nightlife has come a long way from the time when Chet was sleeping days in the walk-in refrigerator to save rent and we had to deal with antivamp protesters on our doorstep. The idea of "night and day" dining establishments is still relatively new. It's been ten years since the Equal Humanity Acts recognized vamps, weres and other "human derived paranormal peoples" as, well, people. The idea that humans and vampires might be willing to sit down together at a table, in public, is one that still gets pooh-poohed around the restaurant world. In fact, the words "freak show" have been used more than once.

What the skeptics miss is that a growing number of families stay in touch with their relatives and friends after they've turned. There's also an increasing amount of crossover in the banking and business communities. This creates a need for a place where everybody involved can socialize, entertain and be comfortable.

Many people still think vampires only drink unprocessed blood. While it's true vampires can't digest solid cooked food, they do just fine with all kinds of liquids, especially those that are protein based. Broth, eggs and milk may not have the psychotropic effects that human blood has on a vampire, but they provide nourishment and flavor. This opens up a whole world for the chef. In fact, the milk-shake tasting on our dessert menu is a big hit right across the board.

Despite our steady growth in food quality and clientele, though, we're still the farm team. We've got heart, we've got talent, but we haven't yet made our move to the major leagues. A good review by Anatole Sevarin could get us there.

Another thing about Nightlife—like most other New York City restaurants, we pretty much run on the ragged edge of disaster. We're located on Tenth Street just around the corner from Broadway, so we fork over a midsized fortune in rent. There've been weeks when Chet went without his salary and I cut mine so we could keep the staff paid. Those times were becoming less frequent, but we had yet to turn our first profit, a fact that was giving our accountant gray hairs. Wimp.

A good Sevarin review could fix that too, and the whole staff knew it. Fortunately, it had the effect of sharpening their game. A professional kitchen is an assembly line with a thousand moving parts. And knives. And fire. Walking in the wrong direction can cause a serious injury. Worse, it can make someone's dinner late. After Chet dropped his news bomb, you could feel the excitement honing the focus of the entire line. Everybody started paying extra attention to basic technique—knife skills, fire, composition, plating—like they were already onstage, which in a way they were. I felt a surge of pride in my people and my place.

One of my jobs as executive chef is to make sure everything moves smoothly and efficiently on a nightly basis. If I have to get in there and push, that's what I do.

I cook, taste, slice, chop, pluck, simmer, butcher and plate. I shout, cajole and praise. I condemn if I absolutely have to. I never, ever compromise on a matter of quality. I revel in the noise, the steam, the scents of onion, grilling meat, fresh herbs and heady spices, as well as the whole control-freak vibe of being absolute mistress of ten people and three hundred square feet for twelve to fifteen hours a day, six days a week.

If I am loud and less than polite, it is because my job demands it. I stand five foot four in my clogs, so I'm not exactly an imposing figure. I'm nobody's waif, though. A lot of what I carry is muscle, but I've got plenty of curves. Part of that is nature and part is a combination of occupational hazard and professional pride. Like the saying goes, how can you trust a skinny cook?

At thirty years old, I have callused hands and my arms carry half a dozen scars. My back has a rough patch that I'm told is the shape of Australia—a souvenir of the burn I got by knocking into someone who was carrying a pot of boiling veal stock. I consider these to be war wounds and wear them proudly. To complete the picture, my eyes are blue and my hair is the shade that goes by the unflattering name of "dishwater blond." I wear my hair long—almost down to my waist, in fact. It's the one girlie affectation that I won't give up, even though it makes my life difficult. I can't wear it loose on the job. Aside from sanitary issues, it's just plain dangerous. Remember those flash fires? So every morning I braid my hair and wind it into a tight coil at the back of my head. That way, even if the roughly fifty pins I use to keep it in place fall out, the braid tumbles down my back and not into the soup.

Which tonight was a choice of a lovely chicken-miso broth with ginger and fresh scallions or a sugar pumpkin soup with either crème fraîche or foamed veal "raw sauce."

"Excuse me, Chef Caine?"

"Yes?" I said without turning around. The voice belonged to Robert, our white-haired English maître d', who was standing back about two feet from me. A veteran of bigger and busier kitchens than mine, Robert knew better than to sneak up too close to someone working an eight-burner cooktop.

"Table two wants to speak to the chef."

"Compliment or complaint? And have you sicced Chet on them?"

"Complaint, I'm afraid. Mr. Caine's out there now, but they insist on speaking with the chef."

I bit back a sigh. This happens. Sometimes it's just somebody trying to impress a date, or a client, but sometimes—despite everybody's best efforts—something's gone wrong. It's the other side of being mistress of all I survey. Mistakes coming out of the kitchen are my fault.

Any other time it would have been no big deal. I'd just go out, smooth things over and offer a complimentary dessert. Tonight, though, we had Anatole Sevarin in the house, and whatever was going on out there, he was watching and taking notes. Notes for publication. Notes to go out on the blogs, and on FlashNews (Online on now!(^{TM})), and even on paper.

Which meant we had to squash this situation immediately.

I motioned Reese over to cover my station, undid my apron, tossed it on the chair at my desk and followed Robert out front.

Nightlife's dining room is a long, narrow space with exposed brick walls, red oak floors and a pressed-tin ceiling that cost most of our meager budget to restore. The building had been a saloon when it opened back in the 1880s, and somehow its magnificent mahogany bar had survived the intervening years, political changes and food trends. The rest of our decor is simple, done in warm shades of brown, cream and gold. The lighting is low for atmosphere, but for obvious reasons we have flower vases on the tables instead of the usual candles.

No matter what restaurant you're in, stepping into the front of the house from the kitchen is stepping into a different world. Not only does the temperature plummet at least twenty degrees, but the noise level drops half a dozen decibels and the atmosphere goes from one of fevered activity to one of leisurely conversation and relaxation.

Tonight, however, not everyone was relaxed. Suchai, our dining room captain, was at the back station where we keep the glasses, water pitchers and bread baskets. His face was screwed up tight.

"What's the story?" I murmured to him as I motioned for Robert to head back to his post by the door. I'd already zeroed in on the problem table. It was table two, up front by the window. When asked if we deliberately sit pretty people there, I plead the Fifth. Right now, Chet stood beside a seated couple: a male vamp with a black jacket, chartreuse turtleneck and thinning hair and an over-fluffed blond woman in white and scarlet, who I could tell, even at this distance, was a complete VT.

That's short for "vamp tramp."

"She's got a problem with the soup, Chef," said Suchai softly.

I frowned. My soup? There was a problem with *my* soup? "Did you offer to replace it?"

Suchai nodded. "And so did Mr. Chet, but she insists on seeing you."

"Okay, then. I got this. You concentrate on Mr. Sevarin's table."

Suchai nodded and I squared my shoulders and put on my sober PR face. My kitchen whites attracted instant attention as I moved between the tables, and everybody in our full house turned to watch the show. I snuck covert glances around me. We had about half a dozen people seated at the bar, most of them with Kevin's specialty martinis in front of them. A werewolf dined alone on the carpaccio at sixteen. The engagement party at twelve and thirteen looked like they were doing all right, although the air was a little strained around the live in-laws. Michele, our wine steward, was pouring more champagne, which should have helped loosen things up. At nine, a pair of African-American vamps I'd been told were up from Atlanta toasted each other with our Special Blend sangria.

In short, except for two, everything looked great.

Except for two and twenty-four. Twenty-four was empty. Completely empty. Absolutely empty. No food critic anywhere.

Can't worry about it now.

"I'm Chef Caine," I said as I reached table two. "Is there something I can help you with?"

The blonde raked me over with her eyes, trying to decide if I was any kind of threat. I also had the feeling that her vampire date was beginning to regret the company he was keeping. You very rarely see a vampire squirm. But this VT apparently had that effect on people. My roommate Trish could have identified the lot number of the dye that had turned her hair that shade of butter yellow. My other roommate, Jessie, could have told me the maker of the scarlet, strappy, sequined stilettos on her feet, but I would have had to go to my publicist, Elaine, to get the designer of the flimsy white dress that was supposed to look like the kind of nightgown that used to be described as "diaphanous," which the VT wore over a red sheath and tights. Elaine also might be able to tell me who was responsible for the too-round-to-be-real boobs that threatened to spill out of the ensemble and into the sugar pumpkin soup with crème fraîche.

"Your werewolf deliberately dropped his filthy hair

into my soup!" The VT pushed the bowl toward me. Yes, there was indeed a black hair in the soup, and yes, that was bad.

I will not look behind me to see if table twenty-four is occupied, I vowed. *I will not cringe, and I will not look behind me.*

Instead, I glanced at Chet. He shifted his weight and I frowned hard. *What's eating you?* I wondered exasperatedly. As front-of-house manager, Chet had dealt with more obnoxious customers than I had mediocre line cooks. One more shouldn't be making him antsy.

"I'm terribly sorry," I said to her, endeavoring to mean every word. I didn't for a second believe there had been deliberate soup sabotage. Suchai is one of our most reliable people. He pays attention to the details of his job and never takes off sick. In return, we make sure he *always* gets his four nights off during That Time of the Month.

"Your soup will be replaced immediately, and for your inconvenience, I hope you'll accept one of our dessert selections, with my compliments." Chet had doubtless said all this to her, but I was the chef. Little Miss Power-Grab wanted to hear it from me.

Unfortunately, she was sharper than she looked. "You don't believe me! She doesn't believe me!" she added to her vampire, in case he hadn't heard the first time.

"It'll be all right, Pamela," said her vamp, attempting to recover some of his lost dignity. The pair from Atlanta was sneering, and I was willing to bet that hurt worse than Pamela's withering stare. "They've already offered to fix the problem—"

"I want him fired!"

I spend my days in an environment that could kill me in multiple ways, dealing with testosterone-poisoned line cooks who all think they're destined to be the next Bobby Flay or—God help us—Anthony Bourdain. I can give orders in a dozen different languages while carving up a chicken in ninety seconds flat. Paranormals do not scare me, and emotionally challenged pretty young things wearing blue eye shadow *definitely* do not scare me.

"I assure you," I said with what I hoped was firm courtesy, "all necessary corrective action will be taken." *Don't look back. Don't look back.*

"I want him fired!" Pamela said again, louder this time. Her vamp looked up at Chet helplessly. I thought I heard a chuckle from the pair at nine, and if I heard it, the vamp most definitely did.

I faced Chet. *Make it good.* Chet, in turn, pressed his mouth into such a thin line you could see the impression of his fangs beneath his upper lip.

"It will be taken care of," he said in the extralow register that vampires can achieve. I knew it was an act, but all the hairs on my arm stood up anyway. Pammy probably thought Chet was going to take poor Suchai out back and make a meal of him.

Actually, there was no way we'd fire Suchai. Not only was he part of the reason we were heading toward genuine fine-dining status, but he and his wife had just had their first litter. Let me tell you, it's no joke to keep six little weres fed and clothed.

However, Chet got the result we needed. Pamela preened, tossing all that hair back and exposing the full length of her pristine, lily-white neck. The corner of her vamp's mouth glistened. I thought about offering him a napkin, and reclassified the woman from vamp tramp to full-blown fang tease. I also considered taking my soup away from her and ordering her out my door. But Sevarin might be back from wherever he had gone by now. He might be seated at his table, taking notes on how I handled this and making a note to tell people not to order the soup. So I simply signaled for Chet to take the dish, which he did.

"Is there anything else I can do for you?" I asked. If that was it, we might just get out of this with whole skins and a decent review. After all, this wouldn't be the only time Sevarin came in. A good critic made multiple visits to a restaurant. Next time, we'd be ready for sure . . .

Then the drunk stumbled in.

Chet saw him even before I did and was in front of him in an instant with a polite "May I help you, sir?" Over Chet's shoulder, I saw dark hair sticking up in all directions and a pair of wild and unfocused eyes in a white face, but that was about it.

"Pamela!" The drunk shoved Chet aside, which meant he was strong as well as completely blotto. "Pamela!"

The engagement party was gasping and guests were shrinking back, if they weren't already on their feet. Pamela had the grace to look embarrassed as everyone, including her vamp, stared at her. I caught our maître d's eye. Robert read me easily and retreated discreetly to the coat closet to call 911.

The Atlanta vamps raised their eyebrows.

"Sir, I'm afraid you'll have to leave," said Chet firmly.

Now I could see that the drunk was a young man, skinny, with high cheekbones and wearing a sports jacket that was probably designer, although it was hard to tell, because it also looked like he'd been sleeping in it.

"Pamela!" he wailed. Pamela sat stiffly, attempting to look as dignified as her fang-tease outfit would allow. I saw triumph shining in her eyes and if I hadn't hated her before, I did now.

"Sir . . ." Chet spread his arms, getting ready to either grab the drunk or herd him toward the door.

The drunk ignored him. "You let her go, you undead bastard!" Nebbish vamp went whiter than dead and knocked his chair back as he jumped to his feet. The drunk swung both arms high over his head.

Whump!

There was a smell like hot kerosene and a ball of flame the size of a watermelon burst to life between the drunk's palms. Chet leapt back. Somebody snarled. Somebody screamed.

Well, shit. This wasn't just a drunk. This was a drunk warlock with lousy taste in women.

And he was threatening to torch my restaurant, and my guests.

In the middle of dinner rush.

This was *not* how I planned to get Nightlife into *Circulation.*

"Put that out!" I shoved past my brother.

The warlock blinked at me. The flame wavered and shrank from watermelon size to cantaloupe size before he caught himself and it flared up again. "Why should I?"

Heat washed against my face. "Because, you idiot, she's not worth it, you're too drunk to have any damn aim, and besides, you're going to . . ."

The alarm blared and in the next heartbeat a driving shower of white foam pelted down on the dining room. Guests shrieked and swore and dove for cover.

"Set off the sprinklers," I finished.

2

At one in the morning, we were still apologizing.

We apologized to the police who showed up ten seconds after the deluge and began to take the deflated drunk-punk-warlock away in the special forged-iron handcuffs they keep for magic workers. We apologized to the firefighters who came to turn off the alarm and the sprinklers. I made a note of their station house so Marie-Our-Pastry-Chef could make up something special and send it over. We apologized to all the guests and took names so we could pay the dry cleaning bills. We called our reservations for the rest of the night and apologized for being unexpectedly closed and offered to reschedule.

I even apologized to the rest of the staff as I called and texted (being especially nice to Marie-Our-Pastry-Chef) to let them know what had happened. I also let them know that tomorrow we would need all hands on deck by noon to get prepped for dinner service.

We tore the kitchen and the dining room apart, looking through every place where the fire suppressant foam might possibly have collected and cleaning it out. By four a.m., we had mopped up and gotten most of the dishes washed and the linens wrung out and bagged. We'd just taken a delivery on Thursday, so thankfully we had enough clean tablecloths and napkins for Saturday dinner service.

At four thirty, I sent everybody home to get a few hours' sleep. I'd just finished shooing Suchai out the kitchen door when I turned around and found Chet waiting behind me.

My brother looked tousled and pale. He hadn't stopped to drink any more than I'd stopped to eat. At least we both had dry clothes. When we designed the place, we made sure there was space for employee lockers and a shower. He was back in his civvies: worn jeans and a BYT ME BEAT-MAN concert jersey. I was still in my uniform of white jacket and black pants, partly, I admit, because it made me feel ready to stay in the fight.

"You get too," I told him. "It's almost sunrise."

Chet shrugged. "I can stay in the walk-in. You look dead."

"Takes one to know one." There was nothing unusual about me making my way home in the small hours. Normally, however, that was from a busy night, not from dealing with the aftermath of a magical assault.

Chet touched my shoulder. "Go home. Get some sleep." I felt him trying to do a little of the vamp-whammy on me, and I shook him off.

"I'm not going to be able to sleep until I do an inventory." This was a lie, although an inventory would be a good idea. But I had something else to do first.

Chet prodded a fang with his tongue, like a kid with a loose tooth. "Okay." He gave me a careful, tightly puckered kiss on the cheek. "See you at sunset, C3."

"G'night, C4." Family nicknames. Our dad was Charlie Caine, so he was C1. Mom was Colleen, C2. Birth order determined my number and Chet's.

Not that we'd been able to get Dad to talk to Chet since he'd been turned, or transitioned, or whatever the hell the current Vampirically Correct term was.

My brother retrieved his hat and jacket from his locker and left by the front door. I locked it behind him. My clogs sounded loud against the hardwood floor as I exercised owner's privileges by going to the bar and pouring myself a very large single malt. Even with everybody gone, tension hung in the air. Maybe it was the fact that every time I looked outside I could see the massive poster for the 3-D rerelease of *Midnight Moon*, the biggest, schlockiest vampire romance movie ever made. Its big red reminder that next week was the fifth anniversary of the actor Joshua Blake's disappearance did nothing to help. We had history—me, *Midnight Moon*, and Joshua Blake—and I didn't need those outsized broody eyes staring at me just then.

On the other hand, maybe the problem was my restaurant just smelled wrong. There should have been a lingering warmth and the scent of spices permeating the dining room. But tonight there was just the odor of cold chemicals, with unexpectedly earthy undertones that made me wonder if we'd left some mushrooms out somewhere.

I'd started the night thinking we were on our way. We were going to get reviewed by Anatole Sevarin. We might *finally* make it. Now, I was wondering how we were going to pay for all the high-class dry cleaning and what in the hell the foodie blogs were going to say about this fiasco.

Tears pressed against the back of my eyelids. My plan was to drink until I was loose enough to start crying. If I didn't get it out of the way now, it'd happen at some less convenient time, possibly in front of witnesses, which would not do my ego or my authority any good at all.

Somebody knocked on the door.

I looked up. A man peered through the glass front door, his expression hopeful.

Oh, *great*.

I mouthed, *We're closed!*

He mouthed back. *I know.* And knocked again.

I do not deal well with slow learners at four thirty in the morning. I made a slashing gesture across my neck and then indicated with two fingers he should walk away. *That way. Now.*

The Guy pulled back a little, reached into his pocket and brought out his smartphone. He tapped the screen, and my heart sank. A couple seconds later, the house phone rang. I glowered at him. He raised his eyebrows at me. I stayed resolutely where I was. After six rings came the click indicating that Robert had remembered to set the voice mail before he left. The Guy frowned at his phone and touched a couple buttons.

The ringing started again. The Guy shrugged, and waited. When the ringing stopped, he hit what must have been redial, and it started again.

At this point, I probably should have just pulled the drapes and taken my scotch back to the kitchen. Unfortunately, it is not in my nature or my training to leave unresolved problems on the doorstep. So, grinding my teeth, I stomped across to the host station and picked up.

"What?" *If you're from the media, I swear to God I will send you back to your editor as fillet of staff reporter. . . .*

The man on the other side of the window smiled sheepishly. "I'm here to apologize. May I please come in?"

This was not what you'd expect to hear from an overeager tabloid writer. "Apologize for what?"

"My cousin the flaming jackass."

That halted thoughts of how I would debone something the size of a human male. I squinted at the Guy. The streetlight didn't reveal any obvious family resemblance between him and the previous warlock. For one thing, I had an impression that the Guy was much taller, and much broader through the shoulders. On the other hand, during the incident, I had been far more focused on the fireball than on the person holding it.

I sighed. "Listen, I appreciate the gesture, but I would much prefer to have this conversation in the morning . . . later in the morning."

"Please," he said. "I need to ask some questions too. It's a family emergency."

My thought processes stopped in their tracks. I understood family emergencies. God knows I'd been through enough of them, and not just in my own family. Since we'd opened Nightlife, I'd watched my staff deal with everything from a line cook's brother being in imminent danger of deportation back to a place stunningly more unpleasant than the dish room of a national restaurant chain to the time Zoe's pet python got loose in the air shaft when her building was about to go condo.

Maybe I shouldn't have, but I put down the receiver, undid the lock and dead bolt and opened the door.

"Thank you." The Guy stepped inside and extended his free hand. "I'm Brendan Maddox, Ms. . . ."

"Charlotte Caine."

Brendan Maddox either worked hard or worked out to get the shoulders that curved so nicely under his electric blue button-down shirt. Nobody came by a build like that naturally. Hats were back in style and he was wearing a sharp gray fedora, which he remembered to take off, revealing waves of black hair cut in a business-chic style. He looked to be in his midthirties, maybe a little older. His tan was natural, and his bright blue eyes were the kind you could spend a long time staring at, especially with the sweetly apologetic little smile he was flashing at me just then. He had a nice handshake too—firm without being pushy. I have strong hands and arms, and I *really* hate guys who act like they're afraid I might break, or worse, like I might break them.

It was a very good thing my hormones were as tired as the rest of me; otherwise I might have had to care about looking like several different kinds of hell just then.

"Ms. Caine, I really do want to apologize for Dylan, my cousin, the one who . . . caused such a scene. There's no excuse for what happened, and I wanted to let you know our family is ready to help pay for any damage he may have done."

That was exactly the right thing to say.

"Thank you, Mr. Maddox." I folded my arms and straightened my shoulders, so he wouldn't think I was *completely* taken in by the charm offensive. "I'm sure our lawyer will be glad to talk to yours and see if we can come to an agreeable settlement." His name was making memories stir. Maddox. They were somebodies, the Maddoxes. . . .

Memory kicked in. Maddox was the name of a prominent witch family from upstate. More. The Maddoxes were also one of the old vampire-hunting clans. I'd seen something about them on FlashNews recently. The name Lloyd Maddox surfaced alongside the memory of an effort to get vampires and vampirism declared illegal again. . . .

"Are you alone?" Brendan Maddox lifted his head, as if he'd just gotten a whiff of something burning.

It was a question that had my hand diving in my pocket for my cell phone. "Yes . . ."

"No."

Maddox leapt for the shadows. *What the* hell*?* I reeled back. For a moment all I could see was a big black blur. Then it separated into two male silhouettes. One man rushed the other and they both toppled to the floor. Tables ricocheted off each other and chairs toppled over. Glassware rattled dangerously.

I yanked out my phone with one hand and slapped on the lights with the other.

Brendan Maddox knelt on a male vampire. The vamp heaved himself backward. Maddox flew through the air and rolled over the bar, taking with him two bottles of scotch, two of vodka and more glasses than I could count. The vamp flowed effortlessly to his feet as glass and booze crashed to the floor. I screamed. Maddox had vaulted back over the bar like a stuntman and raised his hands. The vamp opened his mouth and let out a full-fang hiss.

Maddox froze.

"Sevarin!"

Sevarin? All the strength in my knees gave out, dropping me hard into the nearest upright chair. *No. Oh, no, no, no.*

"Good evening, Mr. Maddox." Sevarin made a small bow toward the warlock who'd been trying to beat the undying daylights out of him.

Anatole Sevarin is still in my dining room.

"What are you doing here?" demanded Maddox.

"This is a restaurant. I am a dining critic." Sevarin adjusted his suit jacket cuffs. He was one of the few vamps I've seen who genuinely looked the part. His face was rugged, with an aquiline nose, high cheekbones and a chin that could have cracked granite. A wealth of fine wrinkles surrounded his green half-moon eyes, and his face was framed by red-gold sideburns that were longer than current fashion. He wore his red-gold hair long too, and it brushed against the immaculate collar of his burgundy button-down shirt.

With a certain amount of internal chaos, I thought, *Anatole Sevarin is still in my just-been-flooded-and-closed-on-a-Friday-night dining room.*

"Dining critic. Interesting career move."

Anatole Sevarin has just been attacked by a warlock in my dining room.

"It pays the rent."

If I commit seppuku in the kitchen, I'll leave Chet with a fortune in catastrophic cleaning fees and no insurance payout. . . .

"And you just *happened* to be in the restaurant where my missing cousin turned up?" The scent of testosterone and quivering one-upmanship filled the room.

"Interesting that your cousin chose to be at the restaurant I was reviewing."

And interesting that they both just trashed my dining room for the second time tonight!

The world suddenly snapped into high definition. I reached up between vampire and warlock and snapped my fingers, hard. "Yo! You two! Down here!"

Warlock blinked.

Vampire lifted one eyebrow, Spock-like.

Both stared at me as if they'd forgotten I was there.

"My staff just spent *three and a half* hours cleaning this room!" I informed them, pointing at the overturned tables and chairs. The wreckage of the bar was obvious, as we were standing in it and the scent of spilled, expensive liquor was overwhelming.

Vampire stared at warlock. Warlock stared at vampire.

Sevarin bowed solemnly to me and glided over to the nearest table. We'd gone for the good stuff, so it was heavy. The vampire set it neatly upright. With one hand.

Maddox frowned hard and picked up two pieces of glass. He fitted them together and blew out a short breath. Light flashed in his blue eyes and I smelled ozone. A warm wind spiraled through the dining room, raising a chime from the shattered glass. All at once, four bottles brimming with liquor assembled themselves in the air, along with a flock of shot glasses that lined themselves up as neatly as ducks on a pond.

Maddox, now perspiring lightly, turned toward Severin and got a nasty shock, because the rest of the overturned furniture was already back in place.

I hadn't even seen Severin move. From the look on Maddox's face, I gathered that he hadn't either.

Vampire stared at warlock. Warlock stared at vampire. Chef stared at warlock and vampire and thought: *Weirdest pissing match ever.*

"Thank you," I said, exercising every ounce of control I had left to keep my voice studiously bland. "Now, you can both tell me what you're doing here."

"I can of course speak only for myself," said Severin. He had a mild, lilting accent. I couldn't place it, but it sure wasn't Russian. "I was here for a working dinner, but that was interrupted—" Severin gestured around the room to indicate the recent drama. "I admit that I succumbed to base curiosity and willfully, with malice aforethought, I did lurk in the shadows to see how the situation would be resolved."

"You admit you lurked?" asked Maddox.

A very, very tiny smile flickered across Severin's face. "I lurked, and I make no apologies for doing so."

"No surprise there."

I turned to the warlock. "And you, Mr. Maddox? You said you had family . . . business here?"

Maddox reached into his pocket. Severin stiffened. Now it was the warlock's turn with the little smile as he brought out his cell phone and touched the screen.

"Dylan said he came in here because he thought he saw somebody he'd been looking for." Maddox turned the screen toward me. "I wanted to know if maybe this was her."

Her?

It was not a recent photo. Her hair was nowhere near as fluffy as it had been tonight, and there was a scowl of discontent in place of the fang-tease simper. She slouched in front of a vista of summer green hills wearing a high-necked black cat suit with a bulky black tool belt around her slender waist—both of which looked a lot better on her than the diaphanous white dress had.

"Pam's my cousin," said Maddox. "She went missing six months ago and my family's been trying to find her ever since." I'd been assuming the missing cousin Maddox had mentioned before was Dylan the Drunk. Apparently not. So, the plot thickened. Joy.

Witch clans, especially the hunters, were rumored to be very . . . strict with their members. A girl like Pamela could easily find herself driven into a case of MSAR (massively stupid adolescent rebellion). Also, contrary to popular belief, witches have a much greater prejudice against werewolves than vampires do, which explained Pammy's overdramatic reaction to Suchai.

"You must be a very *close* family," murmured Sevarin.

Maddox flushed. If looks were stakes, Sevarin would have been very much an ex–dining critic.

"She was in here," I said quickly. "But I lost track of her after the sprinklers went off."

"And that's all you can tell me?" Maddox stowed the phone back in his pocket.

"I'm afraid so. I kind of had my hands full tonight. I wish you luck with your search, Mr. Maddox. Now, if you—both of you—will please excuse me?" I snapped the locks back on the front door and opened it.

This was a hint. But those two seemed to take it as the cue for round three of the Great Greenwich Village Vampire/Warlock Staredown.

Sevarin moved first. "Thank you for a most interesting evening, Chef Caine." He took my hand with cool, callused fingertips and bowed over it. Only old vamps and good actors can successfully perform this maneuver. "I will return for my meal."

"You're welcome anytime, Mr. Sevarin."

Sevarin smiled and I got a glimpse of fang. Then he turned and walked out onto the street, which was just beginning to brighten in the first light of dawn. I tensed involuntarily. Sunrise and vampires do not get on well. But Sevarin just strolled away calmly without so much as glancing at the skyline.

It was oddly impressive. Even Brendan Maddox watched the departure with a strange mix of anger and respect flickering across his features.

"I take it you know each other?" I asked.

"He has a history of . . . annoying my family. My grandfather, my father . . ."

"And you think Sevarin's going for a hat trick in generational annoyance?"

"Maybe." He narrowed those gorgeous blue eyes. "He could have been here for the food, just like he said. But if that's true, he's got lousy timing. . . ." Maddox shook his head, clearly remembering that there was somebody listening.

That memory of the Maddox family name and renewed calls for antivampirism legislation nagged at me again. "Your father wouldn't be Lloyd Maddox, would he?"

"No. Lloyd Maddox is my grandfather." It was not an admission that made him comfortable, which, considering that he was standing in the middle of a vamp-friendly establishment, made plenty of sense. He glanced at his watch. "I should get going. By now the forces of law and order should be about done with my idiot cousin and I can stuff him onto the train back to Ithaca."

"Headfirst?" I inquired hopefully. "In a box?"

"That'd be my preference." There was more bitterness

in those words than I'd expected, and I found myself wondering what was at the back of the family drama that had come so close to torching my restaurant. "I really am sorry about all this," Brendan Maddox added.

"Family quarrels are the worst ones." I didn't want to think about how I was going to have to call Mom out in Tucson to let her know what had happened, in case it made FlashNews, which would surely touch off yet another round of the ongoing fight with my father about how he refused to acknowledge that Chet still walked the earth.

Brendan Maddox was watching me a little too closely and with a little too much open sympathy for my comfort. I looked around for something to do and came up frustratingly empty.

The warlock, still watching me way too closely, pulled a card out of his pocket. "If you hear anything else about Pamela, or remember something that might help me find her, or decide you'd like to have a coffee, would you please call me? It really is important."

I had to replay that speech several times before I could manage the necessary nonchalance to answer it.

"Well, they do say anything can happen." I took the card and handed him his hat.

He flashed a smile that had probably weakened lots of knees, especially as he seemed able to make those amazingly blue eyes twinkle on command. I'd been flattered by experts, however, and therefore was not vulnerable to displays of excess charm, even if his fingertips did accidentally-on-purpose brush mine as he took his fedora. My nerve centers picked that moment to remind me that I hadn't woken up next to a man in well over a year.

Down, girl, I thought. The sudden revival of long-buried hormonal responses to a handsome man was probably just stress.

Brendan adjusted his hat brim, suddenly looking very Marlon Brando circa *Guys and Dolls*. Like Sevarin, the warlock strolled away toward Fifth Avenue, only this time "Luck Be a Lady" threatened to start up in the iPod of my brain.

Along with everything else, Maddox had repaired my glass of scotch. I gulped half of it, welcoming the peat fire burning down my throat.

My watch read 5:40. It was the end of a very long night, or the start of a very long day. Probably both. I thought about going home, but by the time I found a taxi and made it out to Queens, my roommates would be up and fully in the middle of their mutual morning routines. Jessie had one of her house parties today. When I'd left yesterday, she'd already carpeted our living room with a hundred goodie bags from Mary Sue Cosmetics (Show Them the REAL You!). She was angling for Saleswoman of the Month and would be futzing over ribbon curlicues before she even had coffee. Trish was due in court and would be clomping around in square-heeled pumps rehearsing her arguments and citations.

Going home was not the answer I needed. Sleep would be impossible for me until they vacated the place. By then it'd be eight thirty and I had to be back at Nightlife by noon. Add in transit time, and it would probably leave me a grand total of thirty minutes for a nap.

So I decided to do what any overstressed New York woman would do at a time like this.

I went shopping.

People who don't live here are frequently surprised that New York City has multiple farmers' markets, and that they open at five in the morning. This is the time when the food professionals shop. Of course we have our regular suppliers, but the market is where inspiration happens for me. I can roam the stalls, perusing the stacks of fresh abundance, smelling the aromas, seeing nature's glorious colors and cooking in my mind.

I strolled peacefully past luxurious mounds of fruits and vegetables, talking with the farmers and admiring the results of their labor. I became centered again with thoughts of broth of tuna blood vein topped by a lemon-basil pesto as well as warm salad of jicama and baby turnips with bacon, pink peppercorns and fresh herbs.

Of course, some of my peers were already out, every one of them looking a hell of a lot better than I did. Thanks to the tabloid-y Web site FlashNews, some of them had already heard what had happened at Nightlife (part of it, anyway—the postscript with Maddox and Sevarin seemed to still be my secret). Some were just a little too pleased about the whole thing. For the most part, though, the expressions of sympathy and offers of help were genuine. Chefs are a competitive bunch, but if you've got any kind of spine at all, you want your opponents to be at their very best when you kick their asses. Besides, most of us know we're dancing pretty close to the cliff. The bad luck that comes to one of us could come to any of us.

By the time I hailed a cab to take me and my four bags of fresh produce back to Nightlife, the sun was well up and the city wore her gaudy daytime face. My sleepless night dragged at me, but fresh food and the fellowship of my peers had taken the desperate edge off my outlook. I would make myself breakfast and do some experimental cooking until noon. Who knew? Word of our little drama might actually draw in dinner gawkers. We should be ready, just in case.

I paid off the cabbie at the front door and set down my overflowing paper bags on the sidewalk to fish my keys out of my purse. I cranked the lock, shouldered the door open, and froze.

A man's body lay sprawled on the floor, right in front of the host station. His arms were thrown out wide and his blue eyes stared at the ceiling. Two big red holes gaped against the white flesh of his throat.

He was very obviously dead.

He was also very obviously Cousin Dylan Maddox.

3

There are distinct disadvantages to a chef's life.

One of them, as it turns out, is that you've got no time to watch TV.

If I lived like a normal person, not only would I likely not have had a dead body in my foyer but I would have been able to watch the cop shows, which would have given me a better understanding of what the hell the police were actually *doing* about it.

I had vague expectations of frantic action—lots of flash-bulbs going off; guys in clean suits going around dabbing at things with itty-bitty paintbrushes while other guys in trench coats talked in wise-guy lisps while touching their index fingers to suspicious stains spattered on the floor (which, upon reflection, is probably not the best idea; it is a New York City floor, after all). Other guys in white doctor coats carrying black doctor bags would make solemn pronouncements about time of death. Maybe there'd be a skinny chick with great hair, a black leather jacket and high heels moving in to take charge.

Okay, I do get to watch *some* TV.

What I got instead was three white guys in rumpled

suits, one of whom was the shortest, broadest man I'd ever seen. They stood around the body while cops in uniforms blocked off the street outside and wrapped yellow tape around everything they could find. Other guys set up enough lights for a *Vogue* photo shoot and proceeded to take pictures with all kinds of cameras, none of which had flashbulbs and some of which I'm not sure were actually cameras. They kicked at the fresh produce I'd been so happy about just a few short hours ago but now had to watch slowly wilting on the floor.

The ambulance, when it came, didn't even have its lights on. Two attendants in blue jackets rolled a gurney in, confirmed that this was in fact a dead body, and packed it into a zippered black bag with an efficiency that was actually kind of disturbing. When the body was loaded, the ambulance took off at a leisurely pace through the morning rush-hour traffic.

The three suits stood there, writing things down in little notebooks. One of them said, "Huh." Perched on a stool at the bar, I clenched my teeth and waited for "Beats the heck out of me, Bob." The clock hands crawled toward ten thirty, the time Marie-Our-Pastry-Chef and the morning prep staff would arrive.

What'll I tell people? Why the hell did Dylan Maddox get turned into a corpse in my foyer?

And where in God's name was Chet?

Because even if you don't watch cop shows, you know that when a body turns up on your property with fang marks on its neck, the whereabouts of your vampire brother at the time in question will be checked on.

Of course, Chet had nothing to do with the corpseification of Dylan Maddox. Chet wasn't that stupid, or that thirsty. Besides, he'd have sense enough to use the Hudson River to dispose of any ill-considered snacks.

At least I thought he would. God knew, Chet had done

enough stupid things before. Look at how he got himself
vamped.

No, don't. Especially not now.

I was not in the best mental shape by the time the
short, broad, rumpled cop flipped to a fresh page in his
notebook and stumped over to me.

"Chef Caine?" I nodded and he held out his beefy
hand. "Detective Linus O'Grady. Paranormal Squadron."
We shook. *Wow, New York Irish cop,* said the part of my
mind that had gotten stuck in the trivial gear. *Iconic.*

In addition to being short and white, Detective Linus
O'Grady (Paranormal Squadron) was really bald. Neatly
trimmed salt-and-pepper stubble ringed his speckled scalp.
He had a strong, weathered, tired face. His brown eyes
tilted down at the corners to create that droopy spaniel
look that can make a girl go nuts when she's thirteen. He
had a wedding ring on his thick hand, which indicated he
had indeed made somebody go nuts at some point.

"We need to get through some formalities here, I'm
afraid." Detective O'Grady pulled out a chair from table
seven and sat down. He did not ask me to get off my stool.
"Charlotte Cordelia Caine, residence East Seventy-first
Street, Forest Hills, Queens?"

"Yes."

"And you are part owner of this establishment?"

I nodded.

"Why were you here so early?"

"I'd just been to the green market." I looked mourn-
fully at my ruined produce scattered on the tiles. "I was
going to work up the new dinner special."

He looked up at me with those spaniel eyes like he
didn't want to do this. "And the other owner is?"

"My brother, Chet—Chester Calvin Caine—and yes,
he's a vampire, and yes, his registration is up to date."

That he had to be nagged to do it every single year was not something Detective O'Grady needed to know.

"Where was Mr. Caine last night?"

"Until four in the morning he was right here." The good-cop act was getting nowhere with me. Linus O'Grady was not my friend, and he did not have my or Chet's best interests at heart. My sudden impulse to offer him breakfast because he looked like he hadn't eaten or slept in a while was strictly a reflex.

Detective O'Grady flipped through his book again. "All right. Now, I understand there was an incident last night involving the victim?"

I took a deep breath and explained about Pam "Fang Tease" Maddox and Cousin Dylan's drunken fireball antics and the sprinklers.

Detective O'Grady nodded and flipped a page. "I have down here that after that incident, you said you weren't able to identify the perpetrator. How come you were able to give his name this morning?"

Which meant that I had to explain about Brendan Maddox and Anatole Sevarin and the warlock-versus-vamp smackdown that had happened in the wee hours, right about where we were sitting.

"And had you known Mr. Brendan Maddox previously?" Detective O'Grady asked, pencil poised over the paper.

"No."

"How about Mr. Sevarin?"

"No. Sorry."

"Your brother . . ." O'Grady paused, indicating that he knew this was awkward and that he was sorry and that he really didn't want to ask, but . . . "Does he have any connection with the vampire Sevarin?"

"Chet never mentioned him before last night. He—

Sevarin—was going to review Nightlife for *Circulation*.
It's a vampire dining and entertainment periodical. . . ."

O'Grady looked at me until I remembered that as a
detective on the Paranormal Squadron, he probably knew
that.

"But your brother had never mentioned Sevarin before
last night?"

"No."

The detective flipped through his book, paused to read
a note, flipped and paused, flipped and paused. Behind
him, the other two suits murmured to each other and
pointed at things—the door, the host station, the door to
the coat closet. Me. Their voices made a buzzing backdrop to O'Grady's flipping pages. I ran my hands over my
hair and suddenly wished all these people would just *go
away*. Marie-Our-Pastry-Chef was going to be here any
second, and we had prep to start. . . .

Which was when it hit me: there was no dinner prep
to worry about. There wouldn't be any dinner service.
Nightlife had uniformed cops outside in case all that yellow tape fencing off the sidewalk wasn't a big enough
clue that something had gone really wrong inside. A
crowd had formed on the sidewalk. Somebody had their
camera out.

Detective O'Grady twisted around in his chair to see
what made my jaw drop. "Sorry about that," he said heavily.
"I am going to have to ask you where your brother is now."

My mouth had gone very dry. "I don't know."

"Is he on the premises?"

I had to swallow before I could get my throat to work.
"I don't think so. He . . . he sleeps in the cooler sometimes." Except not tonight. He didn't tonight. Because I
saw him leave. He did leave. He was gone. He was not
here. He couldn't have been here when somebody tossed
a body into the foyer.

Except the door was locked when I got here and the windows were whole.

"How did Dylan Maddox get in here?" I blurted out.

O'Grady paused in his flipping. "Sorry?"

"How did the body get in here? The front door was locked and the windows aren't broken."

O'Grady twisted around to look at the foyer again. "The back door was open."

"It was?"

He nodded and there was a brief pause to allow me time to mentally kick myself for extreme carelessness. I was the last person here when we closed. It was my responsibility to make sure the place was locked up when I left.

Detective O'Grady pushed himself to his feet. "Can you show me where Mr. Caine sleeps when he does spend the day here?"

I could probably have made him get a warrant to search the premises for the undead, but that didn't occur to me until much later. It's embarrassing to find out how much you'll do just because somebody with a badge asks. O'Grady followed me through my dining room into my kitchen. The place seemed to have expanded, like in a bad dream sequence. And, for the record? Yes, you really can feel the weight of someone's gaze on the back of your neck. Maybe it's a thing they learn in cop school. How to Unnerve Witnesses from Behind 101.

Unless they learn it in How to Unnerve Suspects from Behind.

I tried not to look at anything as we passed through the silent kitchen. I didn't want any more familiar sights mixed up with this nightmare than absolutely necessary.

"Must be a pain having the fridge down here," he remarked as we headed down the steps to the cellar.

"Actually, we were lucky we could get a space where the kitchen is on the same floor as the dining room."

When we reached the bottom, I hit the code on the security pad, fished out my keys and unlocked the vault-like door to our walk-in.

"Secure water supply?" O'Grady bent down to get up close and personal with the pad for the security system on the wall. Antivamp groups had been known to smuggle priests into restaurants to bless the bottled water, so we have to keep it locked up.

There's nothing in here. There's nothing in here.

I pulled the walk-in door open and snapped the light on to reveal wire shelves loaded with cardboard boxes, wooden-slat crates and row upon row of dated and labeled plastic bins in every size known to man.

"You should probably know, Detective, we keep a lot of blood in here."

O'Grady didn't even blink. "Any of it human?"

I shook my head. "Strictly animal."

"Not even . . . volunteer?"

I thought about Pamela and suppressed a shudder. "Not even. Too many sanitation issues. I can show you our shipping manifests." The words were out before I could stop them and I bit my tongue. You never volunteer information the sanitation inspectors haven't asked for. Too much information made them look at you funny. I had to assume the same rule held good for cops—even aging, iconic Irish detectives with good-cop attitudes.

"Hopefully that won't be necessary," said O'Grady, but he did make another damned note in that damned book.

Detective O'Grady strolled between the shelves, touching nothing, eyeing everything. It was like having somebody go through my closet at home, and I found myself hovering near the panic button we'd installed along with the lock. He paused by one of the five-gallon buckets and pried open the lid to peer inside. I angled myself so I could see the label scrawled in black Sharpie on the side. Ox blood. O'Grady pressed the lid back into place and then straightened up to make a few more notes and flip a few more pages in his book.

"Thank you. And the freezer?"

That was easier. I didn't even have to consider the possibility we might find Chet inside. He didn't sleep in the freezer, as he had no desire to turn into a vamp-sicle. There was very little to see there at all, in fact, except big bricks of meat, both raw and prepped, bundled in aluminum foil and plastic wrap until it could have sat through a Siberian winter without getting frost burn, alongside row upon row of Styrofoam coolers, all labeled and dated. We kept only some of the blood thawed. The rest was stored in here.

"Thank you, Chef Caine. We can go back upstairs now."

Detective O'Grady waited for me to move, and I suddenly didn't want to. I knew what I saw, but I couldn't tell what *he* saw with his cop eyes and cop brain. A dead body followed immediately by piles of frozen meat and buckets of blood—even if it is all neatly labeled—might just make a cop's imagination run off in the wrong direction. But there was nothing I could do, and no question I could ask that would make things look any better.

Back upstairs, Dylan Maddox's corpse was gone, but the other cops were still standing around talking. Detective O'Grady went over to join them, leaving me alone by the bar. The three of them paced the foyer, pointing, crouching, gesturing. I had no idea what they were doing. There was no camera with cuts and pans and close-ups to show me what was really important and no microphone so I could follow the dialogue.

Real life can be *so* inconvenient.

Detective O'Grady lumbered back over, flipping through his notebook one more time. "All right, Chef Caine. I think we're done here. Here's my card." He handed it over. "Call if you have any questions, or if you think of anything new. Officer Randolph is going to give you a ride home."

"It's all right. I can take the subway." I really wanted to get out in the fresh air.

He sighed heavily. "Chef Caine, this is already out on FlashNews. You're going to have cameras on your doorstep by the time you're halfway across town."

I stared at him. *How come I didn't think of that?* Our names were out there—mine, Chet's, and Nightlife's—in connection with the murder of a member of one of the most prominent warlock clans in the state, if not the country.

I snatched my cell out of my pocket. I keep it turned off on the job, and had switched it back off reflexively after I called 911.

126 messages.

Make that 127.

128.

Oh.

129.

Shit.

4

All things considered, the trip home could have gone a lot worse.

Officer Randolph drove me in an unmarked car and I phoned my building super, Georgie "Big Man" Manizotti. After quizzing me for twelve blocks about "what the hell really happened," Georgie agreed to meet me around back. A quick check of FlashNews showed they were mostly using the photo from our write-up in *NYC Bites*, which featured me in my class A chef's uniform and the tightly braided hairstyle that Chet calls my "Swedish helmet" look. So I ditched my white coat and took my hair down.

When we pulled up to the back of the building, Georgie—a mountain of shaved-head white guy from Jersey—stood by the door with his heavily tattooed arms folded. Beside him on the sidewalk lay a smashed smartphone, a crumpled wad of bills, and a much skinnier white guy with highly gelled hair and an impressively bloody nose.

"I wan' do rebord 'n assault!" shouted the gelled guy as Officer Randolph opened the car door for me.

I looked at the wad of bills and then at Georgie. "What'd he offer you?"

"Twenty bucks!" snorted Georgie. "Can you believe this cheap shit?"

Running footsteps sounded from around the corner. Officer Randolph jerked his chin toward the door.

As Georgie hustled me inside, Randolph pulled out a ticket book. The door closed as I heard the word "loitering."

I wondered if Officer Randolph liked lasagna. I make a killer lasagna.

"Sorry about the fuss," I said to Georgie.

"S'okay." He pulled the grille shut on the ancient service elevator and worked the switches. "Gives me something to tell the guys. And don't worry." My super cracked his knuckles and poured on the Jersey accent slowly, like melted butter. "Nobody gets in here for under a hundred. You know what I'm sayin'?"

"Thanks, Georgie." Tuna hot dish for Georgie. With the green peas mixed in with the mushroom soup and potato chip crumbs on top. He'd probably like Velveeta in there too, but even the heights of gratitude had their limits.

He grinned at me as the car lurched to a halt. "Your stop, Chef C."

Georgie hauled the door open to reveal the hallway and Patricia Lehner—otherwise known as Roommate Number One—who stood in front of the open door to our apartment.

"At least you were smart enough to come in the back."

Trish is an attorney in midtown. She lives with two roommates in Queens so she can squirrel away enough money to get her own practice going. Her pastimes include eating Instant Ramen even when it's not strictly necessary and questioning my common sense.

"What're you doing home?" I demanded.

"What do you *think*?" Trish shoved me through the door and slammed it behind us. "Sit," she ordered in a voice that has been known to make wiseguys think twice, and proceeded to slap, turn, click and chain all the bolts.

I sat.

Trish has a frame to match her personality. She's tall and strong, with a figure that would have brought Rubens to his knees. She dressed to impress, even on the weekend. Just then, she wore immaculate black slacks, an emerald green silk sweater and a heavy gold locket. She looked like she was about to very elegantly rip somebody's head off.

"So." Trish folded her arms. "What the hell really happened?"

She'd also clearly been spending too much time with Georgie.

My cell buzzed against my hip. I checked the number, didn't recognize it and let it go. Trish raised one eyebrow.

You know the feeling that comes over you when your mother uses your middle name? Trish could induce that with a single cocked eyebrow.

So, she got to hear the saga of Cousin Pam the Fang Tease and Cousin Dylan the Drunk, alive and dead. If I played down the Warlock vs. Vampire incident, that was my own business.

My phone buzzed again. Again, no name with the number.

"Why'd somebody dump this on you?" Trish asked with a straight face and in total seriousness.

"How should I know!"

"Remember that look of shocked innocence. You may need it."

"What could I know! I'm just a cook!"

"Just a cook?" Now in addition to the brow being raised, her perfectly made-up mouth puckered. One of Trish's few faults was being a walking billboard for Roommate Number Two, Jessie-the-Mary-Sue-Cosmetics-Saleswoman. "You're a New York restaurateur, sweetie, which makes you a bigger shark than I am. But bewildered little sister will play well on FlashNews."

"I'm the bewildered big sister." My cell buzzed again. "And I think we should maybe get a lawyer."

Trish plucked the phone out of my fingers and thumbed it on. "Yes? No. No comment. None. You may contact Ms. Caine's lawyer for any additional information. Yes. Annette Beauchamp at Piziks, Popkes, and Percival. In Manhattan, yes. Thank you. Good-bye."

I blinked. "Trish, did you just give false information to a member of the media?"

"Certainly not. You are distraught and must have misheard me. Do not under any circumstances answer that." She handed me back my cell with one hand and hit a button on hers with the other. "And yes, you're going to need a lawyer."

"Is this the part where I give you a dollar as a retainer?" My smile was pretty weak, but at least it was there.

Trish snorted. "No way am I your lawyer. Too much conflict of interest."

"We're just roomies."

"You got me into a rent-controlled apartment."

She was right. Too much conflict of interest.

"Don't worry." Trish leaned back, crossing one long black-clad leg over the other and circling her ankle thoughtfully. I could all but hear the Rolodex flipping in her brain. "We'll get you in with Rafe Wallace. Best paranormal lawyer in the city."

"Um, do we tell him I don't have any money?"

"We save that for later." She took my hand and held it tight. "It's going to be okay, Charlotte."

I decided to try to believe her.

"Oh my God!"

A good chunk of daylight had passed since my police-

and-super escort into my own building when Jessie Van-Reebek—Roommate Number Two—catapulted through the door with her arms full of party bags that looked like they'd come from the same manufacturer as Dorothy's ruby slippers.

"Oh my God, Charlotte! Oh my—" Jessie pulled up short and stared at me from behind a mass of tissue paper points, white ribbon curlicues and a dozen sparkly bags proclaiming SHOW THEM THE REAL YOU! "What are you doing?"

"I'm cooking."

In point of fact, I was in the kitchen whacking on half a helpless pomegranate to get the seeds out while keeping one eye on my pan of gently simmering shallots.

Jess rounded on Trish. "What are *you* doing?"

Trish had her stockinged feet up on the coffee table and a chunk of dipped bread halfway to her mouth.

"I'm eating." She held out the crock of asparagus Parmesan dip. "You should eat too. It's amazing."

Jessie looked for a place to dump her armload of bags and found our dining table covered with food; there was the lasagna for Officer Randolph and the tuna hot dish for Georgie plus a few other things I'd thrown together.

Despite Trish's insistence and my exhaustion, I'd been able to manage only a brief sort-of nap. After giving up on sleep, I alternated between phoning the Nightlife staff to lie my chef's fundament off about how everything was going to be cleared up Real-Soon-Now, calling Chet even though I knew he couldn't pick up during the day, and clicking through the FlashNews stories, blog posts, and comments. All of these were stupid beyond belief, especially the ones calling for revamping . . . er . . . reworking the paranormal registry laws.

The worst, though, carried the name stamp of Lloyd Maddox, Brendan's grandfather.

"How much longer are we going to permit the undead lobby to blind us to what's really going on in this country?" The news clip showed a powerfully built man, for all that his hair was pure white and his weather-beaten face had more lines than a map of the Jersey thruway. The media called him "the current head of the Maddox warlock clan, one of the oldest magic-working families active in the United States." "We are under siege! Our families, our values, our very identity of a country which cherishes life and the right to life is being constantly undermined by permitting this so-called 'death-style.' Death-style! This style of death caused my nephew to be mercilessly drained of his blood and his corpse thrown aside. . . ."

Any normal person would consider it natural to get a little loud while taking in this ignorant, vitriolic crap. At the end of hour three, however, Trish actually dangled my smartphone out the window and declared it was taking the direct route to the ground floor if I didn't, in her words, shut the hell up.

Effectively cut off from the outside world, I did the only other thing I could think of.

"You found a body, your brother is under suspicion for murder, and you're *cooking*?" said Jessie.

"I made those cheese straws you like."

Trish helpfully rattled the basket on the coffee table. "They are really good with the asparagus dip."

"Asparagus dip?" Jessie leaned sideways toward the steaming crock. "Wow, that smells . . . No." She jerked herself upright. "No!" She dumped her goodie bags beside the coat closet and held up both hands. "This is *not* right!"

I sighed and turned down the burner under the shallots. "The cops have the body. I can't talk to Chet until sundown, which isn't for another fifteen minutes and thirty-three seconds. I've already left six messages for Elaine, our PR rep, but I think she's avoiding me. The only other thing

I'm good for right now is sitting around staring like a deer in the headlights. You want to support me in my hour of need? Eat something." I gestured toward the plates laid out on the coffee table—crostini with olive tapenade, a Mediterranean couscous salad with chicken and green grapes beside a plate of toasted pita triangles, and sliced apples with this killer sour cream, spice and honey fruit dip.

"Oh. Well." Jessie plunked down onto the sofa next to Trish and reached for a cheese straw. She swirled it in the asparagus dip and took a nibble, letting me see that she did this only to humor me. But as she chewed her expression changed. "Mmmm . . ." She took a healthier bite.

Some of the tension left my shoulders and I went back to spanking my pomegranate, which is nowhere near as kinky as it sounds. I'd been playing around with an idea for a warm pomegranate salad with wilted greens and white-wine-and-shallot vinaigrette for the restaurant. Now was as good a time as any to try the idea out. The only greens we had on hand were in the form of a giant bag of arugula, which wasn't exactly what I'd wanted. I was thinking a mix of dandelion greens and micro watercress, but the arugula helped me get the general idea.

I was tasting the vinaigrette and considering if it needed more pepper when the sun dropped below the horizon. Ten seconds later Chet's ringtone, "Bela Lugosi's Dead," sounded on my cell phone. I dropped my spoon. Trish snatched the phone up off the table and tossed it to me. I caught it in midlunge and stabbed at the screen.

"Where are you?" I inquired.

"I'm home. Charlotte, what the hell . . . ?"

I told him about finding Dylan Maddox dead in our foyer. Ever the eloquent one, my kid brother replied, "Shit."

"The cops want to talk to you, Chet."

Over the phone, very faintly, came the sound of a door buzzer. "I think they're here."

My throat seized up. "Don't say anything. Trish's got a lawyer friend who specializes—"

"I don't need a lawyer."

Oh, no. "Those words did not come out of your mouth, little brother, because I know you are not suicidal."

"Charlotte, I didn't *do* anything. I don't need a lawyer."

Nononononono. "This is not about what you did or didn't do. This is about the Paranormal Squadron and the dead Maddox having bite marks on his neck!"

The buzzer sounded again. "I'm going to get the door now. Don't worry, Charlotte. It'll be fine."

It'll be fine. Coming from Chet, those words were as dangerous as "Hey, guys, watch this!" from a frat boy. "Chet!"

"I'll call back as soon as I'm done here."

"Do *not* hang up on me! Chet!"

I was talking to myself.

Trish was already on her cell. "Rafe? Yeah . . . he did. . . . No, I'd go straight downtown. . . . He's going to try to brush you off. . . . Ha-ha, maybe not . . . Thanks. She owes you one."

"I've got to get over there."

"No." Trish put her very solid self between me and the door. "You don't. Let Rafe handle it."

"But . . ."

Trish held up her hand. "You already talked to Linus O'Grady, right?"

That stopped me. "You know him?"

"Gimme strength," muttered Trish to the ceiling. "Every criminal lawyer in the five boroughs knows Little Linus. You go in there to defend your little brother, he's going to look up at you with those puppy-dog eyes and next thing you know you'll be writing Chet's confession for him."

I remembered those eyes. I swallowed.

Trish took my hands. "Let Rafe work. Just . . ." She rubbed a smear of Ricotta off the back of my hand and picked a fragment of arugula off my sleeve. "Just cook something, okay?"

"I've cooked everything." The little undertone of help-lessness was just stress. Really.

"Then we'll have to go grocery shopping." Trish let me go and slung her purse, which was big enough to hold a whole week's worth of briefings, over her shoulder. "Come on, Jessie."

"I don't think she should be left alone." Jessie had picked up a second slice of crostini.

"Your dear friend and roommate is in dire straits and needs food. You are coming with."

A fresh wave of gratitude ran through me. Jessie was a good roommate, and a good person. But if she stayed here, she'd try to get me to release and to start a course of lemon-scented aromatherapy and detoxing bath salts. And I would say what the hell good is a lemon scent not attached to something you can eventually eat? It would all go downhill from there, and probably end with my attacking her with a micro-plane grater.

"All right, all right. I'm coming with." Jessie's purse was a minuscule Kate Spade custom job in Mary Sue Red (sorry, Mary Sue *Scarlet*). It had been her prize for most new facials given in March.

And she thinks I'm nuts.

"Don't answer the phone," said Trish. "Don't open the door."

"Get some fresh spinach. I'll make a frittata for break-fast."

"Will do. Come *on*, Jess." Trish jerked Jess upright from in front of the closet, where she was crouching to set all her little gift bags upright.

"Coming, coming."

The door closed and I stood alone in the middle of the kitchen. The truth was, I'd not only cooked everything, I'd used every pan in the place. This was actually a good thing, because it meant I could switch from cooking to cleaning without having to sit down and look at the clock, or the door, or my phone.

I wrapped up the thank-you foods and stashed them in the fridge for later delivery. Then I dumped the pots and pans into the sink along with hot water and healthy squirts of dish soap. We had an ultra-compact dishwasher, but I needed to scrub.

Two pots and three half-sheet pans later, the door buzzer sounded. I jumped, showering suds everywhere.

You promised Trish.

The buzzer sounded again.

And there's probably still a flock of local media vultures outside.

The spirit was willing, but the flesh was as curious as your average cat. Dripping foam from wrists and fingertips, I crossed to the intercom and leaned my elbow against the button.

"Are you anybody I know?"

"Yes," said the smooth, confident voice.

It was Anatole Sevarin.

5

I stared at the speaker grille. I'd been doing a lot of staring. My eyeballs were beginning to ache.

"Chef Caine?"

"Yes? Yes."

"May I speak with you, please?"

"Errrrmmm . . ." An apartment full of plates, platters and bowls of food suddenly loomed large in the background.

"Is there a problem?"

"Well . . ." Now, obviously, when I promised Trish not to open the door to anybody, that had not included prominent dining critics, who are not just anybody. For this particular critic, however, there were some secondary considerations. "I've been cooking for the last four hours, and there's a trace of garlic in here."

Given the nature of my restaurant, I can't use garlic in my professional life. So when I'm at home, I occasionally go a little overboard. There had been, however, no need for Trish to open all the windows.

"I believe I shall find the resources to endure."

"If you're sure, then come on up." A small voice in the

back of my mind said this was a bad idea, but it couldn't give me a clear answer why.

"Thank you."

That was how I ended up buzzing one of the city's most powerful vampires—from a restaurateur's standpoint anyway—into my apartment.

I took the time until his arrival at my actual door to open the kitchen window again. Trish was exaggerating for regular people, but this was a vampire. The Center for Allergies and Immunology spends millions each year to figure out why garlic and wolfsbane do what they do. The vampire lobby is ambivalent about this, because no one's talking about what'll actually be done with the information once they've got it.

I keep lamb's blood cubes seasoned with rosemary in the freezer in case Chet drops by. He doesn't do it often, so they can get old. The date on the bag said this batch was still good. I dropped four dark red cubes into a wide-mouthed hand-thrown ceramic mug that I'd gotten from a starving artist friend in exchange for dinner. Two minutes on high in the microwave, and I'd have body temperature.

Anatole Sevarin knocked.

Unsurprisingly, Sevarin looked as sharp and unruffled as when I had last seen him. Tonight, he wore a gray sport coat over a dark maroon button-down and pressed gray trousers. A sudden vision of how he would look in black tie swept over me. The sensations brought on by this picture were not fit for public consumption.

Sevarin's gaze roamed around the apartment, taking in the dishes and platters that occupied every flat surface. His nose didn't exactly wrinkle, but I had the distinct impression it wanted to.

I chose to ignore this. "Please sit down. Can I get you something?"

"Thank you." He eyed the remains of the asparagus dip uncertainly.

I ignored that as well, went back to the kitchen, and dipped a knuckle in the blood to check the temperature. I poured myself some coffee so I could be sociable. In the meantime, Sevarin made himself comfortable in the wing-back chair that Jessie had inherited from her grandmother. He sniffed judiciously at the contents of the mug I handed him, sipped and nodded. Relief swept over me.

Yeah, yeah, and like you wouldn't be nervous serving a professional critic.

"So." I set my own mug down on the coffee table. "Can I ask what this is about?"

Sevarin's hand twitched, and he laced his fingers together. "We need to talk about Dylan Maddox."

"*We* do?"

"Yes. Was he actually killed by a vampire?"

Hell of an opener there, Mr. Sevarin. "You could ask the police."

The corner of his mouth twitched. Have you ever seen a twitchy vampire? It's about as reassuring as a twitchy trigger finger. "I'm sure Detective O'Grady would be delighted to talk to me at length on the subject, preferably at the city's expense, but I'm afraid I cannot spare him the time."

I picked up a cheese straw and turned it over. They'd gotten a little too brown on the bottom. I needed a new oven thermometer.

"From what I saw, there wasn't a lot of bruising," I said. "And his throat was intact."

"Meaning he knew his attacker well enough to permit intimacies, or was seduced." Those two tidy holes usually get called love bites or blood hickeys. An actual attack tends to involve a lot more damage, if only because the victim struggles.

I put the cheese straw down before I started crumbling it. I hate wasting food.

Severin swirled the blood in his mug and took another judicious sip. "Lamb?" I nodded. "I like your touch of rosemary here. Very delicate. Dayblood chefs tend to overseason when preparing food for us." "Dayblood" generally means human, but it can be anybody who walks around after sunrise.

Flattery will get you anywhere under normal circumstances, but we'd left normal at least thirty-six hours back. "Mr. Severin, please forgive me for being direct. Why are you here?"

Severin set his mug down. "I want to know why Dylan Maddox's body was left so unceremoniously in your foyer. I assumed you would want to know that as well and thought that we might help each other out." He smiled then and the effect was . . . spectacular. "I assure you, I'm much more entertaining to spend time with than Little Linus."

I'll just bet. "How could I help you?"

"You might have Pamela Maddox's phone number in the reservations computer at your restaurant."

And there it was. "If I'm caught backtracking my customers, it would not be good for business." I thought about that one getting onto FlashNews and shuddered.

"You have a point. However, Detective O'Grady is not going to voluntarily tell either one of us what happened to the unfortunate Dylan Maddox, and the media, if they do get around to discussing the matter, are going to get it wrong. That—depending on how wrong they get it—could be disastrous for your business."

I wrapped my suddenly cold hands around my coffee mug. "Why would you care?"

"Because there have been a series of deaths around the Village over the past six months. All the corpses had what appeared to be bite marks on their necks but were incompletely drained."

I felt a deep chill rising up around my thoughts. There were other people sprawled out on other floors like Dylan? It takes a lot to make me queasy, but the thought of all those staring corpses was doing the job quite effectively.

"There hasn't been anything about it on the news," I said, like I thought that if the media hadn't validated it, it hadn't really happened.

"Detective O'Grady has convinced the mayor there's a danger of panic, and lynchings."

This I could believe. "So tell me again why you *want* word to get out?"

"Word will get out," said Sevarin flatly. "And although Little Linus means well, if word also gets out that there's been a cover-up, the city will go . . . What is the phrase I'm looking for . . . ?"

"Berserk? Ballistic?"

"Both, I think."

Unfortunately, Sevarin made a disturbing amount of sense. "Why is this is your job? You're a dining critic, not a cop."

"I am also old enough to have faced an actual torch-wielding mob, Chef Caine, and I'd rather not do it again. I like modern life," he added softly. "I like being in a time and place where I have recourse to the law and can exist with a relative amount of security. Someone is trying to take that away from me. I want them found, and stopped."

Neither one of us said anything for a long time. Traffic, the eternal New York backdrop, rumbled and honked outside. I glanced at the clock, and at my cell phone on the counter. Chet would have called by now if he could. How long would it take Trish's lawyer friend to get to him? What if Sevarin was right and there was somebody running around trying to frame vampires? What if Chet had been arrested? No. He couldn't have been. Someone would have called me by now about bail.

How much was bail on a vampire suspected of murder? Could he even get bail? Did I have enough in the bank to cover it? God, why didn't I know anything important?

Vampires have dry eyes and they don't blink much. But Sevarin blinked then, and got to his feet.

"Forgive me, Chef Caine. I have chosen the wrong time to speak with you about this." He reached into his inner jacket pocket and laid a plain white business card down on the end table. "The coming days will not be easy. You need to rest."

"Yeah. Thanks."

Sevarin cocked his head, studying my face in a way that made me wish he'd just go back to twitching. "I can help you sleep, if you would permit."

That brought my attention back to the here and now. Fast. "You even think about putting the whammy on me and I will skewer you like a nightblood satay. Understand me?"

"Surprisingly well. Your diction is excellent." He did the bow-over-the-hand thing again. It held up well through a second viewing. Especially since he was smiling again, and giving me a nice close-up of the gold flecks in his green eyes. "Good night, Chef Caine. I hope we'll talk further, and about more . . . pleasant topics."

He let himself out. I stayed where I was for a minute, then slowly keeled over sideways onto the sofa and shoved my head under an end pillow. If my roommates came in right now, they could not be permitted to see my face turning Mary Sue Scarlet. I didn't even know why I was blushing. It's not like I could *do* anything about the fact that Anatole Sevarin was attractive as all hell. And even if I could, now was not exactly a good time.

I meant to get up. I needed to call Chet and to finish cleaning the kitchen. Most of all, I needed to figure out what to do about everything Anatole Sevarin had just told me. I also needed to get his business card out of sight before Trish got back.

Somewhere in the middle of tallying up all the things that needed doing, the world faded to black.

"Charlotte."

Someone shook my shoulder and removed the pillow covering my face. Consciousness returned at a leisurely pace, giving me plenty of time to notice that my mouth was furry, my hair was in my eyes and my back ached. "Ugh. What time is it?"

"Six a.m.," said Trish. Both my roommates stood in front of me, Trish in her turquoise sleeping sweats and Jess in her magenta kimono. "You were totally conked out when we got back, so we decided to let you sleep."

"And you've got a text from Chet." Jessie held up my cell.

"Gimme that!" I snatched the phone away and read: *C3: im ok thx 4 cavalry call 2nite. C4*

Outside, the horizon was brightening. Chet would already be shutting down for the day.

I put my phone down to reduce the risk of throwing it at something. Jessie picked it up immediately and read my message.

"Hey!"

She just passed the phone to Trish, who also decided she could read my private messages.

"Thank God." Trish sighed. I grabbed the phone back, switched it off and shoved it into my pocket. Trish had the sense not to remark on this. Instead, she glanced at the clock. "Who needs the bathroom first?"

Jess raised her hand. "I've got a brunch party. Eight faces, sixteen hands, and nothing packed."

"Okay, you're first."

I should have known something was up. On those occasions when our schedules converge, we do not ever let Jessie go first in the bathroom. Once, Trish and I clocked her at an average of seventy-five minutes over a two-week interval. We keep the chart, just in case she protests.

"I found this when we got in last night." Trish reached into the pocket of her bathrobe. "Next to the leftover blood." She handed me Anatole Sevarin's business card.

"So . . . he came by." I tucked the card into my own pocket.

"And you let him in? After you promised . . ."

There was no way I was standing still for one of my roommate's lectures right now. "If this looks stupid, I'm sorry, but I cannot afford to blow off an influential critic right now." I also was not going to tell her Sevarin wanted my help finding Pam Maddox, or about the other murders. She'd go through the roof, and Georgie would charge us for the repairs.

"You found a bitten body and now you're entertaining random vampires. Yes, Charlotte, as a matter of fact it does look stupid."

I snatched up the nearest bowl and the empty crostini plate and carried them to the kitchen. The water from last night had gone cold and greasy. Plunging my hand in to open the drain woke me up the rest of the way. "You know, you'll live longer if you quit trying to take care of everybody else."

"Yeah, I might, but they won't."

I started the water up, letting it run over my hands. The place was a total mess, and it was my responsibility. Nobody else was going to clean it up. They had jobs to get to.

Trish pinched the bridge of her nose. "All right," she said with a sigh. "But no more, okay? Not until your PR rep's had a chance to work up a decent disaster response for you."

I shut the water off and promised faithfully, but without looking up. Discovering you really are a liar is no fun at all.

Trish retreated to start the long wait for her turn in the bathroom. I cleaned up the kitchen enough to get the promised frittata in the oven. Trish loved frittata. When she came out dressed in her most sincere black suit, she got the first slice, piping hot and perfect.

"Sorry," I said.

"Thanks," she said. "Looks good."

"If you two were wound any tighter . . ." Jess said, coming up behind us.

"Shut up, Jess." I handed across her slice. She shrugged and dug in.

Equilibrium restored, my roommates finished breakfast, got their stuff together and set out to catch the E train, leaving me once more alone in our apartment with nowhere to go.

It's okay. Just like any other Monday. We're always closed on Monday.

As self-deception went, it was pretty lame, but it got me moving. I showered, dressed, brushed and rebraided my hair, cleaned up the last of the detritus from my cooking binge and before I forgot, retrieved Sevarin's business card from the pocket of yesterday's pants.

By then, it was time to try another call to PR Elaine. This time she picked up, which told me Chet had in fact managed to pay her bill this month. So, sitting on the couch and turning Sevarin's card over in my fingers, I let Elaine talk about positive press releases and promised to look for her e-mail with a couple draft statements that could be released to some friendly tastemakers. I thanked her and promised her a dinner when this all cleared up.

I hung up and looked down, realizing I'd blunted every corner on Sevarin's business card. This was ridiculous. Dead bodies in the Village were none of my business—as long as it didn't hit Chet any harder. Even assuming that what Sevarin said about other deaths was true, the Paranormal Squadron officers were the professionals, and they would do their job. My job was to get Nightlife open again.

My eyes slid sideways to my phone. The story had probably already gone away. This was New York City. One dead body wasn't going to take up valuable mediascape for a whole cycle. My personal drama was no more than a footnote to one of the eight million stories in the naked city.

I knew this to be true. I did not have to look.

My phone lay there, gleaming black against the worn green upholstery. Waiting for me. It knew the truth and was just waiting for me to ask.

My fingers were so cold it took me a couple tries to get the screen to light up. I thumbed the FlashNews app.

And between all the Joshua Blake retrospectives and videos of the latest denials from our latest governor, I saw the new headlines wrapped around Dylan Maddox spread out in my foyer with a fresh vegetable garnish. A dozen discussion boards and op-blogs had sprung up overnight, filled with creative insults for my little brother, and for me because I'd "harbored" him. They came complete with calls for boycotts and wails of "What is this city coming to?" As a bonus, there was plenty of speculation that I'd held poor innocent Dylan down while Chet fed on him.

I dropped the phone onto the couch like it had gone rotten and buried my head in my hands. How had this happened? How could there be so much hate spewing out at the place I'd worked so hard to build, and about the brother I'd protected all my life?

Somewhere in the back of my brain reason whispered that it really would go away. This was New York City.

Everything went away eventually. It just needed a little more time.

But the more I thought about Dylan Maddox lying dead in my restaurant, the worse it got. It wasn't just because it had happened in my place, although that was bad, and it wasn't just because the whole mess seemed to be landing hard on Chet, which was worse. It went deeper than that.

These days, chefs talk a lot. They talk about the artistry and passion of food. But in the end, real cooking isn't about art or passion or that fourth star in the *Times* that we all secretly want to see beside our names. It's about the basic, fundamental desire to feed, strengthen and care for other people. Giving the best you have to a guest is a sacred act. If you don't love food on that level, you aren't a true chef; you're just a technician.

Dylan Maddox was dead—pointlessly, needlessly dead—and that offended me deep down, close to where my love of cooking existed. I found I didn't have the strength to just stand back and wait the situation out. I had to find out what had happened, and I had to do something about it.

Severin's card, blunted and bent, lay on the coffee table. There was no way to talk to him until after sunset. Ditto my brother. Little Linus and the Paranormal Squadron, though, would be wide awake and on the case.

Severin had been dismissive about the chance of finding out anything useful from the cops, but when it came to getting information, I had an edge he didn't.

Severin did not make a killer lasagna.

6

There're a couple different stories going around about why the Paranormal Squadron has its own building in the Meatpacking district instead of being housed over at One Police Plaza. The first is that the district was the site of the first publicly identified vampire murder. The second is that the P-Squad likes to keep an eye on who's buying what from the butchers. That might have been true twenty years ago. Since then, the neighborhood's been visited by the hot-trend fairy. Now it has way more hip restaurants—and the Food Network studios—than it does meat distributors.

I emerged from the subway entrance into the pedestrian river, my foil-wrapped lasagna pan balanced on my hip. I eyed the street traffic, thought about jaywalking, decided against it and kept going toward the corner.

As I passed the alley between the Nu Shu Boutique and Wireless Toys, a flash of movement caught my eye and my gaze darted sideways to see Brendan Maddox standing there. Well, he was sort of standing. Actually, he was doubled over, with the knuckles of his right hand pressed against the wall and his face knotted up with anger and pain.

I bit my lip and thought for half a second about how I didn't really know this guy. Then I stepped out of the current to stand next to him.

"Hi."

Brendan glanced up at me and grimaced. "Hi. What are you doing here?"

"Delivering lasagna unlooked-for. You?"

He grimaced again. "Needed a place to beat on a wall."

"How's that working out?"

"Not as well as I hoped."

We both considered this for a moment.

"I'm sorry about your cousin," I said softly. He nodded. His face was twisted up too tight to read easily just then. My attention wandered across the street to the little cluster of uniformed police officers standing in front of the bland, solid concrete block of P-Squad headquarters.

"The cops over there are not happy about this," I remarked.

His gaze followed mine. "No."

We considered this as well. The whole time, Brendan kept his fist pressed against the wall, like he was afraid either the concrete or his knuckles would explode if he moved it. A tiny red smear showed on the beige brick.

"Can I get a look at that?"

"You an expert on stupidity injuries?"

I shrugged. "I've bandaged a lot of hands."

"I guess you would have." Brendan straightened up, cradling his abused appendage. I braced the lasagna pan against my hip again, turned his hand over and prodded around the bloody skin with my thumb. He winced but held still. Good sign. A lot of big guys have never actually had to take a real punch and as a result are total babies about pain.

"You're going to have a hell of a bruise." I let go before I could start liking the feeling of holding that strong hand too much. "But all the bones are still in the right places. Get it cleaned up and on ice and it'll be fine."

"Thanks." Brendan flexed his hand gingerly.

It was one of those strange moments when you're aware that there are crowds of people nearby, but you are ignoring them and they are ignoring you, so you might as well be alone. Brendan Maddox was strained and tired, tall, broad-shouldered and extremely good-looking with his black hair and his too-blue-to-be-true eyes. I don't claim what came next was a sensible reaction, especially under the circumstances, only that it was mine and it was accompanied by wishes that I'd taken the time to put on makeup, or a sexier blouse. But surely the fact that I brought food and was useful in minor emergencies counted for something.

"Are you hungry?"

Brendan tilted his head at my lasagna pan. "And here I thought that might be a bribe for a cop."

"It's comfort food. And you look like you're having a bad day."

This earned me a rueful flicker of a smile. "Yeah. Yeah, I am." It seemed to me that he was about to say something else complimentary, or at least pleasant, but a voice I didn't want to recognize cut him off.

"Chef Caine?"

We both turned to see Little Linus forge through pedestrian traffic.

"Detective O'Grady." A whole string of thoughts dropped into place in my brain, resulting in complete nonsurprise. Of course someone at the *police station* had noticed a guy punching walls across the street. And pretty much the only reason Brendan Maddox would be punching walls on this block was that he'd just had a bad time with the P-Squad. So, of course, someone would have let the detective who had given him that bad time know what was going on, if he hadn't seen it for himself.

"Everything all right here?" inquired the cop.

Brendan flexed his wounded hand, once, twice. "Fine."

O'Grady nodded, as if acknowledging a point, and turned to me instead. "Good to see you, Chef Caine. I was going to have you set up an appointment to do some follow-up with us, but since you're here, maybe you've got a few minutes?"

"Just a couple things to go over?" I suggested.

"Paperwork details mostly, so we can get you your place back."

Well, he certainly knew how to get a girl to say yes. It did, however, leave me in the strange position of not quite knowing what to do with my lasagna. I'd originally brought it for Officer Randolph, but Randolph didn't know that, and I'd just offered it to Brendan. Brendan and I, however, weren't in the kind of relationship where I was comfortable with public displays of pasta.

And in case you've never experienced it for yourself, let me tell you, having a cop staring at you puts a considerable restriction on what you're ready to say to the cute guy whose cousin turned up dead in your restaurant.

So, I looked "sorry" at Brendan and he looked "understand" back.

I hefted my lasagna. "Whatever I can do to help."

Once we got past the cop-filled foyer where I had to pin a bright blue visitor's badge to my shirt, and up the elevator that opened only after the detective swiped a card and laid down a fingerprint, the home of the Paranormal Squad looked a lot like any other office. Well, except for the large number of people walking around with holstered weaponry. The padded blue cubicle walls were a little frayed around the edges. Desk chairs squeaked as the cubicle denizens shuttled between shelves, file cabinets and flat-screen computer monitors. Then I noticed the camera clusters tucked into the ceiling corners and the fact that most of the thresholds had a kind of extra frame grafted onto them that made every doorway look like an airport scanner.

But whatever it was they were looking for, it apparently did not involve basil and garlic. Nothing beeped, flashed or blared as O'Grady led me and my lasagna into a spartan conference room where a whole set of manila folders lay in neat lines on the scarred tabletop.

I sat and put both pan and purse on the chair next to mine. O'Grady leaned across the threshold to say something to a woman going past and then locked the door.

I tried not to be nervous. I did not succeed.

The detective ran one hand over his scalp and looked at the folders. Without saying a word to me, he began piling them up. I tried not to squirm from impatience. I did not succeed in this either.

When O'Grady had all the folders but one stacked and squared off, he sat down.

He opened that last folder. "Now, Ms. Caine, you'll be glad to know that we do not at this time think it's likely that your brother killed Dylan Maddox."

"You don't?" The words jumped out. Of course I knew Chet had nothing to do with this. The relief I felt just then was only because I was so glad the police knew it too.

O'Grady politely pretended not to have heard me. "However, we are left with the question of who thought Nightlife would make a good place to dispose of Mr. Maddox's remains." He riffled through the papers and pulled out a stack of photographs, which he laid out in front of me. "Do you know any of these people?"

Six strangers, four men and two women, stared back at me, each of them thoroughly pissed off at having to face a camera lens. I shook my head.

"And Dylan Maddox had never been in your restaurant before?"

"Usually I don't see the customers. Robert Kemp, our maître d', would know more, or the dining room captain, Suchai Lui."

"We've talked to them, and neither one remembers ever seeing him. Now, about your people . . ." My shoulders stiffened and O'Grady sighed. "Nobody here cares about their immigration status, okay?"

"Okay."

What followed was long, but straightforward. How long had I known Suchai? Four years. He came with me from L'Aquataine when we opened Nightlife. Did I know that Nina, our weekend hostess, was being treated for recurrent possession? Yes. She saw her exorcist twice a week and wore her crucifix under her blouse so as not to disturb the customers. Had Pam Maddox ever been in Nightlife before? Sorry. I couldn't say. What about the vampire she was with? I was really sorry, Detective, but I spend my nights in the kitchen. Did we employ a man named Taylor Watts as a bartender? Not anymore. Fired him a few weeks ago because he couldn't keep his hands to himself and the high-priced liquor was vanishing with suspicious speed. While he was with us did I ever hear him mention an Ilona St. Claire? No, but he worked the front of the house. For the day-to-day business, that was Suchai's territory.

"And your brother's?" the detective prompted.

Yes, and my brother's.

O'Grady frowned at the papers and photographs as if to let them know they did not meet expectations. Then he swept them all into a pile, put the pile in the folder, put the folder on the stack.

"Last question, Ms. Caine," he said. "What did Anatole Sevarin want last night?"

I clenched my teeth just in time to keep completely use-less exclamations from leaping out. Why would I think the police *weren't* watching me?

"He wanted to know if I'd heard anything from you about Dylan Maddox."

"And you told him . . . ?"

"That you hadn't said word one to me." I tilted my head at him. "I don't suppose you'd consider telling me now?"

"Sorry."

"I'd settle for finding out when we can get back into Nightlife."

"We're working on that, Ms. Caine," he said with an atti-tude that would have made a brick wall seem like Kleenex by comparison. "You'll be our first call."

I don't like to plead. For one thing, I'm not very good at it. So I used the only weapon I had at hand. I picked up the lasagna pan and slid it across the table. "Detective O'Grady, I've got a walk-in with a couple thousand dol-lars' worth of fresh food going to rot. I'm not asking you to let us reopen. Just let me get some of my people into the kitchen to find out what we can salvage."

O'Grady ran one blunt fingertip across the edge of the lasagna pan, as if he could ascertain the quality of the sauce and cheese underneath by the crinkle of the foil. "I'll see what I can do." His voice was studiously neutral, but his spaniel eyes softened for the first time that day.

Never, ever underestimate the power of the killer la-sagna.

"Detective . . ." I pushed the lasagna just a little closer. "Was . . . was Dylan Maddox bitten? I mean, we had a lot of nightblood guests when he stormed in, and that was a really nasty fire he tried to start. . . ." I would probably go to some kind of chef's purgatory for pointing a finger at my guests, but I did it anyway.

Lasagna or no, Little Linus took his time deciding to

answer me. "No," he said. "It wasn't a real bite. Our guys think whoever did it might actually have used a syringe."

Can you say creepy? I sure could.

"Which leaves us with the questions of where'd he die and where'd the blood go?"

"And why did somebody go through the trouble of trying to make it look like vampires?"

"That one's on the list too, believe me." O'Grady got to his feet. "Thank you for your cooperation, Chef Caine. I'll be calling you as soon as I have something for you."

I wanted to try to ask more questions, but one look at the detective's bland face and I knew my lasagna had taken me just as far as we were going to go. So I also stood, and let him walk to the door.

But at least I had two pieces of new information. The first was that Dylan Maddox hadn't actually been killed at Nightlife. That was something, I guess. The second was that this was not a spur-of-the-moment act. I know enough about carcasses to understand you couldn't exsanguinate somebody on impulse. Which meant at least one person had planned his murder, which meant it could very well be one of a set.

This understanding didn't make me feel better, because a murder with a plan and an infrastructure behind it is not an idea that puts you in your happy place.

It also meant O'Grady and I now shared a couple important questions.

One: If a vampire didn't drain Dylan Maddox, where the hell *did* all that blood go?

Two: If this wasn't the first murder, could we count on it being the last?

7

When Detective O'Grady finally let me go, it was five thirty. Hunger and exhaustion robbed me of the ability to consider anything beyond an immediate need for food and caffeine. La Petite Abeille, a little Belgian place where they served big buckets of fries and mussels along with very good, very strong coffee, was only a few blocks away.

Etienne clasped my hand as I walked in the door, asked the bare minimum of questions about how Chet and I were doing, and got me a table in the back corner.

The phone rang the second he dropped the menu off. I checked the number and read BRENDAN MADDOX. Had I given him my number? I would have remembered giving him my number, wouldn't I?

Not even Trish could get on my case for taking this one.

"Hello, Mr. Maddox."

"Hello, Chef Caine."

"How's your hand?"

"Sore. Bruised. A little embarrassed, but otherwise all right."

I thought about O'Grady's neat lines of folders and

photographs and the strain of sitting through his long silences. "At least it was only a wall you punched."

"That's what I keep telling myself." Brendan paused. "I'd like to talk to you, if you're free?"

I thought about all the things I had to do before I could crawl into bed. I thought about how nice it would be to share a meal with a good-looking guy with a dry sense of humor and pretty blue eyes.

Then I thought about how his grandfather Lloyd wanted to make my brother illegal, if not permanently dead.

I told him where I was, and he said he'd find it. We hung up and I drank a whole cup of Euro-strong black coffee wondering if I'd finally lost my mind.

I also made the mistake of sorting through my voice and text messages. Unlike yesterday, I recognized most of the numbers. That was because they were coming from my employees, all of whom had one question.

When are we opening again?

"Hi."

I started so violently I almost dropped my phone. Brendan was standing by my table, and I hadn't even seen him come in.

"Hi." I switched my phone off and shoved it into my purse. "Please, sit down."

He did so, taking off his hat as he sat.

"You ditched the lasagna," he remarked.

"Turns out you were right. It was a bribe after all."

"Did it work?"

"I don't know yet. I hope so. If we don't open up in the next couple days, our people are all going to bail on us."

"That fast?"

I grimaced, thinking about all the still-unanswered texts in my phone. "It's a tough business, and most of us

live paycheck to paycheck. Restaurants come and go pretty
fast, and when you've got kids, and maybe family back
home depending on you, you lose your tolerance for extra
risk. I mean, if your boss called up and told you 'it' was all
going to clear up in a couple days, would you believe him?"

"I am my boss, but I get it."

Etienne showed up just then to take our orders. Brendan's restaurant French was solid, and he didn't shrink
from mussels, fries with mayonnaise, or double stout beer.

"So, aside from yourself what are you the boss of?" I
asked once Etienne left.

"I'm a paranormal security consultant."

"Is that security for paranormals, from paranormals or
by paranormals?"

The corner of his mouth quirked up. "Depends who's
asking and what they're paying."

Silence stretched out longer than I meant it to, but con-
flicting conversational imperatives circled each other in
my brain. Brendan seemed to have the same problem, and
we both sat there, elbows on the blue-and-white-checked
tablecloth, sipping our beverages and sneaking glances at
each other, trying to see if the other one was going to get
something out first.

"Look . . ."

"I was just . . ."

And then, of course, Brendan's phone rang. He pulled it
out and checked the number. "Sorry. I've got to take
this. . . ." He scooted himself around sideways in the chair
so he faced the wall and plugged his free ear with his thumb.
"Hello, Aunt Robin. . . . Yes, I did. . . . Yes, of course they
had to come interview the family. I told you that would happen. No. No, please. More of us coming down here will just
complicate . . . *No.* I'm taking care of it."

There are times when you're confronted with the other
side of the story. I'd been so frightened about Chet, and so

worried about Nightlife and the existential insult that was the murder of another human being, the fact that this was Brendan's family that had been violated had . . . not slipped my mind exactly, but it had never felt as important as all the other things being laid on the line.

The urge to drown yourself in coffee can be very strong some days.

"I was just down there today," Brendan was saying. "Tell Uncle Mike we're doing everything we can. No, I promise, whatever happened, it wasn't vampires. . . . Yes, I am positive."

You are? That made the security consultant, the cop and the vampire who were sure Chet had nothing to do with this disaster.

But was that the same thing as being sure this disaster had nothing to do with Chet? I suddenly found myself wondering just where he'd been on Saturday.

". . . just have Grandfather call me if he wants to talk . . . All right . . . I'll call back in a couple hours. I promise."

Brendan listened a while longer and then said something softly, but a crowd of suits and cell phones poured into the narrow little dining room just then, and their noise covered his last words.

"Sorry," he said as he put the phone away.

"That's okay." I wanted to say something sympathetic, but nothing came except regret for my slow brain. Brendan looked tired. If there was one thing that could wear you down, it was family infighting, even when there wasn't a murder involved. "Do you need to go?"

"Not yet."

Silence threatened, but before it could move in for the kill, our food arrived, wreathing our table in steam and the scents of garlic, white wine and the ocean. Mussels are a food you get involved with. You have to go in after the little nuggets of sea-born goodness, but it is so worth it if they're cooked right, and these were. There was plenty of crispy baguette to sop up the salty broth, and of course a range of sauces for dipping the crispy fries— rich mustard, spicy curry, and their bacon mayonnaise, which I kept trying, and failing, to replicate.

Brendan and I spent the next half hour cradled in the uncomplicated glow that comes with sharing warmth and good food. We talked shellfish, sauces, imported beer, places we liked to eat, places we never wanted to go again. This is part of the magic of food. There's no problem it can't smooth over, at least for a while. We talked about eating in New York, in Chicago and Kansas City. Brendan had been to Morocco and Tokyo. I told stories from my summer *stage*—apprenticeship—in Hong Kong.

He was watching me. It was subtle, but it was there. When you work with a lot of guys, you get sensitive to the weight and quality of the gaze. Is it a threat or a challenge? Friendly interest, romantic interest or just stupid lust? If it is interest, is it about who you are, or just about the boobs?

And believe me, guys, the first thing we notice is *where* you're looking. And no, you are not fooling any of us. Ever.

Brendan looked at my hair and at my eyes. He smiled at my smile, and, yes, he looked at my cleavage, what there was showing, but more than that, he looked at my hands— my scarred hands with their short, blunt, unpolished nails. When Brendan Maddox looked at my hands, the premature lines at the corners of his eyes and mouth softened, just a little.

My pulse fluttered at the base of my throat.

But reality had parked itself next to our table, and it wasn't going away.

"So." I dabbed at my broth with a piece of bread so I could plausibly avoid looking at Brendan. "You have a big family?"

He, of course, recognized the lame opening for what it

was, but he also went along with it. "Pretty big, yeah. You?"

"Just my parents and Chet."

"Where're your parents?"

"Arizona." Mom hated the place. Flat and hot and a ticky-tacky stucco house with a ten-by-fifteen patch of grass out front that looked like Astroturf from all the water and fertilizer Dad poured into it.

"Are you from Arizona?" Brendan was asking.

"No. Buffalo. They moved after . . . after Dad retired."

"And after Chet turned?"

The calm question caught me off guard, but I was grateful he asked it. I don't like dancing around subjects. It's something else on the long list of things I've never been good at. Like talking about my dad's refusal to acknowledge Chet's existence, or my reactions to Dad's refusals.

"Yeah. Dad couldn't—or wouldn't—handle it."

"It happens," Brendan said, politely relieving me of having to answer. "When a relative becomes nightblood, some people head for the sunniest spot they can find."

"You deal with that a lot?" I chewed bread and swallowed. My sense of taste seemed disturbingly dull just then.

"Despite all the support groups and self-help books, some people just can't cope, and they want their homes turned into a kind of magical Fort Knox. That or . . ." He stopped and shook his head.

Reality waited. Brendan had invited it over. Now it was my turn. "Your grandfather's got quite the reputation."

Brendan swirled the dregs of beer and foam in his tall glass. "Oh, believe me, I know."

"He thinks a lot of people should be put back in the ground."

"Yeah."

"What do you think?"

Brendan tipped his glass left, then right. He swallowed what was left in the bottom, set it down, and scooted it a little to the right, then back to the left. I tore apart another slice of bread and told myself to just be patient already.

"I think the world's changed a whole lot since my grandfather could name his price for making paranormals go away," he said. "Whether I agree with the changes or not, we're going to cause a hell of a lot more trouble trying to put things back the way he says they used to be than we will trying to figure out how to make the best of what they are. I think some paranormals are monsters. I think some humans are monsters. If you want to know what I think of your brother, I don't know because I don't know him."

"That's honest, anyway. Thanks."

Brendan touched his forehead in mock salute.

We were silent a bit longer, but this silence had a different quality. It wasn't companionable exactly, but it was an acknowledgment that a level of comfort, or at least comprehension, had been reached.

I plucked another fry out of the basket and stabbed it into the bacon mayo. "Should I be scared?" The images I'd seen on FlashNews of the white-haired, powerfully built man yelling at the whole U.S. House of Representatives felt far too close for comfort.

"Of us? Not yet." Brendan scooted his glass to the right again and to my credit I did not smack his hand, or hold it. Truth was, I wasn't sure which would feel better right then. "Grandfather's busy putting out home fires right now. Not everybody in the clan approves of his turning Dylan's murder into political points, starting with Dylan's parents. With any luck, O'Grady will have this figured out by the time he's got all of the family dealt with."

"Sevarin says they've found other bodies."

"Sevarin told you this?"

"O'Grady told me about what the bite marks on Dylan were, but, yeah, Sevarin told me there have been other deaths."

If he had asked how and why I'd been talking with Sevarin, I would have told him, but he didn't. I was beginning to understand that Brendan Maddox had a very good sense of other people's limits. Whether that came from having a warlock family or a career in security, I couldn't say yet, but I was grateful for it. The question he did ask was tricky enough.

"Do you believe Sevarin?"

"I don't know if I believe him or not. He thought I might have Pam's phone number in my reservations computer, and he might have just been trying to get it out of me." I paused. "What's her story? Pam's, I mean?"

"I barely know. When I left for college, she was still a three-foot-tall brat in pigtails, tormenting little Dylan and driving my aunt Robin out of her mind. Then a few months ago, I get a frantic phone call. Pam went on her wander year and vanished."

"Wander year?"

He nodded. "If you want to become a full warlock, you have to take an oath, to the family and . . . Well . . . it's not a normal promise. It binds you, and your magic. So, everyone takes a year off before they go through the ceremony. They live in the mundane world, maybe go to college or just travel and think about what they really want."

"And Pam really didn't want to get with the program? Did she get booted out?" Warlock families, especially the old ones, were supposed to take their traditions very seriously. People like that tended not to deal well with rebellious youth. Not that I could throw stones, considering my father's attitude toward Chet.

"Maddoxes don't kick people out anymore," said Brendan. "Not for deciding against the oath, anyway. It's awkward at family reunions and you don't get a vote on clan matters, but it's not like people stop mentioning your name or anything. Pam didn't just leave, though. She vanished, and we've been looking for her ever since."

"I'd have thought that as a security consultant . . ."

"You and my whole family." Brendan cut me off with that special bitter tone that comes when you're furious with yourself. "Unfortunately, one of the things we still get taught by the family is how to hide from magicians and normals if we have to. Turns out Pam got really good at it."

People think it's so hard to disappear in the webcam world. But any given Sunday, I could give fifty bucks to the right guy in the right bar and come away with a brand-new credit card and a gently used Social Security number. With that and enough cash for a bus ticket to Chicago or Los Angeles, I'd be gone for good.

There had to be a magical equivalent of that guy and that bar, and Pam Maddox probably had a lot more than fifty bucks in her Gucci handbag.

Brendan glanced at his watch and reached into his back pocket. "Listen, I need to get going. . . ."

"Don't worry about it." I gestured for him to put his wallet away.

He blinked. "I'm not going to leave you with . . ."

"Best part of being a chef in New York." I nodded toward Etienne over Brendan's shoulder, and he waved us both toward the door. "Friends wherever you go."

"Must be nice," Brendan whispered and then stood up before I could make any reply.

Outside, shadows threw an early nighttime over the sidewalk. The chilly wind smelled of exhaust and autumn as it hustled down Fifteenth.

Brendan turned his jacket collar up as he faced me. "I have to ask. Do you have Pam's number?"

I shook my head. "Nightlife's still sealed. Anyway, the number in the system would depend on who made the reservation, and that's handled in the front of the house. Sorry," I added.

"Not your fault." He scanned the street for a minute, like he was looking for a cab. Then he said, "Have I apologized enough for my family yet?"

"Yeah."

"Have I said I'm not sorry I met you?"

"No."

"I'm not sorry I met you."

His words left me with no idea what to do next. Sticking my hand out to shake would just be stupid, and yet I wanted to touch him. I had no right to, and no real reason, beyond the fact that we were both tired, both in over our heads, and both aching not to be alone in the middle of this mess.

"You'll be careful, won't you, Charlotte?" he asked. "This—whatever it turns out to be—it's a long way from over."

"I know."

He looked at my eyes and my hair, and smiled. He'd looked at my hands, all through dinner. He'd looked at my hands as if he liked them.

I reached out and laid my fingertips against the back of his uninjured hand. He turned that hand slowly around, until he was holding mine. We stood there, saying nothing. I could feel his pulse beat in his fingers and my own pounded a counterrhythm.

"Can I call?" he asked.

"Sure." Then something occurred to me. "How'd you get my number in the first place?"

"The Google is strong with this one." He winked and my pulse kicked into overdrive.

"Well, good night," he said.

"Good night," I said, before I realized I was still touching his hand.

Brendan swooped down, nervous like a high school kid, and I turned too fast and too far. His peck caught the spot on my cheek right in front of my earlobe.

He straightened up. I giggled. Giggled! Executive chefs do not giggle. I decided, however, I could forgive him this once.

We locked gazes and came to the mutual realization there was no good way to end this . . . whatever this was.

Whatever it might be.

So, we both took the only out the city allowed.

"Taxi!"

8

Chet's building was a few blocks off Bleecker Street; a neighborhood of bars, jazz clubs, Italian restaurants and guys selling art-glass bongs off tables on the sidewalk. He shared a two-bedroom third-floor walk-up with a buddy he met while going to night school for his restaurant management degree. They furnished it out of thrift shops and Ikea, and it smelled like guys, unless Doug had a special guest over, in which case it smelled like scented candles and guys.

As soon as I'd given the taxi driver the address, I got my phone out and hit Chet's number. His voice mail picked up. I cut the call off and hit REDIAL. And again. And again.

This time, the ring cut out in the middle.

"For cryin' out loud, Charlotte, I just woke up."

"Stay awake. I'm on my way over."

Chet sighed, groggy and exasperated. "Is there any point in telling you it's no big deal?"

"No."

"Didn't think so. See you when you get here."

You better believe it, little brother.

When he opened his apartment door, my brother did not look good. He was pale, his lips were chapped and the skin sagged around his throat and on the back of his hands. I handed him the container of chicken blood I'd picked up at a kosher butcher on the way over.

"Thanks, sis." He peeled back the top and took a healthy swig.

"So." I dropped onto the sofa. "Are you going to tell me about it?"

Chet shrugged. "Nothing to tell."

I leveled my big-sister glare at him. "Try again."

"I'm serious! There was *nothing*!" Chet gestured with both hands, sloshing blood dangerously close to the container's rim. "They wanted to know where I was. I told them. They wanted a fang impression and a mouth swab. I gave it to them. Even that lawyer you had come charging in agreed to that much. They thanked me. I came home. No fire hose, no garlic. Nothing."

"So where'd you go after the cleanup on Saturday?"

Chet swigged some more blood and set the container down on the wobbly end table.

"Where'd you *go*, Chet?"

He opened his mouth and was about to say, "None of your business," but I folded my arms and turned the glare up to eleven. He twisted the gold ring on his left hand. Five years gone, and he still hadn't taken off that damn ring.

"I went to Post Mortem," he said.

"Oh, for Pete's sake, Chet!"

"*What?* I was starving, and I needed to blow off steam before sunrise."

"Those dives aren't safe!"

"PM's not a dive," he shot back. "It's a licensed club. Dance floor, DJs, *chicken* blood."

"It's a bite-easy."

It is illegal to sell human blood, or to pay someone to be bitten. But there are plenty of people willing to bend the neck for a good-looking vamp, or for one who can make it into a good time. New Yorkers, never ones to miss an opportunity, have created a whole network of more or less legal clubs where the willing can hook up with the hungry, and whether it's supposed to or not, a lot of money changes hands in those places. This means they get raided a lot, or get stings set up in them. Then there are the vigilante types who hope to get a vamp out back and stake them a good one.

"I can take care of myself, Charlotte." This statement would have been more convincing if he hadn't been slurping down the last of the blood I'd brought him. "And you might want to think before you start complaining. If I hadn't gone, I wouldn't have an alibi."

I caught myself right before asking if he needed one. "I'm just worried, and I spent most of the morning with Detective O'Grady."

"Shit." Chet ran his hands through his hair, spiking it up in a way that made him look even younger than he was. Is. Used to be. I hate verb tenses and vampires. "What did he want from you?"

"He quizzed me about the staff. And about whether I knew the vamp who was there with Pam Maddox."

"Yeah, I got that one too." Chet sat on the sofa beside me. He's so light that the springs didn't even creak.

"What'd you say?" I asked.

"Nothing. I hadn't seen him before."

"He was kind of a nebbish." I have a good memory for faces, but all I had left of the vamp was thinning hair, hunched shoulders and a dazed stare as Pam Maddox flashed her pristine neck.

"Yeah, he was, but she wasn't. They were a complete

mismatch." Chet ran his finger around the bottom of the container and sucked the blood. He used to do that to the bottom of his mac-and-cheese bowl. I resisted the urge to swat his finger out of his mouth like Mom used to.

"Did O'Grady ask you about Taylor Watts?"

Chet frowned. "Why'd the cops want to know about Taylor?"

"Maybe he's taken to ripping off more than the booze from his latest employer."

"Maybe." Chet tossed the empty container into the garbage can three feet away. Two points. "Did they ask you about Ilona St. Claire too?"

"I think so. Maybe. Who's she?"

"Vampire. Runs a theater. Kind of Off Broadway."

"Friend of yours?"

"Not a friend, but I know her name from around. Just wondered who else they were interested enough in to ask us both about."

I ran my hands over my face. Something was wrong with all this. I needed to think, but there was no room left in my brain. It was all taken up with being tired and angry and frightened and dangerously close to being attracted to Brendan Maddox, whose well-connected grandfather wanted to revive his vamp-hunting glory days.

Chet wrapped his arm around my shoulders in a little-brother hug. "It'll be okay, C3," he said. "They can't keep us shut down forever."

That wasn't what was in the front of my mind, for a change, but I didn't bother to correct him. Worrying about Nightlife was more comfortable than worrying about my feelings for Brendan or who had done what to Dylan Maddox and those other nameless strangers.

"They don't have to keep us shut down forever; it's just got to be until we can't pay the bills. Have you had a chance . . . ?"

"First thing I did." Chet pulled back and saw my sour look. "Okay, second thing."

"How are we?"

"Depends. Do we want to keep paying people?" That would be a long way from standard practice, but one of the things we'd determined from the beginning was we'd treat the staff of Nightlife above average in terms of pay, benefits and environment in general. That way we'd not only get the best people, we'd keep them.

"We need to pay the ones who stick around." I brought him up to date on the flood of texts I'd read through at La Petite Abeille. Somehow the fact that I'd been having mussels with Brendan failed to come up. There was probably a good reason for that.

Chet plunked himself down in front of a desk made from cinder blocks and an old door to fire up his surprisingly up-to-the-minute laptop. We had an accountant for the quarterly reporting to the IRS and year-end taxes, but for the day-to-day stuff like paying bills and handling payroll, Chet kept the books. After just a few keystrokes, he was flicking through the spreadsheets that were Nightlife's running accounts too fast for me to follow. He opened a fresh page, plugged in the names I gave him and waited while the new column of numbers filled itself in.

"Without any income, if we keep paying everybody, and if we go through the couch for spare change, we've got four days."

My heart plummeted. "And if we don't pay everybody?"

He hit a few more keys. "In that case we've got two weeks, maybe three if we can get the suppliers to give us an extension."

"Shit," I said.

"Yeah," he agreed.

We sat in gloomy silence for a while.

"Chet?"

"Yeah?"

"Did you see the body?"

He puffed out his cheeks. How do you do that when you don't breathe anymore? "They showed it to me. I don't know, maybe I was supposed to be overwhelmed by an attack of guilt or something."

Or start drooling. But I didn't say that. I also didn't point out how he hadn't bothered to tell me he'd been shown the corpse when I'd asked him what happened at the police station. "How did it . . . look to you?" The question had been lingering in the back of my mind since my conversation with Anatole Sevarin. Brendan had said it wasn't vampires, and he should know, but still . . .

"Based on my extensive experience with dead bodies?" Chet was on his feet before I saw him move.

"Christ, Chet." He winced and I winced, but I stood up so he wouldn't get any ideas about looming. I hate it when people try to loom. "I just meant . . . Look, O'Grady said Maddox wasn't bitten, but they don't know what happened to the blood. I was just thinking . . . maybe somebody used a syringe so they wouldn't leave a fang impression." My voice was very close to trembling, because if I'd thought of this, O'Grady had too.

"So, what? I'm supposed to know how to drain a human without leaving evidence? I'm sitting here drinking *chicken* blood. I'm civilized and safe and registered and I did *not* kill the drunken asshole who tried to burn down my *restaurant* and my *sister*!"

We stood there nose to nose, each simmering with anger. There would be no going back from the next words out of my mouth, so I pushed past him and yanked the door open. He was going to say something to my back, I was sure of it. Something about *Midnight Moon* and Joshua Blake. He was going to say that Nightlife was just another of my screwups.

"Are we going to keep paying our people?" he asked.

I paused with my hand on the doorframe. "Yes. If we're going down, we're going down doing the right thing."

I was out the door and on my way down the hall. I did not take the time to apologize. I most especially did not say, "You didn't kill Dylan Maddox, but you know who did, don't you?" I could not even *suspect* that. Not of my little brother. Never. Because if I did, it meant that my screwups were much, much bigger than I feared.

On the sidewalk, light spilled from clubs and restaurants where people ate other chefs' food and had a good time in other people's homes. Music and voices and all the special energy that thrums through the city after sundown filled the air, wrapping close and warm around everybody but me.

I jaywalked across the street, trying not to think about anything beyond heading up to Bleecker to the subway.

The earthy smell of fresh truffles reached me. At the same time, something tickled the back of my neck, like water dripping from an awning.

Or like somebody watching me.

Pale skin flashed in the shadows of the sunken English porch next to me. I froze.

Anatole Sevarin looked up at me from those shadows and smiled.

9

"Good evening, Chef Caine." Severin's teeth gleamed very white in the city's proto-dark. "Would you care to join me?" He gestured around the little rectangle of space that he shared with the trash and recycle bins.

"You're kidding."

"Never in life." He stretched out his hand, as if I might need help down the stairs. He had worn black for the occasion—black slacks, black turtleneck under long black jacket that could almost have been an old-fashioned frock coat. The final touch came in the form of a black fedora pulled down low to mask his red-blond hair.

He looked dangerous, and ridiculously edible, and he invited me to come down there next to him.

I shoved my hands into my jacket pockets. "Sorry. Lurking in doorways with the undead is against the health code."

"You'll miss the show."

The gleam in his green eyes made me hesitate. *I am going to regret this.*

"I'm still uncertain whether it will be tragicomic or a

bedroom farce," Anatole went on. "But it should be interesting in either case."

"You've got to get better seats next time. Just what show are you talking about?"

He nodded toward the front door of my brother's building.

"You're spying on Chet?" I snapped, but Sevarin just shrugged.

"Why should we limit the fun to the family?"

"I wasn't spying!"

"No. You were interrogating. Please." He held out his hand again. When he saw my murderous glare, he rolled his eyes, looking for any patience that might have been dropped in a dark corner. "If it makes you feel better, let us say I am not spying on your brother. I am spying on anyone who might potentially be arriving to tempt him into further ill-considered behaviors, a set of people whom, as his loving sister, you also should be interested in."

Damn vampire logic. This wasn't what I should be spending time on. Detective O'Grady knew what he was doing, and Chet wasn't under suspicion anymore, which meant Nightlife wasn't under suspicion anymore, right? Right. Time to get these weird Agatha Christie impulses under control. I just needed to wait out the bureaucracy and meet with my damage control expert and worry about building my business back up.

"Not tonight. I've got a headache." I turned my back and started walking. Then I had a thought. I didn't want it. I sped up, trying to leave it behind me, but it wouldn't go.

I stopped, swore, turned and walked back. There stood Sevarin, leaning casually against the wall, and—smart-ass vamp that he was—watching me like he'd never looked away.

He touched the brim of his hat. I opened my mouth.

This was my last chance to back out of this bad idea. I didn't take it.

"Do you know an Ilona St. Claire?"

"In fact, I do. However, if you want to find out what I know, you'll have to come down here."

"Now you're just playing games."

"And you're blocking my view."

I bit down on a whole set of anatomically unlikely suggestions about what he could do to himself down there, gave it up and trotted down the steps. Sevarin made a half bow and a mischievous light sparked in his green eyes.

"So, how do you know Ilona St. Claire?"

"All in good time, Chef Caine. If you would just step back here where it is darker—to avoid attracting attention, you understand . . ."

Riiiiight.

I met Sevarin's eyes, turned sideways, sucked, tucked, and slid into the corner without touching the trash bins or him.

He looked surprised. And disappointed. I smiled pleasantly. "You were saying about Ilona St. Claire?"

"May I inquire, Chef Caine," murmured Sevarin. "Simply for my own information, not to pry, what is your interest in Ilona?"

"You like long sentences."

"It's my Russian upbringing. We are a voluble and flamboyant people."

"Come off it. You don't talk like any Russian I know."

"How many eight-hundred-year-old nightblood Russians do you know?"

There he had a point, and it was his turn to smile pleasantly. "You were saying about Ilona?"

"O'Grady asked both me and Chet about her."

"Interesting. Now, I wonder what could she have done to draw the attention of Little Linus and his merry band this time."

"This time?" My eyes were adjusting to the shadows, but Sevarin remained little more than a promise in the dark. There was no way to tell what was going on behind that calm remark.

Instead of answering me, he murmured, "And here comes another question."

Across the street, a man swung himself onto the stairs in front of Chet's building and hit the buzzer. He was tall and filled with that particular arrogance of someone who knows exactly how good-looking he is. His profile showed a chin that could crack granite.

I'd fired that chin three weeks ago.

The buzzer must have sounded, because Taylor Watts pushed Chet's door open and vanished inside.

"What does the bartender from Post Mortem want with your brother?"

"*Wha—!*"

Sevarin pressed two cold fingers against my lips, and I remembered we were on a—for lack of a better term—stakeout. I shut my mouth and did my best to glower at him to indicate he should stop touching me *now*.

"I sense you are disturbed." He grinned, but he did remove his hand.

"That guy—Taylor Watts—he used to work for us." And he had so tried to turn on the cut-rate charm when I'd called him out back to fire his tight little waitress-grabbing butt.

"And now he works for Bertram Shelby. That is terribly interesting."

"But he . . . but . . . why . . . ?" *If Chet's going to Post Mortem regularly, why didn't he tell me Watts is working there?* My nerves were shriveling up, like they'd been left out in the cold for too long. "I'm going to kill him." I muttered.

"Which him?" Sevarin asked.

"Ask me tomorrow. I'll probably have it figured out by then."

My vampire sidekick settled back against the wall, his expression under the sloping hat brim both appraising and skeptical. "I take it you were not aware of Mr. Watts's current place of employment."

"No." This was bad. This was taking me to all the wrong places via all the wrong streets. I could dig up and screw up way too much doing this.

"And perhaps Detective O'Grady neglected to mention it?" Sevarin cocked his head. "Or was it your brother who neglected to mention it?"

Chet might not have known. Watts couldn't have been working there that long. Chet doesn't go to the bite-easy often. Probably he's never been there while Watts was on shift.

"I have a suggestion," Sevarin went on.

"I'll bet." It was more reflex than anything else at that point and Sevarin sighed impatiently.

"It has been a long time since I've had to seduce a woman in such unpleasant surroundings. I promise if you are still interested later, I'd be happy to attend to the business properly."

"No, thanks."

"Why not? I believe we would both very much enjoy it." His voice dropped to a whisper, and the space between us got both smaller and warmer without either one of us moving a muscle. "Or are you afraid, Charlotte Caine?"

I did not ease away from Sevarin. That would have been more of an admission than I was ready to make.

"I'm not sleeping with a dining critic. It would look bad when Nightlife reopens."

"How disappointingly businesslike of you. Well, we shall continue this discussion later." He straightened up, eyeing the street as he tugged thoughtfully on his hat brim. "Now, it is also clear that stealth is not your métier. I propose that you go to Post Mortem and interview the proprietor about his staffing strategies. I will wait here and follow Mr. Watts when he leaves. It is probable he will be going from here to work his shift. If that's the case, I will meet you there. If not, I will call and let you know where he has gone."

"You are not going anywhere near Chet," I told him.

"Not until I know more about what's going on."

It wasn't the assurance I wanted, but it had the virtue of being honest.

"You have my number?"

"I am ancient among my kind." Sevarin's voice dropped into that dangerous vampire rumble. "So ancient, indeed, that I remember how to use a phone book."

Against all the odds, I had to hold back a laugh. "You are ever so slightly insane. Do you know that?"

He smiled and my heart tried to retreat against my spine. "Ever so slightly. Do we have an agreement?"

I wanted to say something about just for this and just for the moment, but considering the directions my little comments had ended up taking us, I decided to shut my mouth. Besides, he had his eyebrows quirked in a way that in the living and the dead indicates a quip in the chamber, ready to fire.

"We have an agreement," I said.

"Then I suggest you leave before you are seen. Until later, Chef Caine."

"Yeah."

It had been years since I'd been this uncertain about what I was doing, much less what I was feeling. But I walked out of that stairwell and down Bleecker without looking back. Not even once.

Really.

PM was already swinging when I pushed open the dungeonesque door. A hyped-up hip-hop tango instantly overwhelmed the traffic noises. Out-of-towners in heavy goth rig-out shook whatever they had on a dance floor lit primarily by the jumbo video screens flashing video clips from *Midnight Moon*. I averted my eyes to scan the rest of the room.

Licensed vamp bars—sorry, nightblood clubs—come in two flavors: modern goth and traditional goth. Both go heavy on the crimson velvet. There's plenty of lace, leather and mascara on the staff and cheap red wine in the glasses. The difference is that one plays thrash metal and has a lighted dance floor and the other goes in for *Carmina Burana* and chaise longues. Here, however, is the dirty little secret: most New York vamp bars are not run by vampires. They are run by humans, and mostly for the tourist trade. Some of them even pay nightbloods to put in an appearance. As far as I knew, the owners of Post Mortem didn't stoop that low, but they did lean very heavily on the atmosphere.

A waifish, hollow-cheeked young woman behind the polished black bar deftly handled both cocktail shakers and cow-eyed boys in black who lined up for legal absinthe and dirty martinis. Either I'd beaten Taylor here, or he was on his way somewhere else. I thought about getting a seat at the bar, but decided against it. If at all possible, I wanted to see Taylor before he saw me. I don't know for sure what good I thought this would do me, but the maneuver seemed to fit the mess I found myself in.

I took a deep breath and assumed my "I know what I'm

doing" walk as I approached the coffin-shaped podium that served as the hostess station. The wall behind was covered with black and red T-shirts proclaiming I DID IT IN THE PM and priced at $45.

Jesus, Chet, I thought you had better taste.

"Hi!" The hostess's perky level was very much at odds with her predictably funereal color scheme of dyed-black hair, black eyeliner on full blast and black lace dress revealing a lot of very white cleavage. "Welcome to Post Mortem. How many in your party?"

"Just one. And could you please tell Mr. Shelby that Charlotte Caine would like to see him when he's got a minute?" I handed over my card.

"Sure thing, Miss Caine. If you just wanna follow me?"

Hostess Perky Goth led me to a table near the kitchen. Normally this is not a good seat, but as you might expect, it's one I prefer, because it's perfect for spying on what comes out of the kitchen.

I wasn't expecting much in that department. This was a place for drinks, dancing and hookups. The food would be an afterthought. This did not stop me from opening the menu Perky Goth left behind.

When I did, my jaw dropped.

There was a pumpkin soup with a foam of veal "raw sauce." There was a beef carpaccio with scallions and orange zest. The recommended drink to go with it was a pitcher of the house special sangria.

It was the menu for Nightlife—*my* menu all laid out in near-illegible faux-medieval lettering surrounded by a black lace frame.

At that moment I actually saw red.

Chefs steal from one another. You can't trademark your blue cheese dressing, so if it's caught fire you can be sure your "friendly" competition is going to try to figure out how to imitate it, or better it if they can.

But the whole of a menu—that's a chef's signature. A good one takes months to assemble, test and perfect. I put everything I had into designing the dishes for Nightlife. And here they were, reduced to second-rate noshes made with ingredients that probably came frozen from some warehouse, if they hadn't just fallen off the back of the truck.

But what stabbed deep and twisted was that any one of the posers on the dance floor might be planning on going to Nightlife (when it reopened). They'd take one look at our menu and say, "Hey, this is just like that Post Mortem place." Then they'd spread the word about it, and it'd be out there for the world to see. Nightlife, my life, my haven and hard work was just like this made-over tourist dive.

This had to be Taylor Watts's revenge for being fired. If I hadn't been ready to murder him before, I was ready now.

"Charlotte Caine. Great to finally meet you."

I folded the menu shut, placed it carefully down on the table and looked up at Bert Shelby.

Like most of his customers, Shelby was trying way too hard to look the part. He had streaked his hair black and white in a style that didn't look good on the twentysome-things, let alone the headed-for-fortysomething in front of me. He had a long face, and a sharply sloped, pointy nose. The Adam's apple protruding from his long neck bobbed up and down behind the brick red turtleneck like it was trying to come up for air. The hand he held out was long and delicate, with carefully manicured, black-painted fingernails.

"Thanks for agreeing to see me." I got the kind of flabby handshake that makes you think the worst of the person, even if you didn't before. Shelby was checking me out. Whether this was because he was mistakenly interested in me or because he wanted to see if I was going to stuff that tacky stolen menu down his throat, I wasn't sure.

"Sure thing." Shelby sat down. "I heard about your . . ." He waved vaguely toward the door, presumably to indicate the crime scene. "How's that going?"

I shrugged. "Slow. Cops and bureaucracy."

"Sucks." He shook his head. "Have they told you when they'll let you open again?"

"Soon, hopefully. Speaking of Nightlife . . ."

"Yes?" The Adam's apple bobbed a couple extra times.

"I understand you're employing our old bartender."

"Taylor Watts? Yeah. Big favorite with the girls."

"I'll bet."

"We keep him on special for Ladies' Night. Pretty much doubled our take on Thursdays. I was really surprised when Chet said he was out of work—"

The music from the dance floor throbbed painfully hard against my skull for a moment. "*Chet* said?"

"Yeah."

"*Chet* asked you to hire him?"

"No." Shelby's brow furrowed, like he was just beginning to suspect I did not feel friendly. "He just said he was on the lookout for a job for a friend."

"Was this before or after he caught you stealing our menu?"

"St—" The Adam's apple went still and Bert's eyes narrowed. "You think I *stole* your menu?"

"All our house dishes laid out in black and red." I pushed the menu across the table toward him. "Are you going to say it's just a coincidence?"

"I didn't *steal* anything."

"You want me to believe you bought your info off my ex-employee in good faith?"

Bert drummed his fingers on the table, a little flurry of

clicking sounds under the endless pulse of the music. "Well, one of us has definitely got the wrong idea." He pushed his chair back and stood up, menu clutched in his long hand. "You're going to have to excuse me. I've got to get back to work."

"I need to talk to Watts."

"You talk to him all you want. He'll be in for his shift at eleven." Bert shook his head. "I'd heard you were smart." And he walked away.

I sat there at my little empty table near the kitchen. The odors of sweat, blood and cinnamon wafted past on harsh blasts from the air conditioner. The music beat against my ears and squeezed my head.

I'd heard you were smart, Bert had said. I was smart, but I didn't feel that way now. I felt stupid and cheated. Because it was clear Bert hadn't bought my menu from Taylor Watts.

Chet had gotten Watts a job here. Chet was using this place as his alibi for the night of Dylan Maddox's murder. Chet had sold this thrift-store goth-man my menu. Yes, theoretically, anybody could have walked into Nightlife and copied the list of dishes. But if that's what happened, Chet would have said something when he saw it here. He would have raised the roof, or told me so I could do it. He didn't. He kept quiet and gave me no reason to come in here.

All around me, people talked and laughed and swilled bad sangria and watched the dancers. Movement caught my eye. A slim, pale female vampire with a wealth of red hair trolled the edges of the floor under extreme close-ups of Joshua Blake's dark eyes, and I froze.

It can't be. . . .

But the vampire turned and her cold, dry gaze brushed across me. She was a stranger. All the air whooshed out of my lungs. I had to get away from here. Now. I needed air. I lurched toward the side exit and stumbled out into the alley.

Chet was lying. My little brother was lying and covering up and giving away my work, our work. I staggered ahead for about a yard before I fell against the wall and caught myself on my hands. What the hell? After everything we'd done together and everything I'd tried to do for him, what the *hell*? I stood there, bent over, fingers trying to dig into brick, stomach heaving.

It occurred to me this was pretty much the position I'd found Brendan Maddox in this afternoon. What had driven him into the shadows trying to control his sick anger? Who had let him down this far?

"Well, well. What's all this, then?"

I whirled around. A vampire boy, still in his teens but with eyes that were way too old for his gangling frame, grinned at me, letting both fangs shine in the fluorescent light. His skin sagged loose against his delicate bones, meaning he hadn't fed yet tonight.

He wasn't alone. A girl who looked about the same age glided in from the mouth of the alley. I recognized her as the vamp I'd seen near the dance floor. Her red hair hung in ringlets around the shoulders of a white Regency dress. A black velvet band circled her throat, and tattoos circled that. The effect was impressive, and would have been even if I hadn't been able to tell she was hungry too.

"No," I said. "I'm not asking."

"Just relax, honey," said the girl, also giving me the full-fang-effect grin. "I can make it good. You'll like it, I promise."

The boy leaned against the club door and folded his arms.

"No," I said again. *I'm an idiot. A total effing idiot.* My hands were empty. I didn't even have a crucifix, let alone any silver or sharpened wood.

The boy vamp snapped his fangs at me and the girl sauntered forward. They were trying to drive me down the alleyway, away from the street, to someplace nice, private and very dark. Maybe there was even a convenient dead end to back me up against.

So I did the only thing I could think of.

I screamed and charged straight at the girl. My shoulder hit her dead center. Even if she'd been alive, I would have outweighed her by twenty pounds. She went down, and I kept running.

Arms grabbed me and threw me onto the pavement. Concrete pummeled my head and arms as I rolled. My breath was gone, and I saw stars and streaks of light. Before the world stopped spinning, hands had hold of both my arms and had hauled me upright—and I was staring into Vamp Boy's grinning face.

"You should not have done that." He slurred the words around his gleaming fangs. "You've made Angeletta mad." He spun me around to face the girl. Her white dress was streaked with grime now. Her pretty blue eyes glared from deep in their sockets, and all the skin was drawn tight against her bones. She looked like starvation itself, and she was coming toward me.

It was a lousy time to discover I had no survival instinct. "Angeletta? You've got to be kidding me. 'Fess up. You're a Suzy. Or a Jane."

Her bony hand gripped my jaw, forcing my mouth closed. She leaned in close so I couldn't see anything except her hungry eyes. "I am your doom, Charlotte Caine."

My heart banged against my ribs and I squirmed, trying to get free of even one of the vampires. Their flesh was too soft, their eyes too dry, and they were too strong. They laughed at me, and they stank like meat left to rot.

Vamp Boy forced my head back until I was looking up at the dark streak of sky between the buildings. I was going to die, die stupid in an alley. . . .

"Let her go."

Vamp Boy jerked around, taking me with him. A man emerged from the back of the alley. I opened my mouth, expecting to shout for help from Sevarin.

Except it wasn't Sevarin. It was Brendan Maddox.

10

⸻🍴

"Let her go, nightblood."

This was not the amiable man in business casual I had seen before. Here and now, Brendan Maddox radiated danger and the ability to do immediate and painful damage. He stalked forward, hands open at his sides. An electric tingle crawled across my skin, making the hairs on my arms stand on end.

"You don't frighten me, warlock." Vamp Boy tightened his grip on my forehead and chest. I couldn't move. I couldn't breathe.

"Really?" Brendan's lips curled into a tight smile. "I'll have to try harder."

I didn't see what happened. Blinding light flooded the alley, pouring warmth across my skin. Vamp Boy screamed. The iron grip on my head and shoulders vanished. I catapulted forward and slammed against the wall. It hurt like hell, but at least now I could breathe and stand and turn around in the suddenly floodlit alley.

A fiery golden ball floated above our heads, like a miniature sun. I smelled cooking meat, and I realized it *was* a miniature sun.

Impressive.

Whatever else Angeletta was, she was not a coward, because she leapt straight for Brendan. Now that I could see, I snatched up the wooden packing crate lying beside the club door and bashed it over her head. She screamed, staggering back under Brendan's sun. Something sizzled. I smelled pork and my stomach turned over yet again.

But that light did not come without effort. Brendan had one hand in the air, his face twisted in concentration and pouring sweat. Vamp Boy took a swing at him, connected with his gut. Brendan gaped soundlessly and the light went out.

"Oh, this is going to taste soooo gooood. . . ."

Angeletta laughed and I hit her again. This time she went down to her knees. I charged past her, brandishing what was left of my crate. Vamp Boy had grabbed Brendan by the hair and was dropping in for the bite. I screamed. Vamp Boy laughed and someone hollered something I didn't understand.

Brendan shot a hand out. Vamp Boy flew backward and hit the wall. About six feet off the ground. Right over a poster for *Midnight Moon*. Now it was Vamp Boy's turn to scream. He slid down the bricks and the instant he hit the pavement Brendan was on top of him. Metal flashed in the warlock's hand and he pressed the knife to Vamp Boy's throat.

Angeletta's scream joined the chorus. I teetered, clutching the last scrap of my rapidly disintegrating crate.

Turned out I didn't need it. Anatole Sevarin held Angeletta by the collar buttons, at arm's length, about six inches from the ground. She kicked furiously, which might have done some good if she hadn't lost both her stiletto pumps. As it was, she couldn't do anything but pummel Sevarin's shins mercilessly with her bare heels.

Brendan seemed to take this in stride, but that might

have been because he was a little preoccupied with kneeling on the Vamp Boy's back and pressing his pretty, undead face against the concrete.

"Do I frighten you now, nightblood?" Brendan's voice trembled with effort and anger.

"Mrmph!"

"I'm sorry. I didn't hear that." Brendan lifted Vamp Boy's head an inch off the concrete and his silver blade dug deeper into the vampire's sagging flesh.

"Yes," croaked Vamp Boy. "Yes, you frighten me."

"Very good." Brendan glanced at Sevarin, who shrugged. "Now, unless you want this to be your last night on earth, take Suzy and get out of here."

Sevarin unceremoniously dropped Angeletta. She hit the ground, staggered and snarled at him. In response, Sevarin opened his arms, and his mouth. For the first time I saw his bared fangs, long, slim and sharp as a cobra's. But that wasn't so bad. What was bad was the menace that rolled off him like a cloud. This was Death in a dark alley—and he was ready to take on all comers.

Brendan barely got out of the way in time as the vamplette duo fled down the alley. As soon as they did, the warlock slumped back against the wall. The streetlight made him look nearly as pale as a vampire, and he pressed the heel of his hand against his side as he struggled to catch his breath.

And he'd just saved my life. I dropped the crate scrap and wiped my sweating, splintery hands on my pants.

"What are you doing here?"

Probably I didn't communicate as much gratitude as I felt right then, because he rolled his eyes in something that looked a lot like exasperation. "I was following you."

"Why?"

"So I could find out why you were going from hanging out with Anatole Sevarin to walking into a bite-easy."

"I—" I meant to say it was none of his business, but under the circumstances it kind of was. Before I could think of a new sentence to go after that initial syllable, the wail of sirens cut me off.

"Cops!"

The shout came from the roof maybe, or farther down the alley. It was impossible to tell. A second later, though, a flash of red and blue light out front was met by the sound of running feet around back.

"It is time to leave," announced Sevarin to Brendan and me.

"I'm not running. I—"

I didn't get any further. Sevarin grabbed me by the waist and shoulders, tossed me across his back in a fireman's carry, and took off running, right behind Brendan Maddox.

The night had definitely gotten away from me.

So as it turns out, being thrown over a pair of lean masculine shoulders and carried away bodily is nowhere near as sexy as one imagines.

I couldn't see where we were going. Walls rose up close and the air stank of garbage and grease. I felt Sevarin racing around corners and I hung on tight because, as much as I hate to admit it, I didn't know what else to do.

At last we emerged onto the open street. No sirens followed us. The traffic and a few pedestrians passed by with their usual indifference.

I finally found my breath.

"Put me *down*!" I punched Sevarin on the arm.

"If you have the desire to beat on me for this rude abduction, I am prepared to accept my punishment." I heard the grin in his voice.

In response, I grabbed his ear and twisted, hard. His

mouth opened, his knees buckled, and I slid to the ground out of his loosened grip.

A word to the wise: do not mess with an experienced older sister.

"You really should have known that was coming," remarked Brendan as he reached into the pocket of his jacket and brought out a PowerBar.

"I expect you are correct." Sevarin straightened. "Next time I will be prepared."

"How have you survived for centuries at this level of jackassedness?" I asked as I straightened my blouse and tried to find where my dignity had gotten itself to.

"Please. It's roguish charm." Sevarin ran a hand over his hair. He'd lost his hat somewhere during the festivities and his hair gleamed gold in the streetlight. "And I can attest that as a survival strategy it works very well."

"I thought your kind had settled on broody angst." Brendan peeled back the foil on his PowerBar and took an enormous bite.

Sevarin shook his head. "Lord Byron and Bram Stoker between them have a great deal to answer for."

"You can take it up with them when you see them." My head was spinning. I was sure we should actually be talking about something else, but I couldn't get my thoughts to settle down long enough to remember what it was.

"Oh, I have. They've been shacked up together in Budapest since 1904."

"That is not true," I snapped.

Sevarin shrugged. "If it gives you comfort to believe so, please do."

Brendan had the nerve to snicker around a mouthful of granola and preservatives.

"Did you bring enough of that for the whole class?" I asked.

"Magic-working burns calories at an accelerated rate," Brendan told me. He did look pale, and nobody eats the cardboard that masquerades as "power food" that fast unless he's starving.

"I think we three need to talk," said Sevarin. "May I suggest your place, Maddox?"

"Mine?"

"Charlotte has roommates, and while I would love to entertain you both in my home, I think you would be more comfortable in your own."

"Point." Brendan stuffed the last of the bar in his mouth. "I'll get us a cab."

Brendan gave the cabbie an address on Grand between Broadway and Crosby in SoHo. This told me he made way the hell more money than I did even before I saw the place. I'd worked in lofts like his as a personal chef but had never been in one as a guest. Windows opened in every wall. During the day, this place would be filled with sunlight to show off the blond wood floors covered with Persian rugs, the white walls and the framed art—a lot of which I suspected was original. The space had been dressed in butter-soft leather furniture and oak bookcases.

I did notice that only the books looked well used, and my glimpse of the kitchen showed immaculate granite counters reflecting the track lighting. This was a show-piece, and I was willing to bet that the microwave saw more action than the professional-grade cooktop did. Brendan's high-priced loft was a stopping place, not a living place.

"Very nice." Sevarin settled onto a leather sofa, legs crossed at the knee and arm stretched over the back, looking perfectly at home. "You do well for yourself. Or is this a family property?"

"No, it's mine." There was a bar topped with decanters and bottles just like you'd see on a movie set of a rich man's home.

"Can I get you anything?" Brendan reached into the mini-fridge underneath the bar and pulled out a can of Zap Energy Drink.

"No, thanks." I winced and averted my eyes.

"I'm fine," added Sevarin, and smiled when Brendan glowered at him. Then Sevarin turned to me. "Did you learn anything from Shelby?"

I rubbed my arms. *Don't tell them. None of their business. They don't need to know. This is between me and Chet.*

"Did you?" asked Brendan.

I had the uncomfortable impression that Brendan at least was waiting for me to lie. I studied the immaculate floorboards. He'd just saved my life. They both had. What was I supposed to think about them now?

Why did my life even need saving? No. Don't get paranoid. I was in an alley by a bite-easy, even if it was only a tourist joint. I know better.

Brendan sighed and took another swallow of the entirely artificial high-fructose corn-syrup liquid. "Do you know those two from the alley?" he asked Sevarin.

"Actually I do, nasty little creatures that they are. Julie and Tommy Jones. Brother and sister, low-intelligence, longtime troublemakers."

"Wait," I cut in. "Her name is really Julie?"

Sevarin nodded.

"I knew it had to be something like that." Okay, it was a small victory, but I was very short on things to feel good about right then.

Brendan rolled his eyes and took another utterly unhealthy swallow of Zap. My stomach roiled in sympathy. "Professional or amateur trouble?"

"Before tonight I would have said amateur." Sevarin rotated his ankle in a circle a few times, thinking. "But that may have changed. What is your opinion, Charlotte?"

That startled me. "Charlotte?"

"I rescued you from the smiling jaws of death. I think we can be on a first-name basis."

This was probably reasonable, but I was in no mood to admit it. "I bet you were an annoying little brother."

"Incredibly so. But what do you think of the status of your assailants?"

There are times when words are like a door closing behind you. Once spoken, they cut off the last exit. I remembered standing in the dark years ago. I remembered other eyes, livid and hungry, waiting for my words. I'd felt frightened and hollow like this then, my mouth dry and my throat tight. But that other time, I'd spoken the words anyway.

"Chet's got some kind of deal going down with Bert Shelby," I said. "He got Taylor Watts a job in the bar, and he gave them the menu from Nightlife."

"I'm sorry," said Brendan.

"Yeah." I rubbed my arms. "The problem is . . . The problem is, if the attack wasn't a coincidence. . . ." I did not want to say this. I did not want to think this. I wanted this entire evening to just go away. "I can't see anybody wanting me drained just because I found out they copied my menu."

The men remained silent as we all turned this very, very uncomfortable thought over in our minds. Brendan raised the can of Zap to his mouth again, and suddenly it was all too much to bear.

"Gimme that!"

I snatched the can from his fingers and headed for that pristine kitchen. He had to have real food in that gigantic stainless-steel fridge. Everybody had *something*. Orange juice. Great. Strawberry yogurt. My God, the man truly was of the metrosex clan, or he had a girlfriend who came round for breakfast. Don't think about that now. A lime at the end of its lonely life lay in the otherwise empty fruit drawer. Who keeps a single lime in their fridge anyway? He must drink gin and tonic. Ice? Yes. Bananas. On a cute little hook next to the fridge. Fabulous. Blender? Blender, under the counter, with the price tag still on it. Pinch of salt for brightness and to cut the sweet, and squeeze the lime in through the top.

While the blender did its work, I dumped the remains of the energy drink down the sink where it belonged, pitched the can into the compactor and found a glass in the cupboard. I poured it full of smoothie and shoved it across the counter to Brendan.

He looked at me. I looked at him. He wanted to protest, but evidently thought better of it and instead drained a good half of the glass. His color looked better at once. I got myself a glass. It had been a rough night.

"And have you anything for me, Charlotte?" Sevarin let his gaze linger meaningfully on my neck.

"Sorry." The smoothie wasn't bad at all. Needed some herb flavor. Lemongrass? And I could have zested the lime in there if it had been less mummified.

"Ah, how I suffer." Sevarin laid his hand on his chest.

Brendan rolled his eyes and changed the subject. "What do you know about Post Mortem?" he asked Sevarin.

"About what you do, I expect. It has a human owner, but some nightblood investment. Second-rate food, music rather too loud, decor in the worst possible but most expected taste. If you are hungry but not interested in the uncertainties of hunting, it is a place to find volunteers."

"Is that from the review you published?" I poured the dregs of the smoothie into Brendan's glass.

"Some of it," admitted Anatole.

"Do you know who the nightblood investors are?"

Anatole shrugged. "Before this, I never cared. But I can find out."

"Could one of them be Chet Caine?" Brendan asked the question to his glass.

I shook my head. "Chet doesn't have money to invest. He's only been able to make the rent reliably for about six months."

"That you know of," said Brendan gently.

Time for me to change the subject. "What happened with Taylor?" I asked Sevarin . . . Anatole.

Brendan raised his eyebrows, and I explained about my ex-bartender and how Linus O'Grady had dragged his name into this.

"That proved a very interesting time," said Anatole. "Not as interesting as rescuing a fair lady, but still . . ."

"He's not going to lay off, is he?" I said to Brendan.

"Doubt it very much," Brendan replied

"If I may be permitted to continue? After Charlotte left me, I continued my surveillance of her brother's doorstep for twenty minutes before Taylor Watts reemerged. He walked from there to a little bistro on Tenth, where he sat at the bar for approximately one hour, at which point I noticed three things."

"And nothing on God's green earth is going to make him hurry, is it?" said Brendan to me.

"Doubt it very much," I replied.

Anatole ignored us and ticked off his points on his long, manicured fingers. "The first was that he got phone numbers from three separate women with low necklines and clearly low rates of perception. The second was that the longer he sat there, the more uneasy the bartender became."

I cocked my head toward him. "And that couldn't have been because a prominent dining critic was in the house?"

"Their intelligence-gathering operation is not as efficient as yours. I was not recognized."

"How can you be sure?"

"I can tell."

Gimme strength. "Guys always think that."

"Plus, there was the member of the Paranormal Squadron having a beer on the stool by the front window."

"Was he following Watts?" asked Brendan.

Sevarin shook his head. "He was there when Watts came in, and although he tried to disguise it, he was startled by that young man's arrival."

We stood there in that now less than pristine kitchen, drinking our drinks, each turning over the pieces of our own particular puzzle in our mind, trying to make them fit together a little more comfortably. I'd gone to Post Mortem, and maybe made somebody nervous enough to send in the vamplette squad. Taylor Watts had gone from Chet's to a little bistro being staked out by the P-Squad, and the bartender there got nervous. That was a lot of nerves for a Monday night.

In the middle of all this mulling, Brendan's doorbell rang.

I jumped, splashing smoothie across counter, floor and rumpled blouse. Brendan jerked his head around, alert and pale.

Sevarin arched one cool vampire eyebrow.

The bell rang again, followed by a furious pounding that shook the door in its frame.

"You seem to have someone at your door," said Sevarin.

"Yeah," agreed Brendan.

The knob rattled. The doorbell rang, and rang again.

"Are you going to see who it is?" I asked.

"I know who it is." Brendan set his empty glass on the counter and ran his fingers through his hair. "My family."

II

➤—🍴

Anatole pursed his lips. "I don't suppose, Mr. Maddox, that you have a back exit?"

"No."

"How disappointing. Well, we shall have to brave it out." The pounding grew louder. "You could, I suppose, let them break the door down, but I imagine you'd be charged a maintenance fee for that."

For a minute Brendan actually seemed to be considering the trade-off, but at last he walked into the foyer and snapped the locks open.

The pair who all but toppled in could only have been Brendan's relatives. They both had his big frame, black hair and intense blue eyes. Surprisingly, the look worked as well on the woman in the red leather coat, black leggings and red lace-up boots as it did on the man in jeans and black bomber jacket. Better, in fact, because the man had an aggressively receding hairline, one of those obnoxious little chin tufts, and wisps of chest hair sticking out of the top of his black button-down shirt.

"What the hell, Brendan!" shouted Chin Tuft. "What

are you . . ." The sentence trailed off as he caught sight of me and Anatole.

Anatole nodded casually, as if meeting someone at a cocktail party.

"What is this, Brendan?" whispered Chin Tuft.

"Anatole Sevarin is a guest in my house," said Brendan. "You will not give him any trouble, Ian."

Chin Tuft—Ian—looked as if he was exercising superhuman control to keep from spitting on the floor. "You're making guests out of vampires now? Dylan was right. You have gone over."

"Just calm down, Ian." Brendan's weary sigh told me this was not the first time he'd been on the receiving end of this particular accusation. "I haven't gone anywhere."

"And who's this?" The woman sauntered slowly up to me. She was a sophisticate—tall enough that she looked slender despite her sturdy bones—and she walked easily in her high heels. She'd gone light on the makeup, and she projected the particular cat-cool menace of supremely self-confident women. She tugged off her red gloves as she approached. Nice touch.

"Charlotte Caine." I made sure she saw me look her up and down. "And you are?"

But the woman just rolled her eyes. "A vamp and a vamp-lover. Great Goddess, Bren . . ."

"Enough, Margot. Either the pair of you behave or you can come back later."

These new Maddoxes shared a long, eloquent glance that told me there'd be a lot more words as soon as the unwelcome intruders were gone. I started to move. This was no place for me. But Sevarin put a cool restraining hand on my wrist. I should have just shaken him off, and I'm still not sure why I didn't. Probably it was blatant curiosity overriding common sense. Or maybe I just wanted to see how long it'd be before Margot's ice cracked.

Meow to you too.

Brendan walked back into the living room and dropped into an armchair. "So, what couldn't wait?" He did not invite either of his relatives to sit.

"You know what it is," Ian muttered.

"Beyond Dylan being dead?" Brendan shot back.

I slid into the corner between the entrance to the kitchen and the interior hallway and wished for invisibility.

"How can you be so cold?" Ian's chin tuft positively quivered with the force of his rage. "He's our flesh and blood!"

Too late, Ian realized what he had said. Sevarin, who had positioned himself on the threshold where he could enjoy the show, licked his lips theatrically and maliciously. Ian went white and clenched his fist. I got ready to duck. These Maddoxes liked playing with fire. It was a wonder none of them were chefs.

"Ian," warned Brendan.

"He . . ."

"Is doing his damnedest to provoke you. Back off." Brendan surged to his feet and put himself squarely between Sevarin and his relatives. "Sevarin is not our problem. Our problem is Pamela."

"You've found Pam?" Margot cut in.

"No. But I've seen her." This was stretching the truth, and he didn't mention he'd "seen" her in my restaurant a few hours before we got saddled with his cousin's corpse. This was, in my opinion, positively chivalrous.

"And?" Margot tossed her red gloves onto the bar and got a can of Zap out of the fridge. God, had *none* of these people any standards?

"And Dylan was killed a few hours after he did find her," said Brendan quietly.

The Maddoxes digested this. Ian's face flushed as red as Margot's coat, but she shot him a hard look and he kept quiet.

"Pam always thought she was too good to stay down on the farm," said Margot. "But she wouldn't murder one of her own."

"We're not her own anymore. She ran out on us before she could take the oath." The bitterness in Brendan's words startled me.

"She's still family." Margot leaned back against the bar and nestled the can of chemicals in the crook of her elbow.

"It's just a word to some people, Margot."

"To you?"

"You know better."

"I hope I do." Margot kept her gaze on him as she took another swallow from the can. I shivered. I was used to fights that were actual fights. My family hollered. We stormed and slammed doors and got in each other's faces. I once threw a pan at Chet, and he's still damn lucky it wasn't the cleaver. These quiet, faux-polite exchanges bordered on the unnatural.

"So, why the hell haven't you found her yet?" demanded Ian.

"It's a big city, Ian. She might not even be in the city. We've got a hefty percentage of the population of the United States living within commuter distance. This is going to take a while."

"We don't have a while! This was all your idea in . . ."

Unfortunately, Margot remembered that Anatole and I were there. She put her hand on Ian's shoulder and rolled her eyes meaningfully in our direction. Ian gave us another one-eighty-proof poison glare. I couldn't help noticing he checked out my boobs at the same time. *Classy multitasking there, guy.*

"It's too late for this. We'll see you tomorrow, Brendan." Margot reclaimed her gloves and gestured for Ian to follow her toward the door. Clearly being a piece of work was a common trait among the Maddox women.

"Nice to meet you," I called out from my corner. For a moment I thought I'd really done it, because Margot Maddox turned slowly and stalked toward me, inch by inch.

"Don't think you're safe just because my big brother's taken a liking to you, Cookie," she breathed. The leftover smell of the Zap Energy Drink clashed with her Chanel perfume, but her eyes glittered sharp and clear. "Don't think that at all."

Ian almost ruined the menace of her sweeping exit with a smirk and another look at my boobs. Almost, but not quite.

The door closed on the Maddoxes and Brendan snapped the dead bolt.

"Big brother?" I said.

"We don't have a while?" said Sevarin.

Brendan said nothing. But he looked at me, and I know for a fact he didn't see any way out there.

"I can't talk about it."

"So the honesty only runs one way?" *Why should I be surprised?* I wanted to be resigned. I mean, I barely knew him. The idea hurt anyway, like a healing burn under hot water.

"No. I mean . . ." Brendan gestured, expanding and compressing the air between his hands as if he suffered from a sudden urge to play the accordion. I couldn't help noticing that the right hand—the one that had punched the wall yesterday morning—was completely healed. Score one for the warlock health plan. "I mean I *can't* talk about it. There are secrets here that don't belong to just me. It's family. I was hoping you'd understand."

I did understand. I didn't like it, but I understood.

"I think we may safely conclude, however, that Dylan Maddox was not following Pam purely from love and devotion," Anatole mused.

A muscle in Brendan's jaw twitched.

"Yes. Well." Anatole straightened up and cast an eye toward the bank of windows overlooking Grand Street. "As delightful as this has been, I have other places I must be before morning. Charlotte, if you wish it, I would be glad to escort you home."

"I can get a cab, thanks." I had left my purse in the kitchen. I slung it over my shoulder and put the blender carafe in the sink. I was leaving a mess.

"Very well. Maddox, thank you for a most interesting evening." Anatole waited for me to follow. I didn't want to, but I couldn't think of a reason to stay. Saying I wanted to clean up the kitchen would sound truly weird to everybody, even me. So I moved toward the front door. Slowly.

"Wait," said Brendan. "Please."

Anatole and I both turned, and saw Brendan was looking at me.

Anatole gave a small bow. "Good night, Charlotte."

Then he was out the door and the door was shut and Brendan Maddox and I were alone in his picture-perfect apartment. It was late enough and we were high enough up that we didn't even have traffic noise to cut the silence between us.

"I want to apologize for my family," said Brendan. "Again."

"Don't worry about it. You're not responsible for them." I shouldn't be doing this. My brain was filling up with fuzz from lack of sleep and possibly from the emotional overload of having been attacked in an alley by two juvie-delinquent vampires. I shouldn't stay with this man past my ability to think straight.

"Doesn't seem like that most days."

"I know exactly what you mean." I paused and remembered I'd left some important words unsaid. "Thank you."

"For what? Oh. I'm just glad I was there."

"So am I."

I had no idea what to do or say next. I was grateful. So was he. He was tall and handsome and very, very tired. We were both a little frightened and a little tense. We'd stood this close together just a few hours ago. I'd touched his hand, and my brain had filled up with thoughts of kissing him. Now, I found that tide rising again, and I lacked the strength to fight it.

"What do you think of Sevarin?" Brendan asked abruptly.

Way to change the subject. But I was glad he did. "Honestly? I don't know yet."

"Don't trust him, Charlotte. He's got his own agenda."

I hitched my purse strap up on my shoulder. "I know, but I don't have a whole lot of choice. I have to find out what's happening with Chet."

"Are you sure you want to know?"

There's a certain kind of look people get when they've just replayed their words in their head and wish they could hit the DELETE button. "I'm sorry," Brendan said. "I'm just worried. There's a turf war brewing and my family's either starting it or egging it on or . . ." He let the words trail away and just shook his head again.

Which reminded me once more that there was a whole extra set of problems in the background I hadn't gotten a good look at yet. Something else we had in common.

I took a deep breath. "Look. My brother . . . his judgment wasn't fantastic before he was turned, and it didn't get any better afterward. But whatever he's doing . . . it's going to turn out to be more frat house than Mafia."

"I hope you're right."

Me too. "I'll take another run at him tomorrow night. He never could keep a secret from me."

Brendan did not say he'd been doing a good job lately, which was considerate. "So, can I call you tomorrow night?"

Something inside, right under my lungs, lurched. "I'll keep my phone on."

I got a smile for that, the kind that spreads a soft light through the room and makes your bones go all gooshy. Brendan was so close that I could feel exactly how far I'd have to stretch to reach his mouth with mine. I could have done it as a promise, or just to see what it would feel like, or to make up for the fact that I'd been flirting with Anatole right after we'd held hands, or just because I hadn't been this close to anybody I could really consider kissing in close to forever.

But what I did was walk out the door.

12

I left Brendan's in a cab. When I got home, I grunted at Trish and Jess and stumbled past them on the way to my bedroom. There, I toppled over without undressing and slept like the well and truly dead.

Around one in the afternoon, my eyes opened of their own accord. Feeling a lot better, I washed and dressed and went into the kitchen. There, the all-but-empty refrigerator confronted me accusingly. I hadn't had a chance to restock since my cooking binge, and whatever Trish might think, a six-pack of Yoplait, a half gallon of skimmed-to-within-an-inch-of-its-life milk and a brick of cheap Cheddar did not constitute a decent bout of grocery shopping.

I checked my smartphone. Miracle of miracles, there were no frantic messages from staff, warlocks, policemen, my brother, or assorted stray vampires. Maybe I could risk a minute to catch up on personal business. I grabbed purse and jacket and fled with the speed of a teenager handed Mom's credit card.

For an hour, I let myself forget. Juggling a cup of coffee and a warm bialy, I picked over produce; eggs from free-range chickens, good cheese, fresh, crusty bread and

Spanish olive oil. I inhaled fragrances that reminded me about my real life, the one I was going to get back to as soon as this whole mess cleared up.

I most emphatically did not think about what had happened at Post Mortem, or afterward. I was still most emphatically not thinking about any of that when I backed into the apartment, my arms straining to wrap around four overstuffed grocery bags. I turned around to kick the door shut—and saw Jessie.

She sprawled facedown on the sofa with one arm dangling limp and still over the edge. Dark stains crusted her trailing, expensively highlighted hair.

My reaction to this tableau, given the last few days, was perfectly natural. I screamed like a horror movie virgin, dropped the food and rushed over to her.

"Jess!" I hauled on her shoulder, trying to flip her over and find a pulse at the same time.

Jessie opened one badly smudged eye in what I have to admit was a fairly good outraged glower, considering our mutually awkward positions. "What on *earth* is the matter with you?" She swatted at my groping hands.

"Ergh . . . unk." I stumbled backward, plopped down on the edge of the coffee table and proceeded to shake. "Sorry. Startled. Wasn't expecting you home."

"Me either." The smudged eye closed wearily.

For a minute I thought about reading her the riot act for scaring the crap out of me, but the utterly flat way she intoned those two words, along with the fact that she was still facedown took me aback more than a little. If that hadn't done it, the sight of her makeup being smeared would have. In the two years we'd roomed together, I'd never seen Jess with a less than perfect face.

"What happened?"

"The bridal party from hell," she mumbled into the sofa cushions. "Mother-daughter screaming match that graduated to throwing things, which included several pairs of designer heels and half my stock."

"Ouch."

The hand dangling over the edge of the sofa waved, indicating agreement with this particular understatement.

I searched for words of comfort and came up disconcertingly empty.

"You can bill them for the lost stock, can't you?"

"That's not the point!" Jessie rolled over and clutched a sofa pillow to her stomach. In addition to her smoke-gray eye shadow being smudged on both lids, a long green smear decorated one cheek, like someone had slapped her with a piece of wet nori. "I'm supposed to make things better! I soothe nerves, I improve health and outlook, I show them who they want to be!" Jessie pressed the heels of both palms against her eyes.

"What if they want to be raging queen bitches?"

"You're not helping here," said Jessie, without bringing her hands down.

"Sorry."

Jess shook her head. Now I saw the smudges in her foundation that looked way too much like tear tracks. "Go cook something, will you?"

Probably this was a good idea. "You want anything?"

"World peace and a sane clientele."

"Sorry."

Her hand waved again.

I collected my discarded groceries, went into the kitchen and started putting things away. I kept sneaking glances at Jessie, though. She lay there, pillow in a stranglehold, staring at the ceiling. I tried to tell myself this was just Jess's patented emotional overkill, which she applied to any given situation as readily as she applied Paris Rose blush to her cheeks. Except, as I put the bread in its box, I realized I'd never seen her actually in tears before. Then, as I rinsed the fresh romaine, it occurred to me I'd never really thought about what Jessie did during the day, never mind that she might see it as a . . . well, a *calling* of some kind. I mean, all she did was sell makeup, a substance I normally avoided like six kinds of plague. But then, some people looked at what I did and said it was just food and went around happily eating whatever came closest. I did understand wanting to make a place where people could feel better, even in a small way or just for a little while. I also understood how miserable it felt when you failed, whether the failure was your responsibility or not. Especially when it wasn't your responsibility, because that failure remained yours.

I rubbed my hands on my pants and glanced around the little kitchen. Jessie had a sweet tooth and probably hadn't eaten since before her personal disaster. Maybe I should bake something. But as I drummed my fingertips on the counter and glanced at my still-unmoving roommate on our sofa, a new idea stirred in the back of my brain. Slowly and tentatively, fearful of rejection, it crept forward and urged me to look at my drumming fingers. I blanched. No. This idea could not belong to me, and it had better return to the disordered back of my brain. But the idea pulled out a whole portfolio of images I hadn't been letting myself see, mostly involving sitting in La Petite Abeille with Brendan.

I steeled myself. *This isn't for you,* the idea whispered to me. *It's for the greater good.* I'd be spending a lot of time hanging around the apartment during the day until we got Nightlife open again. My having to hang around with Jess when she also was sunk in professional misery would not be good for anyone concerned.

"Jessie?"

"Mmmph?" She blinked at the ceiling.

"Would you . . . could you maybe just this once, you know . . . give me a manicure?"

Jess pushed herself upright and very gingerly set the pillow aside. "Who are you and what have you done with Charlotte Caine?"

The temperature of my charitable impulses dropped precipitously, and I felt my eyes narrow. "If it's going to be a big deal . . ."

"No. No, no, no. No." Jessie was on her feet. "No. No, no." She vaulted the coffee table, something I had no idea she was capable of, and ran over to me, neatly cornering the dining room table. "It's just . . . no, no."

She grabbed hold of my hand and stared at my palm as if she meant to read my future. As she did, the breezy, light version of Jessie faded away. In her place was a cool, serious woman. This new Jess prodded at my cuticles, separated my fingers and ran a delicate thumb across my calluses, taking in the details with a laser-sharp gaze.

This was too much for my timid idea and it tried to slink away.

"Look, I'll understand if you can't do anything here. I mean, you know I can't have polish or scents or . . ."

"Silence!" Jessie commanded. She backed away toward her bedroom, practically daring me to move. As she vanished behind her door, I shifted my weight and eyed the door to the hall, wondering if I could make a dash for it. Too late. Jess reappeared lugging a pair of bright red cases that could have held my entire wardrobe, including the shoes. She plunked them down next to the dining room table and began snapping latches and opening drawers.

"Sit." She kicked out a chair for me and turned her attention to the cases.

I gripped the chair back, watching with numb fascination as Jessie lined up the tools of her trade on our leaf-patterned tablecloth. There were boxes and jars and pouches and towels and a set of what looked like mini chafing dishes, under which she set the heat going. There was also an array of shiny silver instruments with pointy ends that had me wondering if she might suddenly start asking me for missile launch codes.

Jessie turned away from her impromptu lab setup, her hands encased in latex gloves, holding one of those delicate pointy instruments, and saw me still standing behind the chair.

"Oh, sit down, you big wimp."

I will not say that I sized up my roommate and decided I could still take her in a stand-up fight if she got too enthusiastic with any of these strange implements. I will say, however, that I was having some second thoughts. But only because I wasn't sure I had time for all this. Really. If I took a second to think about it, there must be a thousand other things I needed to be doing right now.

Jessie made an entirely unreasonable face for someone ushering a friend into uncharted territory, and tapped the table with the blunt end of her silver pick.

I set my left hand down on the white towel she'd laid out.

She snorted, took a firm grasp of my hand, and leaned in. I tensed. She rolled her eyes, and started digging around under my nails.

Now, I have tough hands. Every chef does. Mine have suffered ten years' worth of cuts, burns, and even the occasional smack with a wooden spoon (it was a French pastry chef, and yes, I probably did deserve it—maybe). But never before had they faced a pick that looked like a refugee from a dentist's office. I gritted my teeth and sat on my other hand. Jess kept digging, firmly and deliberately, her concentration completely on my fingers. Slowly I came to the realization that this might not hurt. Yes, it felt strange to just sit there and let somebody else work, but there did not seem to be any actual pain involved.

In fact, it felt kind of good.

"So, what brought on this sudden change of heart?" Jessie switched from a silver pokey thing to a wooden proddy thing.

"Erm . . ." Was there a nice way to tell her this was a mercy mani?

"I only ask because there was that one time you said you'd rather eat Burger King for a year than sit still and— I'm quoting here—have somebody do strange and intrusive things to your hands."

"Erm . . ."

"Uh-huh." Jessie set down the wooden proddy thing and checked on whatever was brewing in her chafing dishes. "What's Erm's first name?"

"Brendan." I braced myself for the squeeing overreaction. Complete mockery was also a real possibility. Jessie settled for plunging my hand into a warm liquid about the consistency of a loose puree. "Nice name. Cute? Paraffin soak," she added. I assumed that last one referred to the liquid she held my hand in, not to Brendan.

I pictured Brendan's warm eyes and killer smile, and the heat from my soaking hand seemed to spread straight through me. "Definitely cute."

"Employed?" Jess asked, proving her mother had instilled in her a firm grasp of the essentials.

"Enough for a loft in SoHo."

"Definite bonus. So." She pulled my hand out of the paraffin and wiped it down with a warm, soft towel. "What's the problem?"

"What problem?"

"You're making faces, Charlotte. What's the problem? He married?"

"What? No!"

"So, what?" She pushed my hand back into the paraffin. I hoped I never had to admit this, but the soft warmth was actually starting to relax my back and shoulders. Tense is my natural state, but this was affecting me like my trip to the produce market had. Slowly, things inside me were letting go.

"It's complicated," I said.

Jessie gave me another of her glowers. I wondered if this was what Chet felt like when I turned the Big Sister Glare on him. "Pretend for a minute you don't believe I'm a total idiot."

"I don't believe you're a total idiot." Jess pulled my hand out of the paraffin and contemplated it while fingering a little hooky thing and I swallowed. "Really."

"Uh-huh. Hold still."

I swear to God, I don't know how she did it. I'm very good at keeping things inside my own head. But while Jessie soaked, smoothed, massaged and buffed my other hand, I told her what had happened to me yesterday. All of it, including the play-by-play on dinner with Brendan and then what happened with Chet, and Anatole, and afterward.

She was toweling off the fingers on my left hand when my words finally ran out. "You're not going to do the smart thing and call the police, are you?"

I shook my head. "How can I? I don't know what's going on."

"You mean you don't know how much you're going to have to cover for Chet."

That should have been the cue for my famously short temper to rise up and cut loose. It would have for anybody else. As it was, I was wondering uncomfortably how Jess could understand so much about me when we were so different.

"This is so messed up," I muttered.

"You're right about that much." Jessie gave my nails a final swipe with one of her astounding array of brushes and leaned back to consider her . . . handiwork . . . from

farther away. I looked at my fingers. They looked . . .
new. The skin and nails were perfectly clean and had a
healthy pink glow. My hands felt relaxed and ready to go.

"What you need is a once-a-month lunch," said Jess.

"Sorry?" I blinked, and resisted the temptation to
touch that rosy skin just to confirm it was still mine.

"Once-a-month lunch. All the district reps get together
once a month and do lunch, without the district supervi-
sors. You find out everything that's going on."

I was so surprised by this transformation of my work-
hardened hands that it took a minute for Jess's words to
sink into my head, and another minute for them to bloom.
"Dear God," I whispered. "I'm an idiot."

"Really? Why?"

There was a little too much glee in Jessie's voice just
then, but I ignored it. A new idea had come out of the
back room, this one fully formed and fully cognizant of
its own worth.

"If you want to find out what's going on with somebody in the business, you don't just *ask* them."

"What do you do?"

I dove past her, straight for my purse. "You ask Robert
Kemp." I pulled out my cell, thumbed the screen and
waited while it rang.

"Good afternoon, Chef Caine." Robert Kemp, Nightlife's maître d', had a voice that sounded like it had been
delivered fresh this morning from the BBC.

"Hello, Robert."

"Is there news about the reopening?" he inquired
mildly, as if it was a subject of obscure and entirely aca-
demic interest.

"Not yet. Sorry." On the other side of the room, Jess
was tidying her instruments and screwing on jar lids, but
not, I noticed, putting any of them away. She did not so

much as glance toward me. I was not fooled, but shrugged it off. All things considered, I probably owed her a little eavesdropping. "Robert, I need a favor."

"I'll be glad to do whatever I can, Chef Caine."

I'd known he would say that. Robert owed us big-time. Actually, it was Chet he owed. Chet had convinced me that we should hire Robert, and it took him two weeks to do it. Robert's previous place of employment—a four-star establishment called UniQ—had accused him of embezzlement. The charge turned out not to be true, or at least not to be provable, but the gambling problem that made him look suspicious was. Between that bad habit and the recession, no topflight restaurant would take him on. In fact, no one at all would take him on. I gave in only after Chet pointed out two things. First, Robert was willing to work cheap, and second, despite all the problems, Robert Kemp was still was on a first-name basis with every single concierge in Manhattan.

This is really important. Concierges make recommendations to hotel guests on good places to eat out. That they recommend places where friends and acquaintances work should not come as a surprise to anybody. That a maître d' might use some of his tip money to ensure their continued friendship was not something a smart executive chef ever asked about. Plausible deniability is also really important.

"I'm looking for information on Bertram Shelby," I told Robert.

"I am not familiar with the name." He didn't even need to think about that. Robert had a high-definition memory for people.

"He's the current owner of Post Mortem, a vampire club in the East Village."

"Ah." I could picture Robert looking down his very

long English nose. Jobs were transient things, but the true maître d's snobbery was bred in the bone.

"He's been around for a while." Actually, this was a guess, but Shelby wasn't a young man, and as little as I liked the place, Post Mortem just didn't feel like a maiden voyage to me. "Can you find out where, and with whom?"

"I'm certain I can. Is there anything specific you want to know?"

I hesitated and glanced at Jess. She'd given up her non-listening charade and was sitting at the table, arms folded and head cocked. "I just need an employment history and to find out how Shelby got to be running Post Mortem." Clubs in New York are the only ventures riskier than restaurants. The vast majority of them fail before they celebrate their first anniversary. More than one, however, has survived by allowing assorted exciting and highly profitable activities to be conducted on or through the premises. Now, of course, I didn't think Chet was doing anything illegal, but Bert Shelby might be, maybe with Taylor Watts's help. If I'd been living right, that something might be related to whatever had gotten Dylan Maddox killed and we could clear the entire mess up all at once.

"Very well, Chef. I will see what I can turn up."

"Thank you, Robert."

"Not at all. I will call you as soon as I have something."

We said our good-byes and I thumbed the phone off.

Jessie had her eyebrows raised. "So, Charlotte Caine's the new Nancy Drew?"

"Not even close." I ran my hand over my hair. "I just want to know what happened. Chet's keeping something from me, and I need to know if it has anything to do with Dylan's murder and what the hell he thinks he's up to. Maybe he thinks he's protecting somebody, or protecting

Nightlife. Anyway, he's not going to tell me anything if I don't have something solid in my hand already. So I have to ask around. That's all this is." All of which sounded way more like guilty babbling than I was comfortable with.

"Which is of course entirely different than Nancy Drew-ing, especially since there's a dead man involved."

Of course it was, but I couldn't seem to think how. It would have come to me if I'd had a second, I'm sure, but Jessie wasn't giving me a second.

"Come over here and take your shoes off." She reached behind her red cases and brought out a strange-looking bundle of silver sticks that turned out to be a folding footstool.

"What? Why?"

Her smile sharpened, and I'm certain I saw a glint in her eye. "I've got you in my clutches, girl. You're not getting out without the full treatment."

"Jess . . ."

"Don't 'Jess' me. You stand on your feet ten hours a night. You've probably got calluses on your calluses, and if you don't start taking care of them, they're going to split and bleed. It's going to be nasty and you're going to miss work. Shoes off."

It was the "miss work" that did it, just like she knew it would. Clearly, she was a more dangerous saleswoman than I had realized. I went back to my station and obediently took my shoes off. Jess scooted her chair around and set about giving my feet the same kind of work-over she'd given my hands. It could have been the warmth, or that I wasn't used to sitting around doing nothing, or that I hadn't eaten or slept decently in the past couple days—whatever it was, I found myself drifting off slowly toward sleep. Something told me this was not the best idea, but I was tired of fighting to keep my head together, and for once I let go. The nap descended softly, and it felt almost as good as the paraffin soak.

My phone was ringing. I blinked my eyes open and automatically checked my watch. I'd been asleep for two hours. Jess and her implements of destruction were nowhere in evidence. My phone rang again. I swung my feet off the stool and a flash of color made me stop and look down.

While I'd been asleep, Jess had painted my toenails Mary Sue Scarlet.

Brat. I thumbed my phone on without looking at the number. "What?"

"Catching you at a bad time, Chef Caine?" asked Linus O'Grady.

"No, no." I frowned at my toenails. The polish did not evaporate.

"I've got good news. You won't be able to open the restaurant for a few more days, but I can let you back into your kitchen tomorrow."

And just like that, all was right with the world, Mary Sue Scarlet toes and all.

13

All remained right with the world for exactly thirteen hours. I forgave Jess. I called Chet as soon as the sun went down and we whooped and hollered our mutual triumph. It took some effort, but I set aside all my questions about his whereabouts and his connections to Post Mortem. For just this one night I was going to pretend everything could still be all right. If insisting that Trish and Jess come to dinner with me at Pilar's Downtown to drink Dos Equis and eat way too much fresh guacamole was to help keep those questions bound and gagged, I was surely owed at least one night of avocado-and-chile-flavored avoidance tactics.

But then came Wednesday morning, bright and early. Suchai, Marie and Jorgé Sanchez—the only one of the line cooks who could be bothered to show up for the triage—crowded into the walk-in with me as I stared at tub after tub of unusable food.

Restaurants throw out an incredible amount of food. It's a fact and you get used to it, but we were about to open a whole new level of waste. Anything that had been cut or prepped on Saturday had settled into its own ooze. The bread was long past stale. Then there was the produce that had been so fresh and lovely for the weekend, and the stuff that we'd been pushing on the specials because it was about ready to go. . . .

All I could think was this must be what a vet felt like looking at a horse that had to be put down. Thousands of dollars' worth of food was about to be dropped into the Dumpster out back, where we were supposed to douse it in bleach to discourage scavengers. We mostly forget this step. Once you've seen a ten-year-old standing watch while his mom goes diving to try to find something the rats haven't gotten, it does things to you.

That memory turned me back around.

"We're making soup."

"What?" Jorgé moved at light speed when he had a knife in his hand, but he was not exactly quick on the uptake in conversation.

But I had already flipped over into executive chef mode and didn't bother to explain. "Suchai, call the food pantry and find out if they've got some vans, because by four we're going to have dinner for a couple hundred. Jorge, start getting the crates upstairs. Go through them and find out what's edible—I don't care whether it's pretty— and get it into the soup pot. Marie, sort out the breads. Stale we'll use in the soup, or as croutons. Mostly fresh, we can use for grilled ham-and-cheese sandwiches. There's got to be something we can do with those prepped short ribs from Saturday too."

"We can't use the dining room," Marie reminded me. That was still cop territory. O'Grady had been very clear on that.

"But we can use the kitchen and the back door. Grab a bin and let's go." I hefted a tub of not-so-new-anymore potatoes and started up the stairs.

"Yes, Chef," said Jorgé.

"Yes, Chef!" said Marie.

"Yes, Chef!" said Suchai.

After that, it got kind of amazing. First it was just the four of us, sorting, chopping, getting the burners fired and filling that cold kitchen with the sounds and smells that meant life. Then Mohammed, another of our line cooks, came in, towing Marie's apprentice, Paolo, behind him. They said nothing, just washed up, found knives and started taking apart crates of tomatoes. Somebody had gotten busy on the phone, and I hadn't even seen who it was. By the time we got around to turning the toasted bread into crumbs and croutons for the *pomodoro*, the whole line—including all the baby Bobby Flays—was in. Half the front-of-the-house crew took up stations beside them to pack boxes with sandwiches and highly improvised bar cookies, courtesy of Marie and Paolo. The other half had appropriated folding tables from somewhere and set them up out back because the food pantry workers had wanted to know how soon they could start funneling people toward us, and now we had a line.

I did not cry. Seeing my people—who I was sure were getting ready to bail on me—working full tilt to feed their fellow New Yorkers could not possibly make me cry. That would be bad for my authority.

I was backing out the door carrying a stockpot full of pasta carbonara and blood sausage when a woman in a black pantsuit shouldered her way through the line of the homeless, the hungry and the idly curious.

"Oh my ghad! Omighad! It's perfect! Perfect! Charlotte, if I wasn't going to kill you, I'd kiss you."

Elaine West, Nightlife's PR agent, was professionally thin and tastefully blond. She carried a designer bag big enough to conceal a full-grown watermelon and when she didn't have her BlackBerry in her hands, her thumbs twitched.

"Why are you going to kill me?" I passed the pasta off to Katy, who worked the dinner shift the three days a week she wasn't at film school.

"Because you didn't tell me!" Elaine was already thumbing her phone. "Dave? Elaine West. We need a camera down at Nightlife. Now. I don't care where from, just get it here." She hung up.

"I wasn't doing this for the PR," I muttered.

"Well, you are now, sweetie." She linked her arm in mine and smiled. "So let's go over how this extremely generous impulse came to you, so you can get your life back and have a total smash of a reopening."

When she put it that way, I was not only more than ready to be coached, I was doing the face-palm. Why hadn't I thought of that? I guess that's why we were paying her the big bucks, or would be as soon as we had them.

By the time the first camera got there, I was in a fresh-pressed chef's coat explaining how important it was for the city's food professionals to give back to the community and praising my people, who were all donating their time. I meant it, of course, but according to Elaine it also made me look magnanimous and feminine. Well, there's a first time for everything.

We drew an audience as soon as the cameras started clustering around. Suchai put out one of the stockpots with a sign asking for donations to the food bank, and the dollars started fluttering down. More cameras converged and I had to go through my Elaine-prepped spiel four more times, but I did so with a song in my heart. Some days you know that, just this once, you did good.

Sundown found us all collapsed in the kitchen, drinking beers, scarfing down leftover pasta, sandwiches and cookies. We all had our smartphones, BlackBerries and PDAs out so we could take turns reading from the blogs and news Web sites. Every good mention earned a new round of high fives. It wasn't a 100 percent turnaround by any means, but the conversation about us had switched away from murder and vampires, and that felt like a victory.

Every time I glanced at the door to the dining room, though, I knew nothing had really changed. The limits of my ability to play make-believe had been reached. Until we knew for sure why Dylan Maddox had died, and more important, until Little Linus and the rest of New York's finest knew, everything could come crashing down on us again.

So while the crew huddled together, texting their comments to the holdout blogs that still didn't think we were all that plus or minus a bag of chips, I took a fresh beer to Suchai where he was hunkered down on an overturned five-gallon bucket. We raised our bottles to each other.

"Thanks for being here, Suchai."

He shrugged and swigged. This was one of the few times I'd ever seen him in T-shirt and jeans instead of his immaculate white captain's coat. He looked relaxed and easy, except for the dark circles under his eyes that came with being a new parent. "My wife would kill me if I didn't. She thinks you are the next great chef in Manhattan."

"I always did like Surio." I grinned, and changed the subject as abruptly as any blog. "You remember that fang tease from Saturday, the one who helped start this mess? What table was she at?"

"Two up front. She had the pumpkin soup." Suchai grimaced.

"That much I remember. Thanks." He wanted to ask me what was going on, but being Suchai, he just nodded and took another swallow of beer.

"Did you see them come in?"

Suchai shook his head slowly. "I was making sure everyone knew we had Anatole Sevarin in the house, and then I had to help Terry with the service on fifteen. You should ask Robert."

"It's on the list." I looked down the neck of my beer bottle.

Suchai nodded again. "Listen, Chef, I hate to have to ask this—"

"I know. I know." I waved his words away. "You need to know when we're reopening. I've got no answer. If you've gotten a job offer, I won't blame you for taking it."

He looked down the neck of his beer bottle too. I'm not sure what either one of us thought was in there. "We're all right for a while, but I've got the kids now . . . you know how it is."

"Believe me, Suchai, I'm trying to get answers as fast as I can."

"Sure. And if there's anything I can do, you let me know."

"I will." There was a pause I did not want to spend any longer than necessary in, so I reverted to giving orders. This was my kitchen, after all. "You take off, and say hi to Surio and the pups for me."

"You got it, Chef." Suchai got to his feet and joined the others heading for the lockers. I put my beer bottle on the counter and walked over to the desk in the corner that served as my office.

My computer is old, and cranky, but it is also has a (painfully slow) WiFi connection to the other computer out front, where Robert enters the reservations. I sat down and tapped at the keys, calling up the date, time and table. Of course, Detective O'Grady had already dug out this information, but he wasn't the one I wanted it for.

The problem was, the system showed no reservation for table two at eight p.m. on Saturday. We enter the table number after the reservation is seated. It's a bookkeeping measure, and one way we track how busy we've been. Besides, you get the occasional customer who wants their "regular table," and it's good to have a record of what that table is. But table two at eight p.m. last Saturday had no reservation, not for Pam Maddox or anybody else. I swore and scrolled down, then up again. Maybe Pam and her nebbish-date had just walked in off the street. But no, that couldn't be. We'd been booked solid on Saturday. I remembered because it had been our first time as an absolutely full house, and we'd been elated, even before we knew about Anatole Sevarin.

All the other reservations were there—at least, it looked like they were—but as far as the reservations list was concerned, table two had been free.

My first thought was that someone on the Paranormal Squad had deleted the reservation. But that made no sense. They'd need it for evidence, wouldn't they? My next thought was that Chet had deleted it. I waited for guilt to show up, but it didn't. What came instead was a fifty-pound sack of further disappointment.

My crew were coming out of the changing area with their jackets on and waving at me as they filed toward the back door. I waved back and told myself there was more than just me and Chet to worry about. People counted on me. This had to go away. All of it. Whatever it was.

Suchai paused and looked back at me. "You coming, Chef?"

"You go on." I hit a couple keys and blanked the screen. "I can lock up."

"You sure?" Marie leaned out from behind him.

"I'm sure. I'll call tomorrow as soon as there's news."

We said our good-nights and I listened to their footsteps, and how the back door opened and closed again. But instead of silence, I heard another pair of hard-soled shoes crossing the tiles, and getting closer. I automatically sat up and shoved my hand into my pocket for my cell phone.

"Ah, Chef Caine. I'm glad I caught you."

Robert Kemp rounded the corner and I let out a long, slow sigh of relief.

Running a successful restaurant is all about the little things. Decor, table arrangement, and lighting all matter as much as the menu. Every detail affects the guests' response to the space, starting with the person who greets them at the door. The maître d' is the famous first impression, and despite all his troubles, Robert Kemp was one of the best in the business.

Tall and trim and hawk-nosed, he had waving white hair swept back from a clear forehead. Robert dressed in suits made-to-order from Savile Row when he could afford them and the closest Hong Kong copies when he couldn't. His shirts were always crisp, and I'd never seen him without cuff links. Along with the cultivated accent, he had faultless manners, and by the time he handed guests off to their table captain, they felt as if he'd mistaken them for minor royalty.

"Thanks for coming in, Robert. Please." I pushed a chair toward him. He thanked me and sat. I happened to know Robert was closing in on seventy, but his back was still straight as a poker.

"I've been talking to some acquaintances about Mr. Shelby," he said.

"Anything interesting?"

"Some. He came to New York about fifteen years ago with a business degree from Ohio State and apparently a strong desire to make his mark as an impresario. He managed to get a job at the Clientele. . . ."

"I know that name."

"It was on the A-list for a while, but it closed after five

years when it was found that the owners had been laundering money for some Russian oligarchs."

"Heavy."

"Quite. Mr. Shelby was gone before the federal agents moved in. He already had a new job, in fact, managing Le Bon Nuit."

Now that was definitely a name I knew. Le Bon Nuit pioneered the whole concept of haute noir cuisine. That I shamelessly imitated some of its concepts when drawing up the plans for Nightlife is not something we need to discuss. Not all its concepts, of course, because it turned out some of them were really bad ideas, like the casual attitude toward standard accounting practices. "Didn't Nuit have some trouble with, like, not paying their taxes?"

Robert nodded. "But again Mr. Shelby was gone by the time the IRS decided to take an interest. A similar situation occurred with his next management position, at Turcell's."

"So, Shelby's timing is either really bad, or really good."

"It would seem that way, yes."

"These are all seriously high-end places." And some pretty high-priced white-collar crimes. I mean, nothing to impress Bernie Madoff, but still a long way up from, say, robbing the tip jar or, as much as I hated to admit it, stealing my menu wholesale. "If this is Shelby's level of scam, what's he doing running a bite-easy for the young and hopelessly gothic?"

"The general opinion is that Mr. Shelby was too close to too much bad luck and started having difficulties finding work at the best establishments." Robert examined his fingernails, which looked like they'd been given one of Jess's best treatments.

"Yeah, but if Shelby had been setting up the problems and skipping out before the roof came down, he'd either be rich enough to retire somewhere safely out of town, or he'd be . . . in really deep trouble." Nobody likes the guy who gets out with clean hands, especially not the ones who have hired him to do the dirty work.

"It's also strange that he's the owner, is it not?" remarked Robert. "That's never been the case before, not even on paper. Previously, he's always just been a manager, and not the top manager either."

"Huh. Yeah. That is strange." Worry stirred inside. Maybe it was nothing. Maybe this was the best Shelby could do on the straight and narrow. And it wasn't so bad either. Post Mortem had been around for, what? Three years now? Four? For a New York club that was reason to celebrate.

On the other hand, with a work history like this, Shelby surely had some . . . widely varied connections. Which Detective O'Grady would know all about, wouldn't he?

This assumed, however, that Little Linus was even looking at Shelby and Post Mortem. After all, they weren't the ones who had come up with a dead body in the foyer, and I hadn't called yet to tell them about being attacked in PM's alley. That was beginning to feel like a major mistake.

"Chef Caine?"

"Hmm?" I realized I was staring across the now empty kitchen. "Sorry, Robert. It's been a long day."

"I understand. But a word of advice?"

I waved my hand for him to go ahead.

"I've been around long enough to see several waves of immigration into this city." His slightly protruding gray eyes were unfocused, looking inside to his deep memory. "Every wave brings new variants on old problems. There are always shifts in the money flow, whether it's the clean money or the dirty money. This also brings shifts in power. The rise and fall of small-minded men like Shelby tends to be closely tied to those shifts."

"You think Shelby's in on the start of something?"

"It could be." He looked straight at me. "I just hope whatever it is, it stays away from you and Mr. Caine."

This was a hint that even I couldn't miss. He was warning me to stop asking questions, because of those little shifts in the power structure he was talking about. That power was in the hands of people I didn't want to know about, and shifts could be measured in lost lives.

"I hope so too," I told him. I really didn't want to ask the next question, but I had to. "Robert, the night we had the . . . incident. The couple at table two—they didn't have a reservation, did they?"

Robert's flicker of hope died, leaving resignation behind like ashes. "No. Mr. Caine had asked me to keep an eye out for them."

"So he knew they were coming?"

"Yes."

"Was he waiting for the man or the woman?"

He hesitated, and my fingers curled up, looking for something to hang on to. I did not want to have to deal with Robert lying to me.

"The gentleman," Robert said at last, and I knew this was true. "They seemed to be friends. I got the impression this was his first time meeting the young lady."

"Okay," I said, even though it wasn't. "Thanks again, Robert. I appreciate it."

"Anything I can do, Chef Caine." He stood, brushing his suit coat down and straightening his tie and cuff links. "I look forward to hearing from you about the reopening."

We said our good-byes and he let himself out. The back door closed firmly and I sat staring at my computer screen for a long time.

I didn't like what Robert had told me. None of it. Unfortunately, it made sense out of the vamplette attack. If Shelby thought I knew something about whatever extra-curricular activities he was setting up at Post Mortem, that might justify assault with intent to drain. It also meant he might be willing to create dead bodies, or work for those who did.

So had Cousin Dylan come to be one of those bodies? If Brendan was to be believed, he was nothing more than a lovesick puppy determined to bring his wayward cousin home (again I say, "Ew!"). Except Cousin Pam didn't seem to want to come home, and Pammy's squirmy-vamp escort knew Chet well enough that Chet gave him a table without a reservation. Chet also knew Shelby well enough that he got Taylor Watts a job at his suddenly complicated-looking club.

"God Almighty," I whispered to my empty kitchen. "What does he think he's *doing*?"

And what did Anatole Sevarin have to do with it? There was a logical explanation for Brendan's involvement in this mess. This was his family, and he was a security expert. Of *course* he was trying to find out what was going on. But Anatole . . . what was going on with Anatole?

I felt my jaw tighten. I didn't want anything to be going on with Anatole. I wanted things to be just the way he said—he wanted this mess cleared up before the anti-vamp crowd started getting restless. But the possibility that Anatole Sevarin had been up front with me was starting to feel vanishingly small.

I had to call Chet. Break time was over. I had to have it out with him once and for all. I turned to pick up the landline, and another thought struck me hard enough to make me pull my hand off the receiver. I swiveled back to the computer. A few more clicks and I was through to our employee records. We hadn't deleted Taylor Watts's contact information yet because we still owed him his last paycheck. I thumbed his address and contacts into my cell phone.

With Robert's informal background check on Bert

Shelby, we had clearly increased the potential level of stupid that Chet could have gotten himself into. I was going to have to handle this differently. This time I really couldn't just confront my little brother and use a good hard glare to get him to talk to me. This time I would get at least some facts into my own hands so he couldn't weasel out on me.

I dialed the number and listened while the phone rang once.

"Yeah?" came Taylor's voice.

"Hello, Mr. Watts."

"Chef Caine." I could hear my ex-barkeep's oily smile. "Bert said you were looking for me."

"Somehow I thought he'd let you know. Heard from Chet recently?"

"He told me you'd ask that. Communications breakdown in the family, honey?"

Ignore it. Ignore it. "Right now, you're the one I need to talk to."

"So talk."

"In person."

"Why would I do that?"

"Because you've got all kinds of things you want to say to me and I've got your paycheck."

The silence on the other end stretched out a full thirty seconds.

"Say I felt like doing you a favor later. Where?"

"Nightlife. Come in by the back door."

"Maybe."

He hung up. But he'd be here, and I knew it. He wouldn't pass up the chance to gloat at me over whatever-the-hell stunt he thought he was pulling off. Plus, while Taylor might or might not be working for some flavor of the underground, he clearly wasn't at the point where he could say no to $934.22 after taxes.

I sat alone in my office with my paperwork and my old

computer, looking out onto my clean, quiet kitchen. Before long, Taylor Watts was going to walk through the door. In the back of my mind, I opened the mental walk-in fridge where I keep my personal pride, cut out a large slice and swallowed it.

Then I made two more phone calls.

14

"Well, snap, Chef C. You must be moving up in the world." Taylor Watts leaned his pretty-boy butt against my clean counter and folded his arms. "You got yourself hot-and-cold running bad boys."

My ex-bartender was a bulked-out predator, dressed to lounge with in a black jacket and a scarlet shirt with the top three buttons undone. He waxed. No hat, of course, so you could see that his chestnut hair was in fact perfect.

Of course, he had stiff competition in the good-looking-predator department just then, because Brendan and Anatole stood by the cold prep station. They'd both agreed to be my backup for this meeting, and I've got to admit they had the whole menacing-look thing down cold.

I've also got to admit neither of them had been entirely thrilled to see the other.

"I can't believe you didn't think I could handle your bartender," said Brendan.

This made Anatole smile. "While I can easily understand that oversight, I find it difficult to believe you did not think *I* would be able to handle your ex-bartender."

"Put away the macho, guys." I sighed. "If Taylor thinks

I need a warlock *and* a vampire to handle him, he'll get cocky. He's that kind. And if he's cocky, he'll talk."

So far, Taylor was proving me right. Instead of getting nervous when he saw Brendan and Anatole taking his measure across a room full of knives and kebab skewers, Taylor puffed up.

Cue obnoxious sexual comment.

"So," he drawled, "you guys do her separate or together? Or is she the kind that just likes to watch?"

Anatole looked at Brendan, and Brendan looked back at Anatole. A mental game of rock-paper-scissors was clearly being played. Anatole won.

"Mr. Watts, Chef Caine invited you here for a polite talk. A civilized exchange of information and views. I would suggest you remember that."

"Or what? You'll say nasty things about me in your little vamp column?"

Anatole smiled and the temperature in the room dropped ten degrees. "That is one of many, many possibilities." He raised his hand, and Taylor flinched. So did I. I had to hope Taylor didn't notice.

The vampire inspected his clean, well-kempt fingernails. I was surrounded by clean-nail fanatics. He and Robert could exchange manly manicure tips. "So many possibilities," Anatole murmured.

"Look, Taylor, this does not have to be complicated." I pulled the white envelope holding his paycheck out of my pocket. "All I want to know is why'd Chet get you a job with Bert Shelby?"

"Why don't you ask Chet?" Taylor snapped his fingers. "Oh, that's right. Because you're trying to clean up Baby Brother's mess all quiet-like."

But as with his previous snark, I'd been expecting something like this. Taylor didn't get hired because he was any kind of original.

"So enlighten me, Taylor. Explain to me what I don't know."

"Why should I? Like you've got anything on me you could take to the P-Squad."

Now what made you mention the P-Squad? Taylor reached for the check and I snatched it back. Then and there, I decided on a gamble. Taylor liked to think he was in the know. Taylor the Player, he called himself when he was trying to bullshit the more naive waitresses. Brendan had said there was a turf war of some kind going on. Robert said there was a power shift happening, and Shelby had more than once had his digits deep in bad money. Taylor was taking himself a walk on the wild side, and maybe I could work it. Not too hard, just enough for Taylor the Player to get all kinds of wrong ideas.

I'd just have to hope my "bad boys" would pick up and play along.

"Things are going to change, Taylor. You might want to be sure you've got the right kind of friends." I held up the check again.

Brendan, at least, caught my drift. When the easily confused Taylor felt it necessary to look to a fellow guy for confirmation, Brendan nodded.

"You're shittin' me." A little desperate now, Taylor turned to the only other male in the room. Anatole also nodded. "*You're* getting in the game?"

Good start. Which game are you talking about? "Why did Chet get you the job with Bert Shelby?" That the answer would almost surely mean Chet was also "in the game" was something I'd deal with later.

"You haven't got the balls." Taylor struggled to retrieve his attitude, which had been knocked seriously askew.

I shrugged and pushed the check across the counter. "If you're really sure about that, you can walk out of here now. But I will remember this conversation, and more important, Mr. Maddox will remember this conversation." *And I'll apologize to him for this later.*

When it came to personality, Taylor Watts was about one inch deep. That made it very easy to see the possibilities rattling around his brain. The name Maddox worked on him. Something was going on there. At least he thought there was.

"Answer my question," I said to Taylor. "Or quit wasting my time."

Slowly, the new arrangement of reality settled into place behind Taylor's eyes like so many Tetris pieces, and unfortunately, the only set of facts he was comfortable with came out on top. I needed him. He had information, therefore he had power. Taylor grinned at Brendan and Sevarin. The fact that either one could have squashed him like a bug did not seem to be registering. The fact that I could have squashed him like a bug was not even on the radar, although I was itching to put it there.

"Chet got me a job because otherwise I was going to tell you he was cooking the books."

What!

Anatole realized my voice had just short-circuited. Probably those acute undead senses, or the fact that my eyes had bugged out of my head. "Chester Caine was embezzling from his sister?"

"Or laundering money." Taylor shrugged. *No!* my brain howled. *That's* Shelby's *game. Not Chet's!*

"Chet wasn't in a sharing mood when I caught him," Taylor went on.

"*You* caught him?" put in Brendan.

"I'd left my keys here one night and had to come back for them." In Taylor-speak that meant he'd planned on pilfering a bottle of top-shelf vodka again. "So I'm behind the bar, where I leave my stuff during my shift. . . ." *As if I've forgotten we have lockers.* "And they didn't see me when they came out of the office." *I heard the boss coming and I ducked. . . .* "So, there's Chet with this other little vamp. I couldn't understand all of what they were saying. . . ." *I couldn't catch all of it because I was busy trying to keep two vampires from hearing me breathe. . . .* "But they were definitely talking about shuffling around the money in the Nightlife accounts."

The same fierce nausea that had hit me in Post Mortem when I found out about the menu came back with a vengeance, and I found myself wanting to take the smug smile off Taylor Watt's face with the back of a frying pan.

"What then?" Brendan prompted

If Taylor had been chewing gum, he would have popped it right then. "They must have heard my heartbeat or something, because the next thing I know Chet hauls me over the bar and threatens to fire me. But pretty soon he knows it's too late for that."

"Two vampires could have talked you into forgetting," remarked Anatole. "Why didn't they?"

Taylor snorted. "The mental oogity-boogity only works on the tourists."

Silence fell, and so did the temperature in the kitchen by another five degrees. "Would you care to look at me and say that?" Anatole inquired.

"No, thanks, Dracula. I'm fine."

There are things you don't call other people; a whole range of insults that immediately change the game. With vampires, it's the D-word.

For one heartbeat, Taylor was leaning against the counter, full of bullshit and vinegar. By the next, there was a rush of cold wind and Taylor was pinned against the wall, with Anatole's dead-white hand around his neck.

"Gah!" said Taylor.

Anatole barked something in Russian, dry-spat and said, "Look at me, you pathetic little peasant boy."

"Gah!" said Taylor again. I glanced sideways at Brendan. Brendan stayed right where he was, arms folded, watching the proceedings with detached interest.

Slowly, squinting like the lights were too bright, Taylor Watts made himself look at the angry nightblood.

"Be very glad I have changed since my youth." Anatole's voice had gone into vampire basso profundo. All the hair stood up on the back of my neck and Brendan discreetly eased himself a little farther out of range. "Be glad I am no longer the kind who would have already broken your worthless head against this wall and enjoyed hearing the squishy sound your brains made as they dribbled to the floor."

Currents of force leaked out of Anatole. Slowly, all expression drained from Taylor's pretty face. Which was bad enough, but then his mouth stretched out into an empty, mindless grin. "I'm glad."

"Better, Taylor Watts." Anatole let go of Taylor's throat, but Taylor stayed plastered to that wall, up on his toes. My stomach squirmed around as if looking for a quick exit. I reminded myself Anatole liked me. Just then, I had a hard time believing myself.

"Now, give me the truth," said Anatole to Taylor. "What is it you discovered about Chester Caine?"

"I told you everything I know about Chester Caine." Taylor's voice was monotonous, tight and weirdly clipped, like he'd been possessed by the ghost of Stephen Hawking.

"Did you know the other vampire who was there when he caught you eavesdropping?"

"Chet called him Marcus. I'd never seen him before that."

"Why didn't they make you forget what you'd heard?"

"Because I told them I'd already texted myself what I'd heard."

"Smart," remarked Brendan.

"Much smarter than I would have given him credit for." Something was going on in the back of Anatole's mind, but I couldn't tell what. "Tell us more about the second vampire."

Taylor's eyes didn't flicker once from Anatole's. In fact, no part of his face moved except his mouth. Up on his toes like that, he looked as if he had perfected some kind of marionette routine for a talent show or an episode of *The Twilight Zone*. "Second vamp was a little guy. Round face. White. Not real old, but his hair was already starting to thin. Toupee top. Needed a hat."

"Nebbish?" I heard myself whisper.

"Answer her," snapped Anatole.

"Yeah. Nebbish."

My knees decided I needed to sit down just then. But there was nowhere to sit. I pressed both my hands onto the counter, willing myself not to collapse.

Brendan, proving that warlocks also have preternaturally acute senses, rounded the counter to stand beside me. "What is it?"

For all of half a second, I considered not telling him. "This . . . Marcus . . . he was the vampire who was with Pam." And there was no reservation for that table at the time they were in there and we were booked full that night. There was no reservation, because Chet knew Marcus the Nebbishy Vamp when he came in, and took care of the table personally. Because Chet and Marcus were in some kind of business together.

But there might be a way out. It was Marcus who had brought Pam Maddox, and subsequently Dylan Maddox, to Nightlife. Robert had also said he'd thought it was the first time Chet had met Pam. Maybe it was Marcus who was running this game, and just making use of Chet and the fact that he kept our books. Chet would do anything for a friend. He was like that.

I touched Brendan's hand to say thanks, and made myself straighten up. I needed to find Marcus the Nebbish and have a talk with him. Maybe I'd bring Anatole along for that interview too.

"Exactly how was the money being shuffled?" Anatole asked Taylor.

"They wouldn't tell me."

"They did not trust you. Such a surprise. Was that the end of your dealings with Mr. Caine?"

"Caine would come into the bar sometimes after that. Sometimes with Marcus, sometimes with this babe . . ."

"Blond?" Brendan asked before I could.

"No. Black hair and piercing. Vamp, heavy goth, lots of attitude. Wouldn't have minded her wrapping those lips around my . . ."

"Manners. Manners." This time Anatole's voice shook, drawing out the "s" just a little too far. "What was her name?"

"Called her Ill . . . Miss Sin . . . Miss Saint Something . . ."

"St. Claire?" Anatole suggested.

"Yes, St. Claire," Taylor agreed. "Ill-on A St. Claire."

Chet had said he didn't know Ilona St. Claire, whose name I had just happened to hear from Detective Linus O'Grady.

I did not feel so good right then, and Anatole did not look at all good. His face had gone slack, a lot like Taylor's, and his skin took on that waxy corpse yellow color that is never a sign of health. "Why was Ilona there?"

"I don't know. Every time he showed up with her, they'd go into the back office with Bert and lock the door."

Sevarin was quiet for a moment. His hand trembled as he tucked it into his jacket pocket.

"Is there anything you wish to ask?" he turned to me and Brendan. We both shook our heads, and for a split second, Anatole looked grateful.

"Listen to your orders, then," Anatole said to Taylor. "You will leave here without talking to anyone and go directly home. All will be normal, pleasant even. Once home, you will take off all your clothing and fall asleep facedown on your bed. When you wake up, you will have a splitting headache and no memory of what happened. Nod if you understand."

Taylor nodded.

"And the next time you hear the word *Dracula*, you will immediately perform the chicken dance. Nod if you understand."

Taylor nodded.

"And *if* you are ever again with a woman—"

"Sevarin." Brendan interrupted. "That's enough."

I didn't agree. I could tell Anatole didn't either, but he just shrugged. "Obey," he said to Taylor.

Taylor, glassy-eyed and slack-jawed, peeled himself off the wall. He stumbled, and Anatole stepped back. Actually, he staggered back. Taylor, on the other hand, found his footing and straightened up. He adjusted his collar, smoothed down his hair (of course), and walked out the back door without saying a word.

"Are you okay?" To my surprise, Brendan asked the question before I could.

Anatole grimaced. "Contrary to popular belief, 'mental oogity-boogity' takes effort, and it was unusually difficult to get that overgrown adolescent to hold a coherent thought. I will be all right in a moment."

Right. *Macho idiot.* "Hang on." I headed for the stairs.

We hadn't been able to use up any of the liquid product in our cleanout-turned-charitable-event that afternoon. I had five gallons of thawed bull's blood that would not last past tomorrow. When I toted the bucket up the stairs, Brendan actually moved forward to help. I looked him in the eye and hefted the thing up onto the counter.

One-handed.

Okay, so macho is contagious.

I pried off the lid, grabbed a cup from the pile by the dishwashing station (yes, it was *clean*—sheesh), dipped it full and handed it to Anatole.

"Ever the gracious hostess." Anatole's eyes gleamed as he accepted the cup. He swallowed, grimaced at the temperature, and then gulped down the rest. He passed me the cup and I filled it again. Probably he wished I'd just given him a straw.

"Do you know Ilona St. Claire?" I asked.

"I do," he replied between sips. Already his skin was filling out and returning to its normal pallor.

"Can you get her to talk to me?" From what Taylor had said, she would know Marcus the Nebbish. She could give me his name, maybe a contact number.

"To us," put in Brendan. When I turned to protest, he just lowered his eyebrows at me. "You're not the only one with family in this mess."

I couldn't argue with that, and truth was, it would be good to have him there. It's not that I didn't trust Anatole to have my back, but Brendan could make the sun rise on command, which, as we had already seen, could be very useful.

"Ilona might not be interested in talking to either of you." Anatole looked into the bottom of his cup as if he could read hemoglobin like tea leaves. "She has . . . views about daybloods and their relation to nightbloods. However, we have a more immediate concern."

My fingers curled around the edge of the counter. "What?"

Anatole raised his cup. "This liquid I am drinking—it is human blood."

15

"It is not," I snapped at the exact same moment Brendan demanded, "Are you sure?"

"It is, and yes, I am." Anatole smiled at our amazing display of dayblood denialism, and we both got a good look at his bloody fangs. "I am . . . most familiar with the taste. Although it is much better warm."

"I do not serve human blood!"

"I did not say you did." Anatole dipped his cup into the bucket again and took another long, appreciative swallow.

"Then what's it doing here?" Part of me knew I had to get past this, and quickly. There was something I needed to deal with on the other side. But I couldn't make my mind budge from the fact of the bucket's existence.

"Excellent question." Anatole drained his cup a second time, eyes closed, savoring the rare beverage. It might be stale and refrigerated, but nothing acts on a vamp like the true human. Anatole's face, which had been so corpselike a minute ago, wasn't just pink now, it was flushed. If he kept this up, he'd be thoroughly stoned inside of five minutes.

"I've got another excellent question," said Brendan grimly. "Whose blood is it?"

Anatole froze with the cup halfway to the bucket again. Then he set it carefully down on the counter.

"It very much pains me to say this." Anatole eyed my bucket like a drunk eyeing a bottle of Johnnie Walker Blue. "Charlotte, I believe you should call Detective O'Grady."

"No!"

Both of them stared at me. "No," I said again, more softly. I put the lid back on the bucket and pounded it down, hard. So my fist hurt. So I had something to concentrate on besides the feeling of these two men trying to work out how much of my mind I had actually lost.

Brendan grabbed my wrist. We stared at each other over that stupid, mislabeled bucket. He was waiting to see if I'd pull away, I was sure of it. Come to that, I was waiting to see if I'd pull away. "Sevarin's right, Charlotte. O'Grady needs to know about this."

I did pull away then, and Brendan let me go. "I know, I know. Just . . ." I put up my hands to hold him back so I could think. "Not yet, okay?"

"Why?" Anatole ran his finger around the rim of the bucket. Abruptly, I remembered O'Grady and the lasagna. The men I ran into did love their food.

"This isn't easy on either of us, Charlotte," said Brendan. "We've both got someone important at risk here."

You don't know. You don't know anything. You don't know what I've done to Chet. I'm responsible for him. I'm responsible and I will not let anybody take him down like this!

"You must consider that this blood might have been taken from Dylan Maddox," said Anatole. "If it was, it is vital that Detective O'Grady know you are not concealing it. We do not know that Chet can be held responsible for the presence of human blood in your restaurant, but if we fail to report it, we most certainly will be."

"I know, I know." I couldn't seem to stop saying that, which was ironic because right then I felt like I didn't know anything at all. "I just . . ."

I do not beg. Not to anyone, not ever. But while witnessing the nearly inconceivable sight of the warlock and the vampire on the same side, that's exactly what I did. They liked me, both of them. They were attracted to me. We'd flirted. And I stood there working it for all I was worth. I am not proud of it. I don't excuse it. I just did it.

"Please. Just one more day. Let me talk to Ilona St. Claire and find out if she knows what's happening. If Chet's involved, let me give him a chance to explain. Then, if he won't go to O'Grady, I will." The last two words came out in a whisper. "I promise," I breathed. "Please."

Brendan caved first, and Anatole saw him do it.

"This is a very bad idea," he said to the warlock. Why did Anatole care about any of this? Oh, I knew what he'd told me about the importance to the nightblood community of solving the murders, but that couldn't be all there was to this, could it?

"You do not even know that Ilona will consent to speak with you," Anatole reminded me. Us. "She has very definite views about the worth and status of daybloods."

"I was hoping you could help us with that," I murmured.

"Yes, of course you were." Anatole went still the way only a dead man could. There was no way to tell what he was thinking. None at all. I glanced at Brendan, who was almost as still. The difference was that while Anatole was staring at the bucket, Brendan was staring at me.

"Very well." Anatole came back to movement so suddenly that I startled backward. "But only because I also have questions that she needs to answer." Anatole pulled his phone out of his pocket, punched in a number and waited while it rang.

"Ilona," he said and then lapsed into Russian. His

voice went . . . delicious. Smoky, rich and filled with hidden laughter. My toes tried to curl up and I reflexively leaned closer. Brendan caught my shoulder and glared at me, which I deserved.

Anatole finished the call and tucked the phone away. "Ilona has agreed to speak with you," he said. "Both of you. But she wants you to come to her theater tomorrow at midnight."

"Um," I said, "why?"

"I expect it is to make you hideously uncomfortable and to show me how weak and pathetic daybloods are."

"Delightful." Brendan sighed.

"Normally I would refuse. But it is plain that Ilona is involved in something dubious. I would like her to have a chance to extricate herself before she is hurt." I found myself wondering how long Anatole had known Ilona St. Claire and under what circumstances.

"So now we all have a dog in the hunt," said Brendan.

"And we all must follow where they lead," said Anatole.

I didn't have a witty follow-up metaphor, so I just grabbed my bucket of blood and headed down to the walk-in. I would feel better with this locked away. I'd feel best with it poured down the drain. But even I knew that would be a bad idea.

And I could always change my mind later if I needed to. At least, that's what I told myself as I locked the door and climbed back up the stairs. This private reminder did not make me feel better. Neither did the looks I got from both Brendan and Anatole when I returned to the kitchen. Neither did the fact that I was forgetting something. Something important.

Before I could think what it was, my cell phone buzzed against my hip. I pulled it out and saw a text from Chet. Two words. *C3 call!*

My mouth went perfectly and absolutely dry. Total absence of water. Vamp dry.

"'Scuse me one sec," I croaked to the men, who were looking at least as unhappy about this interruption as they had about the blood. "I gotta do this."

I retreated out the back door into our alley with its stacks of pallets, milk crates and the bucket of sand we keep as an ashtray for the smokers. The alley had also been plastered with a solid sheet of *Midnight Moon* posters. I had a dozen copies of Joshua Blake staring at me as I hit Chet's number with a shaking thumb. I stared back at those sad, dark, heavily made-up eyes while the phone rang, and some absurd little part of my mind started to wonder if somebody had it in for me.

It was one of those ideas you shouldn't start in with, because as soon as I thought it once, I thought it again and again.

No. This can't be about him. I swallowed hard. I chewed my tongue to try to work up some saliva. It didn't help.

The ring on my phone cut out, and I got Chet's voice. "Hey, C3!"

He sounded happy. No, elated. The last time he'd sounded this chipper was when he came back to tell me Anatole Sevarin was in the house.

And look where that got us. I swallowed again. "Hey, Chet. What's going on?"

"I just got word. The P-Squad's going to let us all the way back in starting tomorrow. We can open again!"

I swear to God, the alley spun around me. I pressed my free hand against the wall, right over Joshua Blake's aquiline nose. "How did you find out?"

"A friend of mine knows a guy on the night shift. He called in a favor and got a look at the paperwork."

I couldn't take it. It was too much. This was the news I'd been praying for. But as Chet's words sank in, all I could see was that bucket of blood I'd just locked into the walk-in.

"What friend is this?" I asked. Maybe it was Marcus the Nebbish. Maybe I could weasel a full name out of Chet, and then I wouldn't have to go through this business with Ilona St. Claire.

"Nobody you know," said Chet. "Doesn't matter anyway. We're back! If we haul ass, we might even be open for the weekend."

Yes, yes, it does matter! I wanted to scream. *You're trying to distract me, aren't you? You're trying to get into the walk-in so you can get rid of the blood!*

Of course, he could do that anytime. The kitchen was already open, and he had the same set of keys I did.

Keys. That's what I had forgotten. The walk-in was kept locked. Whoever had put what was possibly Dylan Maddox's blood in that bucket had needed keys.

"Charlotte? Are you still there?"

"Yeah, yeah, I'm still here." The words came out as a wheeze. I felt my fingers curl into a fist, scraping against the paper-covered bricks.

"You don't sound so good. And don't say you're just tired," Chet added.

"No, it's not that. It's . . ." *It's that you're scamming me. You're manipulating the accounts and sneaking around with vamps and witches and you won't tell me what's going on!*

"C3?" said Chet again.

"Yeah?" I pressed my fist against Joshua Blake's nose. Hard. Harder.

"It's going to be okay. I promise. Cross what's left of my heart."

I smiled weakly. He sounded so much like the Chet I'd always known. My charming, earnest little brother, the boy king of Buffalo.

"Chet . . ." This was it. Last chance. These next words would open doors back up, or shut them permanently. "I've been asking around about Dylan Maddox."

"Charlotte, is that a good idea? The cops are on it. Nightlife's out of it. We . . . you should let this go."

"Yeah. Probably. But as it stands, I've got an appointment to go see Ilona St. Claire tomorrow night."

There was the tiniest hint of a pause before Chet said, "Who?"

"She's one of the vampires Detective O'Grady was asking about. Turns out she's a good friend of Anatole's."

"Charlotte, you're not going alone into a vampire theater."

"Are you offering to come with me?"

Again, that tiny sliver of a pause. "Look, Charlotte, I'm serious. This is a very bad idea. I've been asking around. She's with the separatist movement. Hell, she practically *is* the separatist movement—"

"Chet." I banged my fist against the wall. It hurt and the wall didn't care. "Just tell me if there's anything I need to know."

"There's nothing, Charlotte. I promise."

He could have said that a hundred more times and I still wouldn't have believed him. "Okay," I said. "That's all there is to it, then." The doors were all closed and locked.

"Now you promise me you won't do anything stupid."

You first, little brother. "Okay," I said, which could have meant anything. I wanted him to call me on it. I wanted him to insist he'd come with me, or keep me from going.

"Okay," he said. "Look, I'm going to start getting hold of the front-of-house staff. I'll have a head count for you before dawn."

"Great. Talk to you soon."

"'Bye, Charlotte."

We hung up. I leaned against the wall of Nightlife. Slowly, my head fell back until I was looking up at the sky. I breathed deep, but that was a bad idea, because that particular alley smell of garbage and grease was too strong, and I was back in a different darkness, with the roll of bills clutched tightly in my hand.

Is that enough? I can get more. I just want to see him. Just for a few minutes, that's all. You can make sure I get to see him, right?

"Charlotte?" Brendan's hand touched my shoulder.

"Yeah," I said, as if I needed to confirm my own name. "Yeah."

"I don't suppose you would care to tell us what has you so upset?" Anatole stood on the threshold, holding the door open for us both.

I looked at my phone dangling in my fingers. "Chet."

"Ah," said Anatole. "I find I am not at all surprised."

"What's happened?" Brendan asked. He hadn't taken his hand off my shoulder, and I was pretty okay with that.

"He says he's gotten the heads-up from a friend of a friend that we're going to be allowed back into Nightlife tomorrow. All the way in."

"And yet you sound rather magnificently unhappy." Anatole leaned against the doorframe. "I will assume, therefore, that that was not all he said."

"That'd be a safe assumption." I stuffed my phone into my pocket and ran my hand over my hair. My braid was coming apart, with wisps and stray locks hanging out all over the place. Great. Now I had metaphoric hair. Just what I needed.

"I will assume you're not going to tell us what else he said." Brendan sounded disappointed already.

I closed my eyes, dug deep, and came up empty. "I can't," I said. "Not yet. Tomorrow night."

Tomorrow night Ilona St. Claire would give me a full name to hang on Marcus the Nebbish, and the Nebbish would lead me to Pam Maddox. Tomorrow night I would know exactly what Chet had done.

I just had to hold on until then. I could do that much. I had to.

16

Once again I caught a cab home in the wee hours. Both Anatole and Brendan stayed to see me get in safely and give the driver my home address. It was like they thought I'd go chasing off after a clue or a suspect or something. The truth was, I couldn't afford it. I could barely afford the cab. These late-night Nancy Drew shenanigans were starting to seriously strain my budget.

I let myself into the silent apartment—tiptoeing in case either of the roommates was not quite asleep—and collapsed in my own bed. This time, though, I didn't fall dead asleep. This time, I lay under the covers watching the sky brighten on the other side of my crooked venetian blinds. I wasn't thinking. I wasn't planning. Brain and body were both gone far beyond that. I was just waiting.

Eventually the sound of running water filtered through the wall, followed by sturdy heels clumping on hardwood and then, unexpectedly, a resonant alto having a bad Queen flashback.

"Weeeee are the champions!"

I pulled on my purple velour robe and shuffled out into the hall in time to see Trish shaking her backside in the living room. As she was also in her best black pantsuit, it was quite a sight.

"Weeeee are the champions!"

"Why have all my roommates lost their minds?" Jess had come up the hall behind me, looking at least as blurry as I felt.

"Because you are looking at the queen of the New York City courts!" Trish executed a tight pirouette and waved her cell phone. "They want to deal! They want to deal!"

I squinted at Trish. How did someone get that happy at seven in the morning? "Who does?"

"The MacMillans of *Preston v. MacMillan Enterprises LLC*, otherwise known as the people who are going to pay through their fraudulent noses *and* kiss some serious and very public ass, starting with my client's!" She spread her arms and waited. Jess and I looked at each other. Trish wiggled her hands in a "give it to me" gesture, and we both dutifully applauded.

"Yea," I added.

"Thank you, thank you. You're too kind." Trish bowed.

"So, this is the rubber chicken case?" Jess slumped onto the couch and yawned hugely. I wish she hadn't, because now I was doing the same thing.

"Dangerously defective novelty products, if you please," said Trish. "Yes, that case."

I looked down at Jess, but had to shove a wad of tangled hair out of my eyes to do it. "She's defending rubber chickens?"

"Actually, she's defending people from rubber chickens." Jess kicked her feet up onto the coffee table.

"Defective rubber chickens," put in Trish. "Rotten latex. Cracks and turns to powder."

As important as this clearly was, just then I remembered something else equally vital and endeavored to muster a glower for Jessie. "You painted my toenails."

Jess shrugged. "You deserved it."

"Can we focus here, people?" Trish cut in. "This is a multimillion-dollar suit I've just fought to a standstill and my firm gets ten percent of the settlement."

"Multimillion-dollar rubber chickens?" I was so clearly in the wrong business.

"Whatever. Look, try this. The firm's going to be throwing a party tonight at Aquavit. You guys should come. Lots of pretty single men, and women who might need makeup consulting."

"Count me in!" Jess managed to sound enthusiastic despite another jaw-cracking yawn.

My roommates both looked at me. "Can't," I said.

"How come?" they chorused.

"I've got an appointment." As an excuse, this might have worked, except I said it too fast and I was halfway to the kitchen before I had the sentence finished. "Who wants coffee?"

"Appointment?" repeated Trish, layering on a full measure of lawyerly skepticism. "And you let Jess paint your toenails?"

"I did not let her paint my toenails. She caught me at a vulnerable moment."

"A vulnerable moment named Brendan," said Jessie. "She says he's cute."

I turned on her, brandishing the coffee grinder. "One more word, and I swear I will be using your party bags as grill fuel."

"You heard that, right?" said Jess to Trish.

"Don't worry. I know a good personal injury attorney." Trish strode over to the kitchen doorway. I got the beans out of the fridge and dumped a full measure into the grinder and did not look at her.

"So you've got a date," Trish said as I started the grinder

and pretended not to hear. "What's the big deal? Bring him along."

"Trish, I swear, it's not a date." I dumped the ground coffee into the filter basket. "It really is an appointment. With a vampire."

"Who? This Sevarin guy?"

"He'll be there." I poured filtered water from the pitcher into the coffeemaker and shoved the carafe into place.

Trish was still looking at me and, incidentally, blocking the only exit. I opened the fridge again and tried to focus on whether I should offer to make pancakes or French toast for breakfast. We were all awake; we might as well eat. I had some really good raspberry preserves that whispered "French toast" to me. I reached for the eggs.

"Tell me this is about Nightlife opening again," said Trish very quietly and very seriously. "Tell me you are not trying to pull a Jessica Fletcher on me."

"This is about Nightlife opening again," I said, pulling my bread knife off the magnetic bar mounted on the backsplash. "I am not trying to pull a Jessica Fletcher on you."

Proving that sometimes the universe does show mercy, my phone started ringing. "That should be Detective O'Grady now." I pushed past her, snatched up my phone and checked the number. "Yep. 'Scuse me."

I hit the TALK button as soon as I had the door to my room shut behind me. "Good morning, Detective." *Thank you for the rescue.*

"Good morning, Chef Caine. I thought you'd want to know as soon as possible. Our team is finished and you are free to enter your restaurant again."

"That's terrific!"

There was a pause on the other end. "You already knew."

Remind me never, ever to try to play poker for stakes any higher than M&M's. "Yeah. A friend of a friend of my brother's."

"Name?" O'Grady inquired, and somehow I just knew that little notebook was out again.

"Sorry. I don't know."

"If you find out, I'd appreciate you letting me know."

"I'll do my best, Detective."

"Thank you. Good luck, Chef Caine. I hope your re-opening goes well."

"Thank you, Detective. You're welcome at Nightlife anytime."

We said a couple more polite nothings and thank-yous and finally hung up. It seemed pretty clear that Detective O'Grady did not expect to be talking with me again, and I sincerely wanted to believe he was right.

I beat Jess into the bathroom by a hairsbreadth, washed up and dressed in my black pants and kitchen whites. I made French toast with warm raspberry preserves spiked with ginger and lemon zest, and topped by a dollop of sweet-and-sour cream. I also spent a good half hour ducking Trish's questions before I was finally able to make my escape down to the station and the E train.

I had the block almost to myself as I rounded the corner and stopped in front of Nightlife. It had been only a few days, but the front windows were already dull and dust-streaked. Trash and autumn leaves had drifted into the corners of the entranceway and the CLOSED sign was badly askew. Three new graffiti tags decorated the west wall.

From the front, Nightlife didn't look closed. It looked dead.

I remembered the night we'd first turned on the sign. It had sputtered for a few heart-wrenching seconds before it lit up the sidewalk in a wash of clean red and orange. I'd high-fived Chet with both hands, and he'd grabbed me up and swung me around in a big circle, just like he had when he came in the kitchen to tell me Anatole Sevarin was in the dining room.

I made myself take a good long look at my dark and silent restaurant. I needed to do more than see. I needed to let the sight take root. Because this was what I faced. This was why I really needed to find out what was going on instead of just letting it all go like everybody from my brother to Detective O'Grady wanted. This was not about any abstract principle. If I didn't find out what had happened to Dylan Maddox, the people who had killed him could take all my work away again.

I sucked in a deep breath and let it out slowly before I crossed the street and let myself in the front door. The dim dining room wrapped around me and a tension deep inside eased, the way it does when you've come home. I tossed my purse onto the bar and put thoughts of my upcoming "appointment" in my back pocket. I would get my sous chefs, Zoe and Reese, on the phone, followed by Marie-Our-Pastry-Chef. They could make the calls to the kitchen personnel and get us a head count of who was staying and who had already found new jobs. If we'd lost too many people, we'd have to get with one of the staffing agencies and bring in a new crew. That would mean training. Robert and Suchai could handle any new front-of-the-house staff, if needed. Reese was a former drill sergeant and could take on a whole new hot line if he absolutely had to. Zoe and I could huddle over the menu. It had to change, top to bottom, before next month, and we had to have at least six new dishes in place for Saturday. Chet was right. If we hauled ass we could open Saturday night. We had to start calling suppliers, see who was still willing to give us credit and—

A sharp rap sounded on the glass behind me. *Brendan,* I thought automatically as I turned around, trying to decide whether I should be annoyed or pleased that he'd come to check up on me this early.

Except it wasn't Brendon Maddox. It was Margot.

Margot Maddox had changed her red leather coat for a basic black trench that fit her well enough to be designer. She'd also swapped her high-heeled lace-up boots for patent-leather pumps. She'd changed her demeanor too. The cat-cool woman was gone, replaced by someone who clutched her slender purse strap and looked over her shoulder twice in the short amount of time it took me to cross the dining room again and snap back the dead bolt.

"Ms. Maddox," I said, summoning my best greet-the-skeptical-client manners. "Can I help you?"

"I hope so, Chef Caine." Margot started to look over her shoulder again, but stopped herself. "May I come in?"

"Certainly." I stood back and let her in. "Although I'm afraid I don't have much time. We're cleared to reopen and we have a lot of work to do."

This was a hint, but Margot didn't even stop to acknowledge it. She walked straight past me, her eyes searching all the shadows in the dim dining room. I remembered Brendan doing much the same thing.

She must have been satisfied, because she turned around. "I'll be brief." She straightened her shoulders, very visibly pulling herself together. "I'd like to buy you out."

Sorry? What? HUH? These and a dozen other exclamations stampeded toward the front of my brain. Fortunately, what got there first was, "Excuse me?"

Margot's fingers clenched around her purse strap. Her knuckles had to be stark white underneath those black gloves. "I will pay you not to reopen this establishment. It will be a substantial sum, for you and your . . . brother both, if you want. Enough so that you can go from here to create any other kind of restaurant your heart desires."

I didn't collapse into a chair this time. I pulled one out slowly and concentrated on sitting down in a controlled fashion. I was glad I'd worn my chef's coat and had taken the time to put my hair up this morning. It reminded me who I was, and that I was on my home turf. Executive chefs do not slump in their chairs with their jaws flapping open, no matter what kind of offer has just been dangled in front of them. I gestured for Margot Maddox to take a seat. She did, but she did not do anything to get comfortable, like remove her gloves or slip her purse off her shoulder. She didn't even let go of the strap.

"What does Brendan think about this idea? Or Ian?" I asked.

"They don't know."

Uh-huh. "And the money would come with conditions?"

"Only one. That whatever establishment you open after this does not serve blood of any kind."

So there it was. Margot and her side of the family wanted to shut us down as part of the Maddox family antivampire campaign. "Listen, Ms. Maddox . . ."

"One million dollars."

The whole of my angry speech died, turned to dust and blew away. "Excuse me?" I said again.

"One. Million. Dollars," repeated Margot. "Cashier's check."

"You have that kind of money?"

She sighed. "I have a trust fund separate from the family money. I also have a very good lawyer of my own and he broke the trust before I came down here. I had a feeling I might need to pay off Pamela and I didn't want to have to get Grandfather's permission to do it. My grandfather, by the way, is very unhappy with me," she added, and this time she did look over her shoulder.

"That'd be Mr. Lloyd 'Stake 'Em All' Maddox?" I peered through the front door, but I saw only the usual range of morning suits, construction workers and women in black going past. "Is your grandfather with you?"

"No. Ian's in the car and—" Margot cut herself off, but I understood. I wouldn't have trusted Ian and his chin tuft to stay where I put them either. "Which is neither here nor there," she went on. "I'm offering you one million dollars, Chef Caine. Today. Your lawyer can draw up papers if you like. I will sign, and I have only the one condition, which you've already heard."

A million dollars. A million, cash. With that as a stake, I could get credit from . . . anywhere. It would mean the ability to open a topflight place and a chance to compete in the big game. It would be the freedom to take my craft as far as I was able to.

Unfortunately, it also left one huge question burning brightly enough to set the sprinklers off all over again.

"Why?" I asked.

"Why do you think?" Margot screwed up her face tighter than I would have thought possible. I had her down for a Botox baby. "My family is being torn apart. I don't care about Pamela," she went on quickly, as I leaned forward again. "At least, I wouldn't if she was just going to hell in her own handbasket. But she's pulling the rest of the family in with her."

"You've talked to her?"

"I wish." Margot exchanged her stranglehold on her purse strap for a similar grip on the table's edge. "At this point it doesn't really matter whether we find her or not. Look what's already happened because of her. Dylan's dead. Brendan's heading into real trouble. . . ." She faltered, and I remembered Margot was Brendan's sister. I met her eyes and saw that in this one way we understood each other very well. We both knew how far we'd already gone to protect our brothers, and we knew we would go further if we had to.

But although I understood that desire, I couldn't see any way it had led to this conversation. "How is keeping Nightlife closed going to help your family?"

"It's obvious, isn't it? Someone wants to use Nightlife for . . . something. I don't know who and I don't care. If I close it off, maybe they'll look elsewhere and maybe that will buy O'Grady and his people enough time to actually *do* something."

"You're willing to spend a million dollars on a couple maybes?"

"Only because that's all I've got right now."

Wow, I thought. *The rich really are different from you and me.* Or this particular rich woman knew way more than she was telling me. As soon as I'd kicked over that mental rock, another nasty thought crawled out.

"If you haven't been talking to Cousin Pamela, have you been talking to Brendan?" Had Brendan told her about the blood? No, not possible. If he had, she'd have been on the phone to O'Grady, not here offering me the bribe of a lifetime.

Margot drew her shoulders back and for a moment the cold sophisticate was back in front of me. "Despite what you and my brother may think, I don't need to run to him with every little question. I have resources of my own."

I could easily believe that. The Maddox family was connected to wealth, privilege and politics. Margot surely knew how to work all three when the situation called for it.

I folded my arms and drummed my fingers on my sleeve. There were too many angles here for me to work out at once. I had to delay her, give myself time to settle down. Get the words *one million dollars* to stop flashing around the margins of my brain.

"If I'm going to agree to think about your offer, I have a condition of my own."

"What's that?"

"I need an answer. What is Nightlife being used for?"

For a minute, I thought she was going to try to tell me she didn't know. I sat back and waited. Now this was a game I could play. It didn't require a poker face, just patience. At various times, I'd had to wait across the table from employees who were stealing the tip money from their fellows, sneaking their illegal relatives in to sleep in the stockroom, and dealing marijuana out the back door.

At last Margot Maddox made her decision. She ran her palm across the tabletop as if checking for wrinkles in the veneer. "Blood running," she said.

"Bullshit," I replied calmly.

"I beg your pardon?"

"The black market in human blood is an urban legend." I elbowed the image of that damn blood bucket back where it belonged. "Warm from the vein works much better. Besides, nobody needs to buy human blood. The live volunteers are lining up." It's what Post Mortem and its seedier cousins made their payroll on. "Check Craigslist if you don't believe me."

Margot cocked her head, and the look she had on her face was one of pure pity. "But there's no guarantee those volunteers are clean, or that they're not FBI stings or vigilantes with stakes. Besides, the kind of person who advertises on Craigslist is looking to be turned, or might be addicted to the thrill or the drain. They turn stalker. Much easier for the civilized vampire"—she spat the words—"to buy a few bags of what they want. Much easier, except, of course, that it's illegal to buy or sell human blood for consumption."

It made sense. It made so much sense my heart was banging against my ribs and my stomach was clenched as tightly as my fists. "Didn't your family have something to do with getting that legislation passed?"

I had the satisfaction of seeing Margot wince. "If I'd been old enough I would have spoken against it. This kind of prohibition never works."

"So you think Pamela's a blood runner?" *Or you know she is. . . .*

"Actually, I think your brother is a blood runner," she shot back. "I think he and his partners have roped Pam in to work security for them."

I thought about the overfluffed fang tease in the see-through white dress and blue eye shadow. "Pam could work security?"

"Oh, yes. It's a family specialty. In fact, Brendan was training her before she ran out on us."

Which, if true, was something he had entirely failed to mention. I really didn't want to think about the implications of that. Fortunately, Margot had given me a deluxe set of other things to think about, complete with Special Offers Not Available Elsewhere.

"You think Chet's in charge of this . . . operation? If there is one?"

"If you don't, Chef Caine, it's because you're deluding yourself."

Why wasn't I getting angry? This smug little rich bitch was sitting here accusing Chet of robbing the Red Cross and selling the stolen blood out the back of *my* restaurant. And she was trying to buy me off.

The problem was, there was still the bucket in my walk-in. There was Marcus bringing Cousin Pam in the front door, maybe to meet Chet. There was how Chet got Taylor Watts a job, and how Taylor was hanging around Village bars to make mixologists nervous. These could easily be the actions of someone checking on things for the boss—things like territory and payment and purchase quotas.

"It doesn't mean Chet's in charge," I said through clenched teeth. "It could just as easily be Bert Shelby at Post Mortem." *Or the Nebbish. Don't forget about the Nebbish. It could even be Pam herself, and Margot here is trying to orchestrate the cover-up.*

Margot smiled, calm and collected for the first time this morning. She rose to her feet. "Think about my offer, Chef Caine. I'll be waiting to hear from you." She pulled a card out of her tidy little purse and pushed it across the table to me. I put it in my pocket without looking at it.

"Tomorrow," I said. She nodded, and left, sashaying across the dining room like she was the one who owned the place.

I couldn't do anything but sit there and think how tomorrow was going to be the first day of the rest of my life.

Shit.

17

The Final Curtain Theater, owned and managed by Ilona St. Claire, is the kind of place that gets referred to as Off Off Broadway. Or, at least it would if a dayblood critic was permitted near it. Such people, Anatole said, did not tend to appreciate the subtleties of vampiric performance art.

"So, what's playing?" I asked him.

"*Blood Slaughter at Sunset.* A newly transitioned playwright, making quite a stir." Nobody can shrug as eloquently as a professional critic. "I find him overly sentimental."

About then it began to dawn on me that this excursion might be a bad idea on more than one level. Yeah, yeah, I know. *Now* it began to dawn on me?

I assumed we'd be catching a cab, but Brendan had a car service he preferred. As he was paying, I didn't object, and before long I was ensconced on the plush seat of a black town car with the expansive blond vampire and the intense black-haired warlock. No way I could ever tell Jess about this. She'd die from jealousy.

My big mistake, though, was deciding to dress for the

theater. I'd borrowed a belted red sweater dress from Jess and a pair of sparkly gold pumps with matching purse from Trish. I was showing way more leg to the guys than I ever had before, and given our crowded conditions, I was beginning to regret it.

I did consider telling Brendan about my . . . meeting with Margot, but not for long. We all had more than enough to deal with right now, and if we didn't we would very soon.

The Final Curtain turned out to be in Harlem, which was gutsy. Unlike most other . . . marginally legal activities, vampirism affected minority and poor communities far less than the white and affluent. There are still too many grandmas and grandpas in those families who grew up when any unwelcome paranormal activity, whether it had fangs, claws or curses, was dealt with by the elders of the clan, and they hadn't forgotten what to do. In fact, despite the stories, if you meet a vamp who says he's from New Orleans, he's probably lying through his fangs. Marie Laveau, who was high priestess there a century back, did not like vampires. The magical wards she left behind still make it hard for them to get past the city limits. She also left behind a whole lot of grandkids, a number of whom had immigrated to New York. Putting a vampire theater in the middle of the city's most famous African-American neighborhood was a big f.u. to that population. It also, Anatole pointed out, kept away the faint of fang.

"So, this Ilona St. Claire has a little bit of attitude is what you're saying?"

"A soupçon. Yes."

"Wasn't she involved in that big public meeting last year?" asked Brendan. "Where the vampires were agitating against more rights? She wanted everyone to scatter out of the city for the rural counties."

Anatole's smile was tight and humorless. "To reclaim the 'unfettered, wild existence that is the true destiny of all nightbloods'? Yes. That was Ilona."

"And this is a friend of yours?" Anatole seemed so fully at home as he was, I had trouble picturing him lurking about the moonlit woods.

"People come together for many reasons, Charlotte." He leaned close enough for me to catch his scent of spiced cologne and fresh truffles. "Look at us."

Brendan coughed hard. Anatole sighed and sat back. I uncrossed my ankles and crossed them again. I should have worn slacks.

As Off-Off-Broadway theaters are not noted for high operating budgets, I expected Final Curtain to be an ex-warehouse or storefront. To my surprise, a renovated vaudeville palace greeted us, standing proud in its evening gown of gilt and neon. Although fully lit up on the outside, the lobby behind the glass and brass doors was absolutely dark. As Anatole directed our driver around the corner, I could see shadows moving slowly back and forth inside. My hindbrain did not like it at all.

It liked the alley with the stage door entrance even less. It was wider than the one where I'd . . . met Tommy and Julie, and didn't have a dead end, but that pair could easily be lurking in any one of the doorways.

"Should I wait, Mr. Maddox?" the driver asked.

"Yes," said Brendan. I ignored the way my hindbrain groveled in thanks.

We all climbed out and Anatole banged on what I had to assume was the stage door. I shifted my weight, trying to find a comfortable way to stand in my borrowed pumps. After a moment, the door opened, amazingly quietly. Despite everything, there's still an expectation that doors into vampire hangouts should emit long, drawn-out creaks.

Of course, there was nobody visible opening it, and the space on the other side was pitch-black. Which in terms of dramatic, nerve-racking effect is almost as good.

If you run away now, you'll never find out what's going on, I told myself. Then, of course, I had to remind myself why this would be bad.

Anatole stepped across the threshold without hesitation. Brendan touched my shoulder, reminding me there was another beating heart nearby. I mentally pulled on my big-girl panties and followed.

Of course the door swung shut behind us. The hollow, metallic thump and instant plunge into darkness more than made up for the lack of distressed hinges. I sucked in my breath and got the smell of dust, mushrooms and that distinctive salt-and-iron tang that you never want to get a whiff of outside a butcher shop.

A woman screamed.

I jumped about a foot and backpedaled straight into Brendan's chest.

"Dead!" the woman shrieked. "All dead! Oh, bloody fate!"

Applause rang out. I heard a distinctive metallic *flick!* behind me and all at once I stood in a small pool of light. Magic? I whirled around to face Brendan, who held his smartphone up over his head. A virtual Zippo lighter blazed on the screen.

"Aye, bloody fate," said a man's doleful overenunciated voice. My eyes had adjusted enough for me to make out a patch of pale gray light over to the right that had to be the stage. "For what else can our fate be but to die, should they who are free of death choose us?"

"Nice app," I said. Brendan grinned and although there was probably no reason to, I suddenly felt better.

"But our children!" wailed the woman. "We must avenge them!"

"There is no vengeance for us. They were taken by one who is as far beyond us as the shifting moon."

"*Blood Slaughter at Sunset*," murmured Brendan.

"Really, Ilona." Anatole addressed the interior darkness. "This is an abundance of drama, even for you."

"Occupational hazard, I'm afraid, Anatole."

Ilona St. Claire glided out of the darkness. Unlike Anatole in his sharp, modern dress, Ilona was working with expectations. Her high-necked black evening gown looked demure, until you saw the back, which wasn't there. At all. Her rose and bramble tattoo was . . . impressive, as were the gold rings on her gloved fingers and wrists, and dangling from her ears, and pierced through her eyebrow and nose. In the light of Brendan's cell phone Zippo, Ilona St. Claire glittered as brightly as her theater's exterior.

"Anatole." Ilona slipped up close enough to him that her bodice brushed against his chest. "You must to speak with your theater critic at *Circulation*. He completely misunderstood Raymond's work." She ran a gloved palm across his cheek.

". . . Rip out my heart and lay it at his feet . . ." the actress added.

Anatole gave that critic's shrug of his. "You know my feelings about romanticizing the good old days, Ilona."

"Your time will come soon enough!" warned the man. "Look! Even now the sun sets as the world turns to offer itself again to *him*."

"Then give us your story, Anatole." Ilona drew her fingers along his lips. "Tell us what it was really like."

Anatole took her glittery finger, kissed it, and returned her hand to her side. "Perhaps I am holding out for an offer from Hollywood."

"Don't be ridiculous."

"Don't say that to my agent."

All Ilona's seduction vanished, replaced by a simmering

frustration. She suddenly looked a lot younger too. "If you must play the fool, Anatole, could you avoid doing so in front of the daybloods?"

Anatole leaned in. "It keeps them off their guard." It came to me that he was deliberately provoking her and I wondered again about the pair of them. The two of them, I mentally corrected myself.

Wait. What did I care whether they were a pair or not?

The patch of gray light at the corner of my vision turned deep red. Applause broke out again.

Evidently having failed to get the kind of reaction she wanted from Anatole, Ilona turned her attention to the "daybloods." She glided up to me. Neat maneuver. Must have taken a lot of practice too, as the hem of her backless dress puddled dramatically on the floor and she didn't once stumble. "You are Charlotte Caine. The vampire chef."

"That nickname was not my idea." I held out my hand. "Thank you for agreeing to talk to us."

"It is Anatole you should thank." Ilona looked at my hand like she wondered what it was doing there. I shrugged. Okay, now I knew where we were. "Without him, you would not be here."

"Will I blot out the sun itself with the strength of my hunger?" inquired a new actor with the heaviest Eastern European accent since the master himself. Clearly, it was monologue time in *Blood Slaughter*.

I found myself with absolutely no desire to prolong this weird little encounter. Time to be direct. "I'm trying to find out why Dylan Maddox's body was dumped at my restaurant. Your name's come up a couple times, so I thought you might have some ideas about who or what was behind it."

Ilona swiveled her head to glare daggers at Anatole.

"I was surprised as anyone, Ilona," he told her. "You have always been so discreet." The last word came out heavily laced with grade-A sarcasm. "Is there somewhere else we could have this conversation? Somewhere perhaps you would feel comfortable providing a little illumination for your guests?"

"What do I not dare? I hunger. I thirst! These are mine, and if their bodies shall feed the soil, so their blood, their lives be reborn in the fire of my vein. . . ."

"Is this . . . normal?" I whispered to Brendan.

"I've heard worse," he whispered back.

"You're kidding."

I should have kept my mouth shut, because now I got the full brunt of vampire glower. Studying the floor became very interesting just then, and a whole lot safer.

"Come with me." Ilona's disgust was plain. Keeping up the smooth, swaying glide that made me wonder if she was on Rollerblades under that dress, she led us deeper into the theater. Anatole followed her and I followed Anatole, with Brendan bringing up the rear and keeping his virtual lighter held high, so he and I could actually see where we were going. As we passed the stage wings, I could just make out the shifting backstage action—actors doing quick changes, stagehands ready with props or wheeling new bits of scenery into place. We passed a heavily pinked-up young vampire in a tight-laced, translucent nightie (white), who adjusted a corkscrew curl. Something nagged at me, and I did a double take, and staggered. Damn stupid heels.

Brendan caught me. I gripped his wrist for a split second, and then hurried ahead on tippytoes, as if that could keep a vampire from hearing me.

Because the pinked-up vamplette in the blond wig was Julie.

"Take me, then!" She announced in high, quavering tones that made her sound like a cross between a valley girl and an anxious hamster. "Reveal to me the awesome purity of your thirst!" Arms held out in front of her, Julie paced onto the stage.

Brendan was still holding on to my arm, helping guide me up the stairs. I bit my lip. I wanted to tell him what I'd seen, but not within vampire earshot. At least, not within Ilona's earshot.

There were no lights on inside Ilona's office, but one velvet drape had been pulled back enough to reveal half of an arched window, and enough city light entered to see by. We stepped onto plush carpet, and I could have sworn I heard a door close.

Brendan stowed his phone without looking at it. His eyes swept the room, methodically searching the shadows. Unlike its owner, the room was done up in an ultramodern style. An angular silver and crystal chandelier hung from the vaulted ceiling. The desk, tables, sideboard and chairs were all glass, steel and white velvet. No wood, I noted. Anywhere. Except that other door behind the desk.

"What's back there?" asked Brendan, nodding toward the second door.

"A closet," replied Ilona. "Something to drink, Anatole?" She unstoppered a square decanter on the sideboard. I smelled warm blood as she poured a healthy measure of dark liquid into a matching crystal goblet.

"No, thank you." Anatole, of course, seemed perfectly at home and settled into one of the white plush chairs. "I have imbibed sufficiently this evening."

"Really?" Ilona eyed me over the rim as she sipped. To be precise, she eyed the neckline of my borrowed dress.

Oh, help.

"Mind if I look in that closet?" Brendan was already halfway across the office.

Ilona shrugged and sipped her blood. Brendan opened the door. It was a closet—complete with black dresses in various styles on padded hangers and lots of stiletto heels arranged in tidy pairs. He closed it, frowning.

A sense of familiarity crept over my skin like a cold draft. At the same time every synapse I owned was telling me I didn't want to be here a split second longer than necessary.

"Listen, Ms. St. Claire, you were the one who insisted on a face-to-face. I've just got a few questions, and then we'll be more than happy to get out of your way."

"Will you, indeed?" Ilona said the words in that special musing tone that telegraphs something bad is about to be attempted. I had a split second to drop my gaze before she drifted into my space.

"Look at me, Charlotte Caine," Ilona whispered. It was a loving, dangerous sound, and as much as I hate to admit it, I almost did what I was told.

"I don't know you that well."

"You are afraid?"

"Absolutely." Few things throw a bully off like honesty.

She snickered and drew back with, I'm pretty sure, a snide sideways glance at Anatole.

"Ilona . . ." He sighed.

She waved him away and knocked back the rest of her blood like a shot of tequila. "My information has a price."

Color me unsurprised. "What is it?"

"I want a drink from the warlock."

That unsurprise? I take it back.

Anatole rolled his eyes. "We all want a drink from the warlock, Ilona." I was about to say I didn't, but decided to keep my mouth shut. Anatole saw my confusion. "Warlock blood carries a certain amount of power with it. It is highly prized."

"That is my price." For a minute, Ilona resembled Taylor Watts, standing there like she owned the world. "Agree, or you can leave."

Tension thrummed through the room, lifting the hairs on my arms and neck. I rubbed my arms. My skin was trying to tell me someone else was watching me. I tried to tell it to calm down. We had bigger problems. Ilona had agreed to see us only to get Brendan down here. To get Anatole down here. Everything else must have been a setup. I was . . . extraneous at best. I should have told her to go to hell right there.

That I hesitated even a split second is one of my worst moments. But I did, and Brendan saw it. The sensation of being watched deepened, and goose bumps prickled down my arms.

"On the wrist," Brendan said.

"No!"

Ilona shrugged. "If that is your pleasure." I didn't imagine the greedy gleam in her eye, or the little bit of moisture at the corner of her mouth.

"Ilona," said Anatole sternly. "This is unnecessary."

"But it is most enjoyable." She smiled, making sure Brendan and I got a good look at her stained fangs.

Brendan turned to me and took a deep breath. I grabbed his arm before he could say anything. "No. Don't do this. You can't trust her not to mess with you." *Chet, when I get hold of you I'm going to kill you really dead this time for getting me into this.*

Tension shifted. My skin crawled. Something was wrong. Really, really wrong.

Brendan smiled and laid his hand over mine. God, did he have to look so much like a hero? It made my heart twist. "I can take care of myself, Charlotte. It'll be okay." He squeezed my hand, and my heart constricted in sympathy. "But you'd better wait outside."

"Oh, no. Sister Chef stays to watch. That also is part of the price."

"Ilona." Subsonic warnings filled Anatole's voice and

the rest of my goose bumps came out to get a better listen. "This is not reasonable."

But Ilona waved words and warnings away. "It is entirely reasonable, Anatole. The little girl needs her eyes opened."

"What are you talking about?"

"I am talking about this dangerous naïveté that day-bloods like you carry about."

"Like me?" She wanted to bite Brendan because of me? "You got it in for chefs?"

"The *families*." Ilona spat the words. "The 'loved ones' who can't let go when the transition is complete. You want so much to believe your brother has not changed, that he is still the living high school boy he used to be."

Wait. What? How is this suddenly about Chet? "I accept what my brother is."

That was a tactical error. I knew it as soon as I saw Ilona's big, fangy smile. "If you truly accept our kind, then you will not mind seeing this. You are, as you remind me, a chef. Why would you be bothered by the sight of someone enjoying a meal?"

"I won't do it with Charlotte in the room," said Brendan flatly.

"Then we have nothing more to discuss." Ilona draped herself gracefully over the nearest chaise longue, revealing a pair of black stiletto shoes on her feet. How many decades of practice do you need before you can *glide* in stilettos?

"Ilona, you are being ridiculous." I had thought Anatole would be angry, but he just sounded tired. The kind of tired your father turned on when you were six years old and it was nine o'clock and you still wouldn't get undressed for bed.

Father? I looked at Anatole. I looked at Ilona. *Father?*

"I'm being ridiculous?" Ilona rounded on him. "You're

tailing around after a *Maddox*, playing boy detective, and *I'm* the one being ridiculous?" Rage poured off her in waves. I wanted to run. I needed to run. There was the door. Time to go.

Except that would mean leaving Brendan alone with two vampires. That this was enough to make me hold my ground made me feel slightly better about myself.

Not that Ilona was paying any attention to Brendan or me. "You could be magnificent, Anatole. A leader, a *king* among our kind!" She spread her arms wide. "But what do you choose to do with yourself? You consort with a creature who would not hesitate to kill you. You write *trivia* in a squalid little paper for fools who like to call themselves UV-challenged, and you say *I'm* being ridiculous!"

"Excuse me." Brendan cut in. "It's my blood you want, and I'm not objecting. But," he added, "because it is my blood, you answer all my questions as well as Charlotte's."

Ilona's eyes narrowed. "You do not set the conditions here, warlock."

Brendan did not look away. He undid the cuff of his button-down shirt and rolled it back, just enough to expose his forearm with its strong tracery of veins. A thin, straight scar ran from his wrist up his forearm and disappeared under his sleeve.

He held his arm out.

Anatole smiled, and I got the feeling he was impressed. "Your move, Ilona."

I thought she'd refuse. I hoped she'd refuse. Whatever Brendan was playing at, this game was not safe. I didn't care what magics he could pull out or how he thought he could shield himself. This wasn't like giving to the Red Cross. This was the Feeding and it was *different*.

Ilona stared at Brendan's wrist and licked her lips. I started forward, but Anatole gripped my shoulder, holding me back as effectively as if I'd been leashed to an iron post.

Brendan went down on one knee in front of Ilona. She took his arm in her graceful, dead-white hands, running her fingers over his veins.

"No." I struggled, and Anatole's fingers dug in hard. "It's not worth it!"

No one was listening to me. Brendan's attention was all on Ilona. Ilona opened her mouth, fangs glittering in the streetlight.

But before she could get any further, the shadows shifted. Glass shattered and a silver missile shot between us and thudded on the carpet. I had just enough time to see a battered canister roll to a stop.

Pop!

Yellow-white gas boiled into the air, carrying with it the unmistakable scent of garlic. Anatole stumbled toward the window, hand clamped over his mouth. More glass shattered and the light was gone. Two dark figures swung in through the window.

They had stakes, and crosses.

18

"Die, vampire!"

Anatole threw himself backward. The two ninja-style silhouettes hurtled past and landed in the center of the carpet, stakes and crosses held high. Ilona snarled. Ninja Silhouette One charged her, but Anatole snaked his long arms around its waist and flung it aside. The Ninja Silhouette howled in outrage and slammed against the wall hard enough to shake the chandelier. The vampires' contagious fear and anger swirled through the air like the garlic smoke, so my throat burned as much from the need to scream as from the rank gas.

Brendan roared something and tackled NS2. The garlic grenade popped again and another wave of gas filled the room. Anatole hit his knees, hands pressed tight against his eyes.

I dove for the spitting canister, wobbling badly on my stupid borrowed heels, and scooped it up. Pain bit hard through both palms.

"Hot!" I dodged Brendan, who was sprawled full length on the floor, grappling with NS2. "Hot coming through!" I hurled the garlic grenade out the shattered window.

"What the hell!" came the New York echo.

"Sorry!" I swung back around toward the fight.

Ninja Silhouette One towered over Anatole, who was now on hands and knees. Ilona screamed in Russian.

"Light!" Brendan struggled to hang on to NS2's ankle while he waved his smartphone in the air. NS2 kicked free of Brendan and grabbed Ilona by the knees, toppling her. Above us the chandelier shuddered, clinked and flared to life. I and the vampires all yelled as the sudden light hit our eyes.

Now I could see faces. Margot—Ninja Silhouette One—held Ilona down with one hand and wielded an industrial-sized silver crucifix with the other. Ian—NS2—had the stake.

Chet stood by the curtains, crouched and ready to spring.

Chet stood by the curtains.

Chet.

Brendan stared wildly at his cat-suited relatives and gave what I can only assume was the traditional Maddox family greeting.

"You *morons*!"

Chet straightened up and avoided my pedestrian-in-the-headlights stare.

Anatole didn't waste time on salutations. He snagged the neck of Ian's unitard, dragging him away from Ilona.

"What do you think you're doing?" demanded Brendan.

"Rescuing you, you idiot!" Ian clamped onto Anatole's wrist and threw himself sideways so they both rolled across the floor in a mass of flailing limbs and multilingual curses.

I still couldn't move.

"Rescuing!" shouted Brendan.

Vamp and vamp hunter banged against the metal desk legs and came to a halt with Ian very much on top. He brandished his stake and grinned like a teenager about to get laid. Ilona scrambled to reach under her desk. I jerked back into motion and jumped to stop her, but I collided with Chet hard enough to bounce, and lost my balance on those stupid, stupid heels. My brother caught me by the shoulders before I could fall and grimaced apologetically.

"You were getting bitten, Brendan!" Margot dove toward Ian and Anatole.

"You followed me?" Brendan grabbed Margot and hauled her away from that tomcat fight.

In a split second Anatole rolled Ian under again. He came up kneeling on Ian's chest and holding the stake under the warlock's tufted chin. I gotta say, Ian now looked considerably less enthusiastic about being on the floor.

"You were having us followed!" Margot tried to yank her arm out of her brother's grip.

"Brendan! He'll kill me!" squeaked Ian.

"No, he won't. Unlike you two, Sevarin's not a moron."

"Thank you for the compliment." The words would have sounded much smoother if Anatole hadn't bared his fangs at Ian right then. "But I do feel grievous bodily harm is a viable option at this time."

The door flew open. A pair of male vamps in black turtlenecks and slacks charged in. Now I knew why Ilona had gone for her desk. Whoever thought of a vampire office with a panic button?

"Kill them!" Ilona drew herself up straight. "They laid hands on me!"

Chet shoved me behind him, but he didn't need to bother because Anatole turned his head to look at Ilona. May I never see such a look leveled at me. It froze the two new vamps right in their tracks, and even Ilona seemed to shrivel.

Slowly, Anatole stood up and backed away so Ian could scramble to his feet. Even from where I stood peeking behind my brother's back, I could see the balding warlock tremble.

"Yours, I believe." Anatole held out the stake to Ian.

"Anatole . . ." began Ilona. You could have heard the threat in Hoboken.

"No." Anatole brushed his suit coat down. "Despite appearances, Ilona, you are not a moron either. If three dead Maddoxes are found in your theater, you will start a war."

Vampires do not stare daggers at each other. They stare AK-47 full automatics and rocket-propelled grenade launchers.

"Ilona, I have reached my limit," said Anatole. "If you do not care for your personal safety, you might at least remember how many of your secrets I hold, and that I have access to more kinds of media than you ever knew existed. The Paranormal Squad would be very intrigued by your latest moneymaking scheme, and your separatist movement friends would be most interested, I'm sure, to know about your current lover." He looked right at Chet.

My voice, which had abandoned me about the same time as my power of voluntary movement, came rushing back.

"Lover!" I grabbed Chet by the ear and dragged him around to face me. "She's your *girlfriend*?"

"Ow!" answered Chet. "Charlotte! Ow!"

"You said you didn't know her!"

The color left Ilona's face so fast that even her lipstick turned pale. "You wouldn't—" she started saying to Anatole. Then my words caught up with her, and she wheeled toward Chet. "You told her *what*?"

"Ow!" said Chet. "I told her . . . Ow! Charlotte, let go!"

"Charlotte, let go," suggested Brendan.

Reluctantly I did. Chet backed off, rubbing his ear and looking around wildly to find where he'd left his dignity.

"I'm sorry," said Chet, to me and then to Ilona. "I thought it was for the best, considering . . ."

"Considering what?" Ilona and I both demanded. Then we eyed each other, freaked out by being even this close to the same side. At least, I was freaked out. Ilona just looked ready to chew iron and spit nails.

Anatole, however, was not interested in watching Chet's attempt to weasel out of this one.

"Ilona, I am taking the Maddoxes and Chef Caine out of here," he said with a seriousness that pressed hard against my brain. "You and I will discuss this evening later, in private, and in detail."

Ilona drew herself up to her full height. "Get out of here." She said from so deep in the vocal dead zone that my skin tried to crawl off my body. "*All* of you, get out!"

"Ilona." Chet stepped toward her, hands out. Ilona bared her fangs at him.

"I would do as she says." Anatole cast a significant glance toward the vamp stagehands who flanked their boss.

No good reason to argue presented itself to me, or to Chet either, evidently, because he slumped toward the door. Margot and Ian seemed less convinced.

"You're just going to walk out of a theater full of vampires?" Margot planted her fists on her hips and glowered at Brendan.

"No, I'm going to run out," replied Brendan reasonably. "Are you coming, or do I get to explain to Grandfather how you committed suicide?"

This seemed to finally reach the other Maddoxes, so they didn't struggle too much when Brendan grabbed each of them by an arm and dragged them forward. Anatole held the door. I waited for Chet. He'd stopped at the threshold to look back at Ilona, searching for words to charm her down off her mountain of anger. But judging from the cold look on her face, Ilona wasn't, excuse the expression, going to bite.

Under other circumstances I would have liked her better for that. Right now, I was just interested in getting my idiotic, undead brother out of there so I could yell at him properly. Maybe I could borrow one of Margot's stakes and save us all a world of trouble. Because Ilona was Chet's girlfriend, Ilona had gone with him to Post Mortem, where they had talked to Bert Shelby, separately and together, and fang-for-rent Julie Jones was downstairs somewhere. This was all adding up to Something Very Bad.

Chet must have realized Ilona was not going to budge and he walked out behind Anatole and the Maddoxes, with me right on his heels. I felt Ilona's anger burning through the closed door all the way down the stairs.

On the main floor, the vamp stagehands were striking the show, all of them too busy to pay much attention to our strange little procession. We made it outside without being molested, although I did pull an Orpheus and look back once. I saw nothing, but I knew Ilona was there, making sure we left, waiting for us to try something, anything at all.

Anatole closed the stage door firmly behind us. In front of us, Brendan's driver climbed out of the car, cell phone in hand.

"It's okay, Kyle," said Brendan. "Just a few party crashers." I could tell Chet was not happy to be included in the sweep of Brendan's gaze. Good. I wanted him unhappy.

"Party crashers. Right." Ian yanked himself away from Brendan. "You go into a vampire lair, with a vamp and a vamp-lover, and by the time we get up the fire escape, you're on your knees and about to get drained. I know it's a huge stretch, but we thought you needed help!"

"Oh, and by the way, that guy you put on our tail?" Margot smoothed her ninja suit down. I found I had enough unoccupied brain cells in my trivia lobe to wonder what kind of foundation garment she was wearing. Because that thing was pretty much painted on and she didn't show so much as a panty line. "You're going to need to bail him out. He got picked up for indecent exposure."

"You didn't," said Brendan.

Ian smirked. "That was Margot's idea. You should hire uglier private dicks."

"Thanks *so* much for that image," I muttered.

"Charlotte," whispered Chet, "just stay cool. I'll explain as soon as we get out of this."

"Oh, you'll explain all right," I hissed back at him through clenched teeth. Anatole cocked an eyebrow in our direction, but said nothing. Fortunately, the Maddoxes were too busy with their own family dialogue to pay me and Chet any attention.

"Did Grandfather put you up to this?" Brendan knotted his fingers in his hair like he was trying to keep the top of his head from blowing off. "Did he say go down to the city and completely screw things up for Brendan?"

"You were supposed to find Pamela!" Ian threw up his hands. "You said you had a way out for the family, and what have we got? Dylan's dead, Pam's still nowhere to be found and you're hanging with Anatole Sevarin!"

I recognized the look on Brendan's face. It was the look you get when you have no good answer for the person currently getting in your face.

"We're going home," Brendan announced, pushing his sister and cousin toward the car. "Right now."

"I will look after Charlotte," said Anatole.

"That'd be my job," announced Chet.

"I don't need looking after," I reminded the testosterone-heightened segment of the studio audience.

"A theater full of vampires is on the street looking for

an after-performance snack," said Anatole. "You need looking after."

That no-good-answer look on Brendan's face? Now it was on mine.

"Oh, but she would enjoy being somebody's little snack," sneered Ian. As an insult it would have worked better if the idiot wasn't *still* checking out my boobs.

"Get in the car, Ian," barked Brendan. "Now!"

Somewhat to my surprise, Ian did as he was told.

I needed to apologize to Brendan, and let him know I was finished. It had all gone too far. I wanted to explain so he would understand. But I couldn't, not in front of Anatole, or Chet, or the Crazy Maddox Relations, especially not with Margot fixing her eyes on me, clearly trying to telepathically remind me of the million dollars still on the table between us. I could only stand there and be sorry.

But Brendan was already in the car with his family. The door shut and the driver started the engine. I watched until they turned onto the next street, trying to shake off the weight of things I should have figured out how to say. This was not made any easier by having to turn around and face Anatole and Chet.

"Get your sister out of here, Caine," said Anatole. He sounded tired, and disappointed, but I couldn't tell if it was with one of us or only with himself. "Ilona is very angry and she might easily do something we will all regret in the morning."

"Yeah." Chet ran his hand through his hair. He looked tired too. So that made three of us. "Let's go, Charlotte."

Something in me didn't want to just leave Anatole there. Ilona was angry at him too, and she had backup. Serious, muscled, well-fanged backup. But even while I was thinking this, Anatole shot me a blood-drinking grin, then backed away slowly until he mingled with the alley shadows and vanished.

Classy.

Chet tugged gently on my arm, and I fell into step beside him as he started down the alley, following the path Brendan's limo had taken. Emotion surged through me like a food processor on high, chewing up my ability to think. There'd been too much fear and too many reversals in what I thought must be true.

We reached 124th and Chet turned us east. My brother was absolutely quiet beside me. It was like walking with a shadow. For days now, all I'd wanted was to get hold of Chet—by the throat if necessary—and make him tell me what he'd really done and why he'd done it. Now here he was, and I couldn't make a single sound.

"I've been an idiot," said Chet.

Well. This was a promising start. I looked up at him.

"A total idiot," he went on. I kept looking up at him.

"A total and complete selfish, egotistical idiot," he said, warming to the theme. "If I had any real sense of how much I put my sister through—my sister who has loved me and looked out for me even when she had every reason to shove my pathetic carcass into the sunlight—I'd stop in the nearest tapas bar right now, get a bamboo skewer off the shrimp kebab and commit hari-kari. But I'm such an unbelievable idiot I'd probably miss my own heart and have to call up one of the vampire-hunting Maddoxes to do it for me."

I blinked. "Would bamboo even work?"

"How would I know? I'm an idiot!"

My laugh came out as a single sharp bark. Another followed it and another until my chest hurt and tears streamed out of my eyes. I had to laugh. There was no other response to the mental stew inside me all churned up by the sight of Chet throwing his hands out in surrender. Chet, who was still in once piece and who, God help me, I was still glad to see, even while I was pissed as all hell at him.

He grinned and shoved his hands in his pockets and paused at the corner and turned north, walking without looking. "If you're going to hug me or smack me stupid, maybe we can get that out of the way now?"

Which squashed flat anything good in my gigantic bag of mixed feelings. "You're messing with Nightlife's books, you're involved in some kind of blood-running operation *and* sleeping with a vamp you told me you didn't even know, and you think I want to smack you!"

"I'm sorry, Charlotte. I can explain." There it was: the pleading look, the hunched shoulders, the whole ashamed-little-boy attitude accompanied by a silent plea to be understood; to be given just one more chance. But I knew what would happen. He'd start spinning his story with heavy layers of smiles and charm and I'd let him get to me, just like he got to everyone else.

I couldn't let that happen. Not this time.

"You've been stealing from Nightlife, Chet." My voice sounded deader than a vampire at a Maddox family barbecue. I was going to have to call Linus O'Grady. I was going to have to hand Chet over.

"No."

"You've been juggling the books to hide the fact that money's leaving the accounts. That's why you keep a copy on your laptop. You've got a second set you send to the accountant." And me.

"No. I haven't been taking money out of Nightlife. I've been putting it in."

I mentally rewound that last statement, and played it again. And again.

"Jesus, Chet, that's a stretch, even for one of your stories."

"You want to see? Come home with me. I'll show you

everything." I walked right past him, trying not to see, trying not to hear. If I listened, I might begin to believe.

"So how did you find yourself with enough extra cash you could start making donations to Nightlife?"

Chet's shoulders rose and fell in defeat. "Ilona and I . . . We were both sitting around complaining about the money thing, you know, for Nightlife and her theater . . . and I was joking and said what we needed was the nightblood version of the organic foods movement to bring in the cash. We could make a killing. Metaphorically," he added swiftly as I frowned up at him. "Ilona said she knew this guy with some land up in Connecticut. He'd been planning on developing it as a kind of nightbloods-only community, but with the financial crash and everything, he couldn't get people to buy the parcels. So we turned it into a retreat."

"A retreat?"

Chet nodded. "For people who want healthy, natural lifestyles. For the duration of their residence, each member gets a balanced, all-organic, chemical-free diet, a custom-designed exercise program, stress-management counseling, a personal life coach and full telecommuting facilities."

"And in return?"

"They donate a pint every six weeks."

Ilona the separatist, advocating a return to the good old days of free-range vampires, was financing her activities with a human-blood farm. That was either terminally warped or totally brilliant.

"How much are you paying the 'residents' for being drained?"

"Nothing," said Chet. "They pay us."

No. There was no way. No one would pay to be comfortably housed and bled like that. Not even with organic meals, a 24/7 spa lifestyle, and total catering to for their health and comfort . . .

They wouldn't, would they?

"We've got about two hundred residents right now," said Chet. "And we're booked through next June. Average stay is three months."

Focus, Charlotte. Focus. "Who buys the blood?"

"We don't sell blood." Chet lifted his nose in the air. "That's illegal. We sell shares in the spa. The blood's a free perk for shareholders."

Shareholders. Of course. Nightblood investment. They put in their money, they got a steady supply of human blood. No seedy bite-easies, no chance at stings or blackmail, because they all knew Ilona St. Claire would never collaborate with dayblood cops or any other kind of dayblood. And because Chet could sell as much snake oil to the undead as to the living.

"It brought in a quarter million last year," Chet was saying. "We've got a superior product to the blood runners and we're probably legal—"

"*Probably* legal?"

"Beats definitely illegal," he countered. "Look, you've been talking to Taylor Watts, haven't you? What Taylor caught me and Marcus talking about was filtering money *into* the account, not taking it out. There was no way he was going to believe that, and I couldn't tell you—" He stopped when he saw my disapproval and started again. "I didn't *think* I could tell you, so I figured I'd pay him off while I got everything sorted out. I got him the job at Post Mortem because I didn't trust him and thought Bert Shelby could keep an eye on him."

"And what about my menu? When I stopped by Post Mortem the other night I couldn't help but notice how they've ripped mine off, ingredient for ingredient."

"Charlotte, I swear on my own grave I did not sell him your menu. I'm an idiot, but I wouldn't do that to you. Taylor probably sold it to him because he was pissed about being fired."

I didn't know where I was anymore. I didn't dare stop to look for an address or landmark. I had a hoard of nightmares behind me. If I broke stride, they'd catch up.

"So you have been blood running out of Nightlife," I said slowly. "And that's where this money's been coming from."

"No. This is not blood running. It's not even close—and none of our product goes through Nightlife."

"Then why didn't you tell me what you're doing?" I shouted.

Chet stopped in his tracks and turned to face me. He was completely white and his dry eyes didn't even flicker as he loomed over me. "What's the real problem here, Charlotte?" he demanded, and I felt the question hammer against my brain. "Is it that I might actually have an existence without you? Or is it just because I didn't ask your permission to go get an afterlife?"

"You're in the middle of a of blood scam with a girlfriend that you won't even tell me about—"

"Because you have this great history of letting me manage my own relationships!"

"This isn't about that!"

"Of course it's not! This is about you finding out that maybe I don't *need* you! No, sorry. That's not it either. It's about you finding out *you* might need *me*!"

My hand swung out toward his cheek and the world blurred. Pain reverberated up to my shoulder like I'd struck an iron bar. My brother had hold of my wrist, and I couldn't have shifted his grip any more than I could have picked up a crosstown bus.

"No more, Charlotte," Chet said, and I saw his fangs flash in the streetlight. "Not now. Not ever."

My eyes locked with his, and he held nothing back. Chet pushed hard against my mind, willing his way inside, willing me to give in, to believe, to obey. My wrist felt like glass in his hand. He could snap it in two if I didn't obey. This wasn't my brother. This was the night-blood, the vampire. My brother was dead and gone, and I was the one who'd killed him.

"Charlotte?" Chet whispered, and his grip loosened just enough for me to pull away. The blood had run out of my face and my heart was racing a mile a minute. I backed up until I stumbled against a parked car. I had to get away. I had to.

Chet stood there for a moment, his hand held exactly in the same position as when he'd grabbed me.

Then he took two steps back, turned, and ran away into the dark.

19

Things got kind of disjointed for a while after that. I made it home somehow. I remember my phone ringing in a shifting stream of discordant tones until I shut it off and threw it against the wall. I remember telling Trish and Jess to leave me alone four or five times each before they finally took me seriously. I remember standing at the kitchen counter and crumbling farmhouse Cheddar into little pieces. Somewhere in there, there was also a certain amount of curling up into a tight little ball and sobbing myself sick.

Eventually, however, my brain got tired of the hysterical shtick and came back home—bleary-eyed, shamefaced and wanting to know if there was any coffee left. I forgave it and made the coffee. I melted cheese crumbs onto a piece of toast and ate that with an apple and some slices of prosciutto. I took a shower and put on clean clothes. By then it was ten a.m. and I went to work.

I know this sounds either utterly cold or utterly ridiculous. But for me it was an affirmation. I had to believe there would be a way out of this mess, for me and for Chet. Because I had to believe that, I also had to be sure there was something for us both to find our way out to. If I didn't get Nightlife back up and running, that something wouldn't be there.

Besides, if I kept busy, I wouldn't have to think about Chet's hand around my wrist, or the fear I'd felt when he looked down at me on that dark and empty street.

So I worked. First it was two solid hours of sweet-talking suppliers. We couldn't open without food, and we had no food. We also, despite what Chet claimed to have been doing, had no money. The amount of tap dancing I did around that little tidbit could have gotten me the lead in the Broadway revival of *A Chorus Line*.

Then I sat down with Robert and Suchai and the schedule pad to hash out the front-of-the-house situation. We had just enough hands to make it through a Saturday rush, if it was a light one. Suchai knew some experienced servers who might be looking to pick up some extra cash, and I told him to call them. Then it was the PR hour with Elaine West. We needed to let people know we'd opened again, but not too many, in case we stumbled coming out of the gate. To my surprise, she agreed that Saturday should be a kind of test opening and we held our announcements down to just the old Internet—she would reach out to a couple well-known foodie bloggers and big mouths.

Zoe and Reese, my sous chefs, and Marie-Our-Pastry-Chef showed up right on time at four p.m. Then came the time I needed more than I needed food or sleep or even answers.

We went into the kitchen and we started to plan the menu. We'd make it simple—keep the best sellers, like the pumpkin soup and the carpaccio, but switch up things around the edges. Anatole had complimented the lamb-and-rosemary combination; we could work that up pretty easily. We could add my warm pomegranate salad as well. Zoe sketched out an idea for what she called a night-and-day duck tasting. Reese thought the emergency blood-sausage-and-pasta dish that we'd made to help clean out the walk-in had legs, especially with winter coming, and I told him to run with it. Marie had an orange-hazelnut milk shake she wanted to try for the dessert menu, and I had to agree when she said now was the time to add in that Mexican drinking chocolate we'd been talking about, in a formula that could be spiked with booze or blood, depending on the guest.

It was a marathon. Possibilities started getting inside us and opening up the hope we'd all been keeping on ice. It was like the time before we opened all over again, when everything was new and anything could happen. Arguments broke out and had to be settled by a trip to the market to bring back fresh product so that the experiments could be cooked up and tasted, and dissected and tasted again.

Sometime after midnight, we sent out for Chinese food. The plum sauce gave Zoe some new thoughts for her duck tasting. Marie considered kumquats as milk shake flavoring, while I sketched out plating designs in the battered notebook that had languished in my desk drawer since the disasters started. It felt so much like my normal life I found myself having to bend low over my carton of noodles with cloud ear mushrooms and sugar snap peas to hide the way my eyes were leaking around the edges. I kept eating and talking and sketching, because I didn't want to stop to think about how the sun had gone down outside. Chet would be awake by now, and he wasn't calling. It was okay, I told myself. If Chet was still too pissed to talk to me, I was still way the hell too pissed to talk to him.

Because he was wrong. Beginning to end, top to bottom. The fact that he was involved in something so huge and massively screwed up that it created at least one dead body and he *still* couldn't tell me about it was proof positive exactly how wrong he was.

"Chef?" Marie had been out to the bar to get a bottle of cognac and now she pushed through the swinging doors.

"Oommpk?" I asked, caught in inelegant midslurp of some very long, very good braised noodles.

"Somebody out front asking to see you." She handed me a business card. I swallowed, and took it.

The name on the card was Anatole Sevarin.

He couldn't just text me like a normal person? No, of course not. I wiped my mouth and tossed my napkin on the desk. "I'll be right back."

Anatole waited beside the host station, looking as cool and immaculate as if last night had never happened.

"Good evening, Chef Caine. I'm glad to see you made it home all right."

"Me too, to tell you the truth." Which was the sum total of my available pleasantries. "Has something happened?"

"You mean something new? No. But as it has become clear that you will not be leaving before the early hours, I thought I would extend an offer to see you home."

I stood there for a while, rearranging those words into an order that made sense. "You've been watching the door?" No, not quite right. "You've been watching *me*?"

"Between the Maddoxes, Ilona and the fact that you have not yet called Detective O'Grady, I feel I was perfectly justified in my actions."

"How did you know I didn't call O'Grady?"

"Because if you had, you would not currently be holding staff meetings in your kitchen."

Score one for the vampire detective. "Are you going to call him?" I asked.

"Are you?"

I bit my lip and glanced toward the bar. For obvious reasons, we don't keep a mirror there, just glass shelves full of imported liquors, waiting for the thirsty and the curious. "Not yet," I said.

"How long are you going to ask for this time?"

That cut, deep and clean. "I don't know." If I called O'Grady we wouldn't have our opening. I'd have to tell him all about Chet, and the accounts, and Margot's million dollars. This last shouldn't have bothered me, because of course I wasn't going to take it. I'd already decided that, because I was going through with the Nightlife reopening. Right?

But then, I hadn't called the number on her card and told her absolutely no yet either. Of course, I hadn't dumped that blood down the drain yet either. I was keeping my head down, thinking about food, pretending I'd already gotten past the disasters and the nightmares. I jammed my hands into my pockets. Unfortunately, as a strategy, my putting a fine dice on denial was not making things any less messed up.

I saw movement out of the corner of my eye and glanced toward the kitchen door just in time to see somebody duck away from the portal. Probably Marie. It occurred to me that the last thing I wanted was for my staff to overhear this particular conversation.

"Perhaps we should continue this on the way home?" suggested Anatole.

"Yeah." My shoulders slumped under the weight of the inevitable. "Perhaps we should."

It went against the grain to go home while my sous chefs were still working, but I hung up my kitchen whites, collected purse and jacket and headed out, with Anatole Sevarin right behind me.

"Shall we walk?" he asked as we stepped onto the pavement.

I shivered, but nodded. The air was damp and the sky clouded over, the particular pale gray of city clouds reflecting the lights back down on us. It was going to rain soon, but right now the fresh air would feel good.

Anatole held out his arm. I held out my best "you've got to be kidding me" look. He shrugged and started up the street. We strolled along for a few blocks, ignoring the passersby and being ignored. Nothing to see here. Move along, city. It felt surprisingly soothing.

But silence isn't my natural mode, and slowly the press of questions in my head was too much to ignore.

"So, that thing Ilona said . . ." Not the best opening, but it was all I had. " 'You could be a king of our kind'?"

"Ilona, in case you had not noticed, is a little dramatic."

"I did notice, yeah, but king?"

"How to explain?" Anatole pursed his lips. I would have bet my next paycheck (which would probably be nonexistent after we paid off our suppliers) that he already knew exactly how to explain, but Anatole did like his little show. "Dayblood culture is obsessed with youth and beauty. These things are equated with power and wealth. They are to be sacrificed for, worshipped, and extolled in story and song."

"Yeah, yeah, yeah, we're shallow."

The corner of Anatole's mouth curled up briefly. "As are we. But where daybloods worship youth, nightbloods worship age. Age is all the things to us that youth is to you. And I—as I believe I have mentioned—am very old."

"How old?"

"My first master was Ivan the Terrible."

He had to be joking, but he just looked down at me with that all-too-familiar raised-eyebrow challenge, waiting for me to try to make him deny it.

"Wow," I said.

Anatole shrugged.

"But why an obsession about age? You're immortal."

"We have the potential to be immortal," he corrected me. "The truth of the matter is that most of us have a shorter existence than you do."

"But . . . but . . ."

"Think, Charlotte. We are helpless during the day when you own the world. You can stay up late into the night, but we cannot remain conscious after sunrise. You can form a gang, a mob, an army. We can congregate in a large group, but for more than a few of us to cooperate for a long time is nearly impossible. And despite our boasts that we are the very pinnacle of the food chain, daybloods are exceedingly dangerous prey. In a group, appropriately armed, there is nothing more deadly than your kind."

"Why don't you stay away from us, then? Do like the separatists say and scatter into the countryside."

"That is the other thing we don't talk about. We don't just want your blood, we want your presence. We crave it."

"You love us and are doomed to destroy us?" I meant it as a joke, but considering everything that had happened lately, it maybe fell a little flat.

"You have been watching too many bad movies." Anatole's flicker of a smile came as a relief.

"So, how old is Ilona?"

"She was turned about forty years ago."

"Kids these days."

Anatole stopped in his tracks and turned toward me. The light caught in his golden hair but left his eyes sunken in shadow and turned his skin uniformly white. He was not human. He was Other and the fear that had come over me the night before when it was Chet I walked home with struggled to make its prime-time comeback.

"With the young Maddoxes running about the city

with their stakes, I am less than amused about that at the moment."

"Sorry."

Anatole nodded his acceptance of my apology and we walked on. Cars rolled past. Lights flicked on and off in the windows over our heads. The city was going about its business and expecting nothing more than for us to go about ours.

I probably could have let things lie, but I didn't. "Something's going on with the Maddoxes." There's no way Margot Maddox offered me a million dollars because it might stop a blood-running scam that her cousin might be helping out with. "It's not just Brendan trying to keep his relatives under wraps."

"Something else to inquire into."

"I hope he's okay," I whispered. I should have found time to think about him today. I should have checked in.

"Have faith, Charlotte. I have a feeling your Brendan has been looking out for his family for a long time."

It was a measure of how far out of it I was that I didn't say anything about the "your Brendan" remark. Anatole noticed it too, and got a very strange look on his face before he turned toward the eastern horizon.

"It is almost sunrise. I will find you a taxi."

God, is it that late? I glanced at my watch. Yeah, it was. "Thanks. I'll let you."

"Ah!" Anatole laid his hand over his heart. "The lady accepts my gifts. My heart may dare to hope. . . ."

"Don't get carried away."

This time the smile was real, and it held. "It is not to be helped. Russian, remember?"

He stalked over to the corner and stood, staring down the street like he was willing it to produce a taxi. I let him be. I was not ready to handle what looked like a touch of jealousy from Anatole Sevarin. Not that it was warranted.

Between the debacle at the theater and the fact that he
hadn't called me any more than I had called him, it was
pretty clear Brendan didn't want anything more to do
with me.

He hadn't called me, had he? I pulled out my phone
and found I'd accidentally switched it off at some point.
At least, it probably was an accident, or maybe reflex.
Unless it was more of that fine-dice denial I'd been working on all day.

I pressed the POWER key and checked my messages.
There were three new ones, none of them from Brendan.
I stomped on my disappointment. Two were voice mes-
sages from Elaine West, and the other was a text from
Chet. It had been sent back at 7:18. I immediately thumbed
that one. A single line appeared on the screen.

Where the hell is he?!

I swallowed around my heart, which seemed to have
filled the back of my throat, and hit Chet's number. It rang,
and rang, and I got voice mail. I hung up and hit REDIAL.

The fourth ring cut off in the middle. "Chet, you asshole, what are you doing?"

It took me a minute to recognize the outraged voice.
"Doug?"

"Charlotte?" I could picture Chet's roommate wrin-
kling his Neanderthal-grade forehead.

"What're you answering this phone for? Where's
Chet?"

"Fuck if I know. I was out last night and I got back in
from work and half his stuff is cleared out and his phone
and keys are on the table."

My brain, which was already imploding from adrena-
line and lack of sleep, froze solid. I could make no sense
of this. None whatsoever.

"I gotta go, Doug," I whispered.

"I wouldn't care. You know, whatever, but rent's due."

"Yeah." I hung up and stood there, a statue on Lenox Avenue. A yellow cab pulled up, waiting, and I still didn't move.

"Charlotte?" Anatole was beside me as though he had materialized there. "What is it?"

"Chet." I was still staring at the phone. "He's gone. That was his roommate, Doug. He said Chet's cleared out his stuff and gone."

Anatole took me by both shoulders. "Charlotte, listen to me. I am almost out of time. Who is Chet's sire? If he thought he was in real trouble, that's where he'd go."

"We don't know where she is." The lie I had spoken for five years came easily to me, even with Anatole's eyes looking straight into mine. "She vanished."

"That is not possible," he said sternly. "A sire does not abandon the ones they deliberately turn. There is a connection, a need."

Memory dragged me under. The dark alley, hungry, eager eyes, the tightly folded wad of bills in my hands. *Just a few minutes . . .*

Anatole made a strangled noise deep in his throat. "I do not have time to understand this now. Go to O'Grady. Immediately. You must tell him what has happened."

"But—"

"Charlotte!" He shook me, and I felt how much he was keeping a rein on his strength. "This is not a game! Promise me you will call O'Grady!"

"Why do you care?" Tears trickled down my face. When had they started?

"Does it matter?"

"Yes!"

"Preserve me from daybloods. Charlotte, I do not want to see you arrested and thrown in jail because your brother is too stupid to exist! Now will you promise to call O'Grady?"

I nodded and Anatole straightened up and let me go. "Thank you. Now, get in the cab and go home."

I hesitated. "Will you be okay?"

"If I am not delayed by more foolishness, yes."

I climbed into the cab, awkward and one-handed because I couldn't manage to put my phone down. The door closed behind me, and when I looked back, Anatole was already gone.

"Where we goin'?" asked the cabbie.

"Fourth and Bleecker," I said.

I'm sorry, Anatole.

20

I had to lean hard on the buzzer for a full minute before Doug let me in.

I never liked Doug. When not actually out on the street he tended to dress in torn T-shirts and crumpled boxer shorts. He never learned the art of the clean shave, and he had a forehead that proclaimed direct descent from the Clan of the Cave Bear. Chet said my real problem was that the one time I'd offered to make him dinner, Doug had dumped catsup all over my steak au poivre. But Chet also said Doug paid his rent on time, he didn't mind sharing an apartment with a vampire, and whatever he was into, it never came home except in the form of the occasional hookup.

"So where is he?" Doug shuffled into the kitchen, pulled a can of Mountain Dew out of the fridge, popped the top and chugged half. I watched, unable even to muster a queasy feeling.

"I don't know." Chet's cell lay on the table, along with his apartment key, just like Doug had said. There was also a stack of junk mail, old copies of advertising flyers and a few issues of *Circulation*. I sorted through it all, vaguely hoping to find a note, or a business card, anything that might tell me where my brother had gone.

"Well, if you don't know, who does?"

"I don't know." There was no note. I pocketed his cell phone and keys and turned to the living room. The laptop where Chet kept Nightlife's books was gone. The books that Chet admitted he was cooking, just not in the usual way. He said. Except I couldn't exactly trust what Chet said right now.

He's not dead, I told myself as I moved away from the empty makeshift desk. *If someone had killed him and wanted to make it look like he took off, they wouldn't have taken the computer and left the cell.*

Unless they didn't care what it looked like. Unless all they really wanted was to know what he'd been doing with the money. From where I stood, it looked like he was working with Shelby and Taylor Watts as well as Marcus the Mystery Nebbish. Maybe he was putting money into the Nightlife accounts not to help the restaurant but to hide it from his partners. Maybe they found out about it. Or maybe he just got mixed up with someone who was out for undead blood, like the Maddoxes. Maybe Margot Maddox got tired of waiting for me to accept her payoff and had decided to take a more direct route to stop the reopening, right through Chet.

"Can I see his bedroom?"

Doug waved me past with the Mountain Dew can. I nodded my thanks and walked into Chet's room.

It was not entirely a sty. The bed was unmade, but the sheets were clean. The hamper was full, but nothing overflowed onto the industrial beige carpet. One of the two dressers had its drawers pulled out. I recognized a couple of Chet's sweaters and his BYT ME BEATMAN T-shirt.

He's not dead. My hand wrapped tight around his cell phone. *He's running. He thought somebody might be able to trace him on the cell, so he left it. He didn't think about how much information it's got in it. Or maybe he did. Maybe he wants me to be able to figure it out. Maybe he's counting on me being able to help him.*

Maybe this is about you finding out I don't need you. . . . I tried not to hear his voice echoing in my head, and failed.

"Anything?" Doug yawned like he was calling down moose from Vermont.

"Not really." At least I didn't think so. I poked through the drawers. It looked like stuff was missing, but that was all I could tell. Some empty hangers dangled in the closet, but the dark blazers and white button-down shirts that he wore when he was running the front of the house at Nightlife were all still there.

"Thanks, Doug." I pushed quickly past him.

"Yeah, well. Listen, Charlotte . . ." I stopped in the middle of the living room and squeezed the cell phone hard.

"Chet's a good guy," Doug said. "I hope he's okay."

"Me too." I couldn't get the words out in more than a whisper. "I'll take care of the rent, okay?"

"Don't worry about it," he said. "We've got a week."

"Thanks." I squeezed the phone again. "I'll let you know what's going on once I know."

"Cool."

I walked out thinking I owed Doug another shot at dinner. I'd even spring for the catsup.

Chet's block of Bleecker, though, was mostly a night street. First thing in the morning, it was just me, the autumn leaves and some restless fast-food wrappers on the sidewalk. The pigeons hadn't come off the ledges yet, and the cars lumbered down the street like they hadn't had enough caffeine. Another couple blocks, and I was into the student area surrounding Washington Square. Hip young things strolled past, hanging on to their backpacks and texting the entire world. I glimpsed the name on a diner as I threaded my way between them, and a memory jogged loose.

Friends wherever you go.

I scurried across the street and through the door of a long, low dining room done up in rattan and glass. Big windows let in the sun and an espresso machine the size of a VW bus waited up front for carry-out customers. The pass-through to the kitchen was large enough that I could see the head line cook, and when she turned around to slide a steaming omelet onto a pristine white plate, she could see me.

"Charlotte!"

"How's it going, Nicki?"

The hostess in obligatory black jeans and T-shirt smiled and let me by. Nicola Papandreos and I clasped hands through the pass. We had worked the line together at Caliente. It was my first serious restaurant job in New York and Nicki'd helped me navigate that particular minefield. But I had my executive and owner ambitions, and she said she just wanted to cook, so we went separate our ways.

"It's good." Nicki reached for a squeeze bottle and laced hot sauce across the omelet. "Better than it's been for you." She had no idea, but I managed to keep my answer down to an eye roll. "Word's out that they're letting you open again, though?"

"Fingers crossed." A server shouldered past, gave us both dirty looks and pulled three loaded plates off the pass. "Listen, Nick, I'm dying here. Can you . . . ?"

"Sit." She pointed me toward a table by the window. "Breakfast's on its way. Coffee?"

"You're a goddess."

I slid into a table by the window where I could see the front door, the kitchen door and who was going past outside. I also took a moment to hate the fact that I was thinking like this. A server brought me coffee and I downed a big slug too fast, letting the burn clear my mind.

I pulled out Chet's cell and cradled it in my hand for a long moment. Then I called up his texts, rearranged them so they'd read in the right order and scrolled through the ones from last Saturday, before this whole debacle began.

My mind tried to shut down again, to shield itself from comprehending what my eyes read.

Set for Sat.?

Not loving this. What about CCC?

Can't play this out longer.

I bit my lip hard and brought up the recent calls. All of them had NYC area codes or no area code at all. I scrolled down. Last week my brother had been making a whole lot of calls over to Connecticut. That'd be the spa. There was also a number in New Jersey.

I touched the Jersey number and held the phone to my ear as it rang.

Outside, a black-and-white police cruiser rolled up the street, followed closely by a beige Crown Vic. The cruiser stopped at the corner light, which put the Crown Vic almost level with my window. I blinked hard, sure I was imagining things, then scrunched back into my booth.

Linus O'Grady was driving that Crown Vic.

Chet's phone stopped ringing and clicked over to voice mail.

"Leave a message," said a woman's voice that I'd first heard last Saturday night. "I will call you back."

I dropped the phone like I'd been burned. It clattered on the cement floor, and I stared at it, heart pounding, lungs heaving. It beeped and the call cut out.

Robert had been wrong about Chet knowing the lady who'd walked in with Marcus the Nebbish. Chet had called Pamela Maddox at least ten times since Dylan Maddox turned up dead in Nightlife. Now Chet had vanished. Linus

O'Grady was outside, and despite all the warnings from Brendan and Anatole, who were way more used to dealing with Badness than I was, I had left a bucket of human blood sitting in my walk-in.

There are times when overreacting is the only option.

I snatched up Chet's phone and dialed.

"Maddox," Brendan picked up after the second ring.

"It's Charlotte. Get down to Vieux Cafe on East Eleventh and ask the head line cook, Nicki Papandreos, for the phone."

"What . . . ?" But I hung up and jumped out of my seat, dodging little tables and skinny waitstaff to the pass-through.

"Nicki." I grabbed her hand and slapped the phone into it. "Hang on to this until Brendan Maddox asks for it. Got that? Brendan Maddox, nobody else."

"What—"

"Sorry. Need to be elsewhere." I bolted out the door.

I wasn't trying to run away. Not really. I just didn't want what was coming next to happen in Nicki's place.

I only made it half a block. The black-and-white and the Crown Vic waited for me at the curb, just like in the movies. And just like in the movies, Linus O'Grady stepped out of the Crown Vic, right into my path.

"Charlotte Caine, you are under arrest."

"What's the charge?" But I already knew.

"The murder of Dylan Maddox."

21

Like all the other police procedures I'd had close encounters with recently, getting arrested was nothing like I thought it would be. After I got my rights read to me, there was no snide commentary, let alone any witty conversation with O'Grady. It all happened so fast, we barely even stopped traffic. Two uniformed officers (apparently taking people in is not something actual detectives do) handcuffed me, sat me in the backseat of the black-and-white and drove me to the Sixth Precinct. In handcuffs. They walked me up to the big desk. In handcuffs. The bored lieutenant with a comb-over and a serious doughnut-belly looked me up and down.

"Whaddaya got, kid?" he demanded of my escort. They told him. Details were written down and I was put in the holding cell.

They did take away the handcuffs at this point. In fact, they took away my purse and everything I had in my pockets, which wasn't much, but did include my phone. They also took all my hairpins. So I had a tangled mass of blond hair falling down around my shoulders, getting in my eyes and my mouth and everything else it could find. I felt like a Nordic Medusa.

Oh, and they don't do the ink-and-roll thing to get your fingerprints anymore. There's a nice clean screen that lights up when they hold your hand down on it.

There was, however, a strip search. And there was a rubber glove involved. And that is absolutely all you're going to hear about it.

Afterward I got a whole bunch of receipts for the stuff they'd taken away.

Eventually, the same uniformed officers who'd put me in the cell came back, with the handcuffs and put me back in the same black-and-white cruiser car, which still smelled like coffee and disinfectant. They didn't talk to me and I didn't talk to them as we drove through the city once more lit up in her nighttime splendor. I had no trouble recognizing the meatpacking district when we got to it, or the headquarters of the Paranormal Squad.

This time I got walked to the basement and all my paperwork got handed over to another bored lieutenant. This one was a gray-haired lady who looked like she could be somebody's grandma when she was off duty. But not the nice kind. The kind that pinches your cheek too hard and orders you to stand up straight all the time.

I got searched again.

Finally, they put me in an interrogation room, which was clearly for "special" cases. It had polished stainless-steel walls where it didn't have one-way mirrors. There were pressure plates on the floor. Before my arresting officer took the handcuffs off again, I was put in a wooden chair at a wooden table. The two dead bolts on the steel door were black iron, and when I rolled my eyes toward the ceiling I saw three prominent old-fashioned sprinkler nozzles protruding from the ceiling. I was willing to bet they had five or six local priests in to say the blessings on whatever came out of those.

They'd taken my watch, so I had no idea how long I sat there. I just knew it was cold. They'd taken my jacket when they took away my purse and phone, so I had on only the plain green T-shirt I'd worn under my chef's coat. I watched all the variations of my own reflection in the steel walls and thought about how I didn't know where Chet was. He'd run away. He'd run away and left his phone and key behind. Phone, key, sister and a bucket of blood. He had Pamela Maddox's phone number, something her security consultant cousin hadn't been able to track down.

But all I could really think about was that this once he must have really told me the truth. This scam, with Ilona, Marcus and the rest of the wacky gang, it really was his scam.

My baby brother, all grown up.

But that wasn't the real problem. The real problem was that there were only a few people who could have gotten the human blood into the walk-in, because whoever'd done it would have needed a key. Unless they'd managed it on the day we were feeding people out the back door. And that would eliminate all the nightbloods. I felt a surge of hope. It couldn't have been Chet who smuggled in the blood. It *couldn't* have been.

Except it could, because Chet had a key. Except it couldn't, because Nightlife had been police-sealed and watched and there was no time for him to get the blood in between when we were there working and the little chat Brendan, Anatole and I had with Taylor Watts. I'd been in Nightlife that whole time.

Which brought us back to daybloods; the Maddoxes, Bert Shelby and Taylor Watts.

The smell of metal polish worked its way down my throat. I needed to pee and my heel started to tap nervously on the floor from the strain of sitting still and looking calm for whoever watched from behind the mirror.

As if this were the signal, the door opened to let Linus O'Grady in. "Okay, Sergeant," he said to my bored uniformed escort. Bored Uniform nodded and left. Then it was just him and me.

Linus didn't look so little anymore. His bulk filled that cramped, shiny room and his spaniel eyes took on a German shepherd quality, the professional, bomb-sniffing kind. He slapped his folder down and planted his hands on the chipped and splintering table. I hadn't really looked at his hands before. They were big, callused paws with scarred knuckles. He'd hit things with those hands. A lot.

"You have officially blown all your chances with me, Charlotte Caine." O'Grady's words were quiet and cold. "I trusted you. I said to myself, anybody who can make a lasagna like that, she's got heart. Real passion. Plus, she's smart. She wouldn't jeopardize her life's work."

Don't say anything. They'd allowed me a phone call before they put me in the first holding cell, and I'd called the apartment because it was the only number I could remember without my cell. Fortunately, it was Trish who answered. We had a very short conversation, but even so, I'd lost count of how many times she told me not to say anything. I clamped my mouth shut now.

O'Grady shoved a piece of paper toward me. It was covered in black-and-white lines and lots of tiny print. "This is a DNA analysis of a five-gallon bucket from your freezer, Chef Caine. Labeled 'ox blood'. Except it's not ox blood. It's Dylan Maddox's blood mixed with cow blood. Nice touch, that, by the way. Must have killed you to dilute the merchandise."

I didn't do anything.

"Where's your brother, Chef Caine?"

I don't know.

"Did he hold Maddox down for you? Is that what happened? He holds your victim down over the bucket while you get him twice in the neck with one of those big kitchen syringes and let the blood drain out. The walk-in would be a perfect place to do it too. No way to hear the screams. Did you drain him out into the ox blood, or did you dump that in on top?"

No. That's not what happened. I don't know what happened. I didn't do anything.

"What I don't get is why you dropped the body in the foyer. Why didn't you cut it up? Or at least dump it in the river. We wouldn't have found it for weeks, if ever. Did you get interrupted by somebody? Like maybe Brendan Maddox?"

"I didn't *do* anything!" My chair banged against the metal floor as it toppled backward. "You actually think Brendan caught me draining his drunk cousin and didn't do anything about it?"

I was on my feet, leaning across the table, nose to nose with Detective O'Grady. He smiled, a thin, satisfied smile.

"Where's your brother, Ms. Caine?" Little Linus asked calmly. "Why'd he leave you holding the bag and me looking at Brendan Maddox for a suspect?"

I opened my mouth, and closed it again. All my protests banged against my skull, demanding to be let out, along with days' worth of guilt, fear and anger.

"Detective?"

Slowly, Linus turned his head. Bored Uniform was leaning in the door I hadn't even heard open.

"What?" O'Grady didn't say it out loud, but he managed to leave "this better be good" hanging in the air.

"Her lawyer's here, Detective."

My lawyer?

"Hello, Detective O'Grady. Good to see you again so soon." Rafe Wallace, the man Trish called the best paranormal lawyer in the city, walked into the room.

I stumbled backward, because relief sucked the last of

my strength out of me. Rafe Wallace was a tall, immaculately dressed man with deep black skin, the barest hint of a Jamaican accent and salt-and-pepper dreadlocks pulled into a neat ponytail.

O'Grady sighed and gave me a look that said he was conceding the point, but just this once. "You taking on this whole family, Rafe?"

"Liberty and justice for all, Detective." Wallace dropped his briefcase onto the table, picked up the chair I'd knocked over, and motioned for me to sit down. As I did, we locked gazes.

Shut up, his dark eyes commanded me.

Yes, sir. I studied my hands in my lap. My recent bout of cooking had seriously marred the effects of Jess's manicure. The green pepper stains weren't helping.

Apparently satisfied with my show of submission, Rafe Wallace opened his briefcase and pulled out his own folder, plus a legal pad. "Detective O'Grady, two days ago my client was feeding the hungry on the streets of our fair city, and now you have her in jail. Why is that?"

"Your client has Dylan Maddox's blood in her freezer."

"My client had been barred from her establishment for days."

"Except for the day she was so philanthropically feeding the huddled masses, which was a whole day before we decided to allow her access to the crime scene. Plenty of time to shift a few things into the cooler."

"So what? Do you think she actually put incriminating evidence into her restaurant cooler sometime in the last two days? Or is she just a Mrs. Lovett, peddling suspicious meat pies to the city's poor?"

"You said it, Wallace. I didn't."

Rafe clicked the button on his mechanical pencil several times and started jotting down notes. "Then I am also saying someone might think the Paranormal Squad has a problem with the Caines. Or perhaps you just have a problem with not being able to close the case of one dead Maddox."

"Not going to work, Wallace."

Rafe didn't even bother glancing up from his writing. "What's the matter, Linus? The mayor's office putting pressure on you to make this go away? Or is it old man Maddox himself? You and he go back a bit, don't you? And neither one of you is exactly a big booster of the city's nightblood population."

The mayor's office?

There's a turf war brewing, Brendan had said. *And my family's egging it on.* And it was worth a million-dollar bribe. Which Margot said was coming from a broken trust. Or maybe she added that detail because she thought I wouldn't even consider taking money straight from a powerful antivamp crusader like Lloyd Maddox.

"Nice try, Counselor." O'Grady folded his arms. "But it's no good. The blood was in the refrigerator the night Maddox was killed and I've got all the paperwork I need to prove it."

Rafe waved his hand. "Sure, sure, sure. Because backdating a report and giving orders to your own lab techs is so difficult." He paused, and I felt the next shot being leveled. "And of course, if you'd actually found such valuable evidence when you had complete control of the premises, you'd naturally leave it right where it was."

O'Grady turned back to me. "Ms. Caine, you'd better hope this guy has something better by the time he gets to court. Otherwise you're going to be working the chow line at Rikers—you and your brother both. As soon as we find him." The point on Rafe's pencil snapped. O'Grady's scary smile—the thin, satisfied one that did not belong on the face of a man who appreciated a good lasagna—slid back into place. "Why, Mr. Wallace, didn't you know your other client had fled the jurisdiction?"

Rafe met the detective's gaze and clicked his pencil twice, slowly and deliberately. "We are discussing Ms. Caine, not Mr. Caine."

"We are discussing a dead man, a bucket of blood, and a missing vampire. And frankly, I'm getting tired of how many items are getting tacked on to this case."

"What about the other bodies?" asked Rafe quietly.

O'Grady's smile faded, and Rafe clicked his pencil once more, like he was racking up a point.

"You're sitting on four other Greenwich Village murders, Detective," he said. "All of them drained while alive, but none of them bitten. Did you also find their blood in my client's freezer?"

"What are you playing at, Wallace?"

"Nothing at all, Detective. Only I wonder what the media will think when they find out you've been engaged in a cover-up and that you're trying to railroad the Caines because you've been unable to find the real killers."

I wasn't sure whether I was in the middle of a high-stakes poker game or a full-fledged Mexican standoff. I just tried to make myself small, as if I could avoid the shrapnel when one of these two exploded.

"Now we're into the cheap threats?" inquired O'Grady.

But Rafe bent back over his legal pad and started in on his notes again, as if the detective had ceased to be of interest. "I'm just saying there are all kinds of things to take into account here."

"And I'm sure the district attorney and the judge will be just thrilled to go over them all with you. But none of them make up for the evidence found in your client's— both your clients'—place of employment."

"Which also does not explain why she was attacked outside the Post Mortem nightclub."

"*What?*"

Now it was Rafe's turn with the satisfied smile. "My

client was attacked by two vampires outside Post Mortem in the West Village."

"And she didn't think to *report* this?"

"An oversight, I'm sure. She's been very concerned about her brother's welfare and the situation with her restaurant."

"And I'm supposed to just believe this attack?"

"There were witnesses."

Anatole. Sometime while I was in here, the sun had set and Rafe Wallace had talked to Anatole. He was the only one who knew about both the attack and the other deaths. No, wait. I'd told Brendan too.

Somehow, I had acquired my own damn cavalry. They ran to my rescue in alleys, escorted me out of vampire-filled theaters, and came to my aid in police effing head-quarters. Why did that make me want to shrivel up inside?

Because I took care of other people. Nobody took care of me, and I liked it that way. But it was more than that. It was because no matter which way I looked at it, both Brendan and Anatole could have reasons for helping me that were very different from the ones I thought I knew.

"Things starting to look a little more complicated?" inquired Rafe.

Oh, yeah.

Linus drummed his big fingers on the tabletop. Rafe clicked his pencil. I bit my tongue to keep from yelling at both of them to knock it off.

"Changes nothing," said O'Grady at last. "We've got the blood."

Rafe shrugged. "Circumstantial evidence, but go spin your wheels if it makes you happy. I need to talk with my client."

O'Grady got to his feet, but I got no sense of retreat from him. He was heading out that door because he had to. He'd be upstairs, sorting through his folders, until he had a nice neat paper trail leading from me to Dylan Maddox's blood. My wrists burned where the handcuffs had been and I felt my chin shake as the door closed.

"No need to look like that, Ms. Caine." Rafe clicked his pencil once more and made another note.

"Why not?"

"Because it is very obvious you are being set up." My lawyer picked up the other chair, moved it around to my side of the table and sat. Even sitting, he had at least six inches on me. "And Detective O'Grady knows it."

"He does? 'Cause before you got here, he sure acted like he thought I was doing a Lizzie Borden on the neighborhood."

"Among his many other talents, Linus O'Grady is a one-man good-cop-bad-cop show. It doesn't help that he thinks you're being set up by your brother."

I was not ready to discuss how many times that same idea had crossed my mind. "What do you think?"

Rafe considered his words carefully, and considered them again. "I've represented a lot of nightbloods with something to hide, Ms. Caine. I don't think your brother has the patience to pull off something like this, especially if you add the other four bodies into the equation."

"How'd you know about that?"

Rafe touched the side of his nose and pointed toward the mirror.

I sank back into my chair and waited while Rafe went back to his notes, occasionally clicking that pencil. At last he looked up at me.

"I'm going to ask you one more question and I need a straight answer."

"Okay." I was pretty sure I knew what was coming, and it gave me a sick feeling in my empty stomach.

"Do you know where your brother is?"

Straight answer. Right. "I wish to God I did."

Rafe held my gaze for a long moment, clearly waiting to see if I was going to change my mind. I don't know if what he saw satisfied him, but he didn't make any notes about it. "If you do hear from him, you have got to convince him to turn himself in. At this point, Linus O'Grady and the holding cell here are about the only things that are going to keep him safe if the Maddoxes decide to get their vigilante on."

"I know." Memory of Anatole's dead white face and shadowed eyes looked down at me. *With the young Maddoxes running about the city with their stakes out, I am less than amused about that at the moment.*

"I know you think O'Grady's on the dark side now," Rafe said. "But I've been dealing with the man since the P-Squad was formed. He's fair and he's clean. Your brother will be treated right."

"I believe it. I just . . ." *Don't say it. Don't say it.* "I'm really worried about Chet." Which was true, as far as it went. I was not going to say out loud that I didn't even know for sure he was alive. So instead I asked about something Rafe had said to O'Grady.

"What was all that about the mayor's office?"

"You don't know?" When I shook my head, Rafe hesitated, but only for a moment. "The Maddoxes—in the form of Maddox Security, LLC headed by one Brendan Maddox—are up for a major city contract to provide magical and paranormal protection services to public buildings and monuments."

I sat up straight. That explained a lot, including what Brendan couldn't tell me and Margot's bribe. A citywide contract—a million dollars would be the budget for coffee and Danish on something like that. How on earth had they kept this off FlashNews? The nightblood community would go ballistic if they found out the city was contracting security out to the Maddoxes.

What if it was Brendan who had given Margot the money for my bribe? But it still didn't explain *why*. Why the hell would it be worth a million dollars to any given Maddox to keep me from opening a nightblood-friendly establishment?

"Do you think Detective O'Grady knows about the security contract?"

"I'm sure of it. I haven't seen Little Linus so mad in . . . forever."

"Couldn't be because everybody keeps calling him Little Linus?"

"Actually, no. But it might have a lot to do with a city that underfunds his team and then gets ready to hand millions over to a private contractor." Rafe tossed his notes and folder into his briefcase. "Hang tough, Ms. Caine. I will get you out of here as soon as humanly possible." He put a hand on my shoulder and gave me that little reassuring shake. I thought about swatting him away, but couldn't seem to muster the strength. "Did you say anything to O'Grady before I got here?"

"No."

"Good. You have the right to remain silent, and I want you to keep using it. Now, from here, they're going to put you in a holding cell. You're actually fairly lucky. As a thauma-typical in the paranormal lockup, you should get a spot to yourself."

"Lucky?" A hysterical laugh threatened, and it had backup. I swallowed hard.

"Trust me, Ms. Caine, you do not want to be locked in with the kind of nightbloods who end up here."

I thought about the other daybloods I had shared my previous city-sponsored accommodations with, and I shuddered. Seeing that I'd gotten the point, Rafe went on. "Hopefully, we will get ourselves a judge with a healthy sense of skepticism, and a reasonable bail. If so, you will be out of here in eight to twelve hours."

"Bail?" I'd been so wrapped up in sorting through all the things I didn't know, I hadn't stopped to think about much of what might actually happen next. "How much are we talking?"

"It depends on what charges O'Grady and the DA think can be made to stick. But don't worry. You can get a bond. That will mean you only have to put up ten percent of the total."

My mouth had gone very dry. "I think I've got fifty dollars in my checking account."

That, of course, was exactly the wrong thing to say to a man who charges by the hour. I had an abrupt vision of him shaking my hand, wishing me luck and heading out the door. As it was, a muscle in his cheek twitched and he made another note.

"Well, we'll cross that bridge when we come to it."

I smiled up into my lawyer's eyes and tried to project confidence. He didn't believe me, but I let that go, because honest to God, what else was I going to do?

22

Exhaustion is a useful thing. With my brain and body fully anesthetized by its effects, I was able to fall asleep in the little holding cell, despite the fact that the narrow bunk had a mattress about one inch thick over a solid metal shelf.

When Bored Uniform came and got me for my "desk appearance," he took me to the bathroom first. He did not, however, let me have a comb, or any of my hairpins. I walked into the courtroom stained and rumpled, with bloodshot eyes and the mother of all bad hair days. If I'd been the judge, I wouldn't have believed a word I said.

Fortunately, Rafe Wallace wasn't about to let me do any talking. I stood beside him and kept my mouth shut while he explained how all the circumstances were, well, circumstantial, that I was an upstanding member of the business community, and could not even possibly be considered a flight risk. (Thank God for Elaine and her cameras. He actually pulled out his smartphone to show the judge how I had fed the hungry.) The demonstration of all of this innocence and virtue proved that I should be released on my own recognizance.

The DA, a skinny, faux-redheaded woman who evidently believed that eighties-width shoulder pads were back in style, had a different opinion. She brought up the bucket of blood seven times, and Chet's disappearance twelve.

After she finally ran out of synonyms for "heinous," there was a wait while the judge shuffled papers and sucked on a cough drop.

At last the gavel came down. "Seventy-five thousand, cash or bond. Next."

My basic math is good, especially when dollar signs are involved. Ten percent bond meant I needed seven thousand five hundred dollars to get out of here.

"No contest, Your Honor," Rafe said.

"I can't raise that much." Panic flitted around the edges of my mind. I was going back into that silent, empty, windowless cell and Bored Uniform was going to turn the key. . . .

"It's taken care of." Rafe closed his briefcase and herded me toward the edge of the courtroom.

"What? How?" If this was Trish again, I was going to have to leave town. How could I look her in the face after she'd done so much?

Rafe glanced to the back of the courtroom. Premonition prickled the back of my neck as I turned.

Brendan nodded to me from the back row of benches.

I opened my mouth. I closed it again.

"Come on," said Rafe. "No time to be standing around."

Fortunately I didn't have to deal with Brendan right away, because I got heavily involved in another hour of following Rafe around. More papers were exchanged between tired, hard-eyed people both in and out of uniforms. Down at the desk for the holding cells I got my stuff back in a manila envelope: purse, hairpins, cell phone, all the little things I carried around to feel prepared for life on a daily basis. Rafe waited while I counted and sorted. All the while, one question spun around the back of my mind:

How am I ever going to pay Brendan back?

"Now, Chef Caine, there're some things you need to know," said Rafe as I slung my purse over my shoulder. "Word of your arrest has gotten out, and we're going to have reporters waiting when we leave here."

I should have known. I was sure the thought had passed through my mind at some point during the last—I checked my watch—twelve hours. "How bad?" I asked.

Rafe handed me his smartphone with FlashNews already active.

First headline shone in screaming red: VAMPIRE CHEF HAS BLOOD ON HER HANDS.

It went downhill from there. FlashNews had compiled tons of articles and videos. I saw myself smugly staring up from the thumbnail graphics, looking like I deserved all the puns being applied to the ruin of my life.

CAUGHT RED-HANDED.

BLOODY DISASTER FOR PHILANTHROPIC CHEF.

FANGS, BUT NO FANGS?

I thumbed the screen off. It was gone. Everything I had worked for my whole adult life—family, job, reputation, all of it. All gone.

Rafe took back his cell phone. "Let's get you out of here."

"Yeah." But where could I go? The vulture flock waited on the courthouse steps, cameras, mics and smartphones held high.

"Chef Caine!" they shouted. "Chef Caine!"

"No comment!" Rafe gripped my arm as he shouldered between them.

The way ahead filled with exploding lights and a blur of voices. They shouted questions, but I couldn't tell one from the other any more than I could see where I was going.

"Chef Caine!"

"Chef Caine!"

"Chef Caine has no comment!" bellowed Rafe.

He was wrong. I had plenty of comments. I just didn't have the strength to deliver them, and if I had, they'd've all been bleeped out on the networks. Which really made me want to open my mouth and give them a taste of what my line cooks got on a Friday night when we were all in the weeds.

Used to get.

"No comment!" Rafe propelled me toward the black town car with tinted windows that waited by the curb. The door opened, and I was folded and pushed into the plush seat. The second the door slammed shut, the driver simultaneously blew the horn and gunned the engine. We squealed away from the clicking, popping, shouting curbside crowd.

"Are you okay?" asked Brendan.

Of course it was Brendan occupying the other half of that plush seat, managing to be spruce, clean, in control and concerned all at the same time.

"For certain minimal values of okay, probably." I pushed my hair back. I hated everything about myself right then—the way I looked, the way I felt, where I was, and most of all where I had just been. More than any of that, I hated what I had to say next.

"You were right. I should have gone straight to O'Grady." One more total screwup by Charlotte Caine to add to the list.

Brendan didn't say "I told you so," despite the fact that he'd more than earned the right to. But I'd known he wouldn't. It was so very much not his style. He was a class act all the way, the kind of customer I'd have been glad to have in my place, when I had a place. He would treat the staff well, enjoy the food for what it was, tip generously, and treat his date with consideration. He probably rescued puppies on the weekends and tutored underprivileged orphans.

Whereas I got arrested and terminally fouled up other people's lives trying to help.

"It'll be all right, Charlotte."

"Chet's gone missing," I told him.

"I know."

"Somebody could have killed him, Brendan. Somebody—"

"I don't think so." Brendan cut me off before I could work up more than a small head of hysteria.

"Why not?"

"Because if someone did kidnap Chet, it would be the same people who killed Dylan, and they would want to make sure you knew about it so you would be good and scared of them."

A thin river of hope trickled into my tired heart. "You sound very sure."

Brendan opened his hand to show me Chet's cell lying on his palm.

That thin river swelled into a decent-sized stream. "Did you find anything?"

Secrets gleamed behind Brendan's blue eyes. "Your brother was trying to set Pam up."

"Set Pam up? With who?"

His face went blank for a second before comprehension dawned, along with a look that was dangerously close to amusement. "Not that kind of setup. He was trying to pull off a sting operation."

"*What?* Are you sure?"

Brendan nodded. "He's been recording conversations, e-mailing the files to his home computer and then deleting the recordings off the phone."

"You can tell that?"

"Security consultant, remember?"

I did remember. It just hadn't filtered through my admittedly overworked brain what that might actually mean. "I thought that was with paranormal things."

"You would not believe the number of paranormal things you can do with a cell phone."

Very few answers existed for that statement, and none of them would make me sound intelligent at all. "What else did you find out?"

"Chet had been calling Dylan as well. Given the timing of the calls, and the text messages you found, it looks like Chet and his partner talked Pam into coming to Nightlife. Then they let Dylan know where she'd be. My best guess is they thought Dylan could take Pam back to Ithaca."

"But why are they involved with Pam at all?"

Brendan clearly didn't like any of the ideas he had on this score. "That depends what's going on in Connecticut."

"Connecticut?" Once again I was several conversational steps behind.

"Your brother has been making trips into Connecticut about once a month."

"How'd you know . . . ?"

"The GPS and the Google cache. Your brother's been buying his train tickets and renting the car online."

I sat back, overwhelmed by the urge to go home and run my cell phone through the food processor. For a while, I didn't say anything, just looked out the window, trying to digest everything he'd said. It was then I realized I hadn't asked a very important question.

"Brendan?"

"Yeah?"

"Where the hell are we going?"

"Oh. Sorry. I got you a room at the Ritz-Carlton until

the Flash vultures are done making little messes all over your front stoop."

"The *Ritz*!" I shot up so straight the belt dug into my shoulder. "I can't afford—"

"You're not paying."

"I already owe you for my bail!"

"Unless you're planning to skip out on me, I'll get that back." He saw me getting ready to protest and made a "be reasonable" face, the kind that instantly makes you want to stop being reasonable for a long time. "You need to be someplace, and unless you want to brave the feeding frenzy and make your roommates put up with the loss of privacy longer than necessary . . ."

"Nice use of the flanking guilt maneuver."

"Thank you. And wherever you end up it's got to be someplace that neither my family nor your two playmates from Post Mortem can get into."

"And they can't get into the Ritz?"

"Not anymore."

"Client of yours?"

"Yes."

I settled down. This was another one of those times when struggling would just make me look ridiculous. I had nowhere to go and we both knew it. This was my own damn stupid fault. We both knew that too.

"Given what we found on his cell, it's possible that Chet's gone to Connecticut now," said Brendan before I had a chance to serve myself up another full portion of self-loathing. "Charlotte, have you got any idea what he's doing up there?"

I told him what Chet had told me, about the spa and about how much money he said it was making. So much, in fact, that he was funneling the extra into Nightlife.

Brendan didn't say anything. He sat there next to me for a long time, not saying anything.

There was something else I needed to know. Though asking the question meant taking the risk of insulting the man who was once again saving my skin, it was not something I could leave alone.

"Tell me you're sure Margot and Ian had nothing to do with Chet vanishing."

Brendan sighed and looked away. He didn't want to answer me, but I was not about to let him off the hook. Not for this. We were way past the small stuff.

"I'm sure. They only found one of the tails I put on them."

"You had more than one. . . ."

"Security consultant, remember?" he snapped. "We were just talking about it? Yes, I put two tails on my own sister because right now I do not trust her. I shouldn't have to tell you how deliriously happy that makes me." He looked down at his own smartphone and thumbed the screen. "My last update is from an hour ago. They're at their hotel, probably on the phone with our grandfather. I just hope to God they aren't telling him it's time to go all Bruce Wayne on the city's nightblood population. And before you say it, yes, I know she came to talk to you, and I've been really, really wondering when you'd get around to mentioning that."

A wave of nausea at my own helplessness rolled through me. There was nothing I could do, nothing I could say to make this better, or to find the way out. Brendan already had plenty of reasons to be angry, at me, at Chet, and at this situation we were only making more complicated. That we were witnessing a private family struggle become painfully public only made it worse.

"I know about the city contract," I said, because at that point honesty was all I had to offer him. "Rafe told me."

My admission did not seem to surprise him at all. "This could save my family, Charlotte. It's a way to put their skills to work legally on a large scale. It'll also bring them out of the shadows, make them rein in . . ."

"Margot and Ian?"

Brendan sighed. "A few facts about the Maddox clan. My grandfather and his siblings made a lot of money—and I mean a *lot*—dealing with problems nobody could openly acknowledge. We were one of the few families able to defend the daybloods against the encroaching nightbloods. Then came the Change Time, and the Equal Humanity Acts, and all that income dried up. Granddad and my great-uncles started spending their time down in Washington lobbying to get the acts repealed, or at least softened. A few bad investments got made, and all of a sudden we were beyond broke.

"Going for the city contract was my idea. I was making good money in paranormal security, so why not bring the whole family into it? There are people in high places who know how much we can do. The connections my grandfather forged are still in place. All this, and it still took months to talk him around to letting me put in a bid."

Brendan watched the city roll past behind the permanent twilight of the tinted windows for a long time.

"We need a way out," he said finally. "If the family is disgraced, if Grandfather decides to call for revenge . . . it'll be a free-for-all."

"How many of you are there?"

"Enough to go toe-to-toe with the whole P-Squad and come out ahead."

I tried to imagine the kind of havoc that could be wreaked by a clan of warlocks turned paranormal Mafia. Then I tried not to let Brendan see me shudder.

The owners of the Ritz-Carlton must have been very satisfied clients. When we pulled up to the entrance, the manager waited beside the doorman to hand over my special key card for the elevator, usher us up to the VIP floor and show us to a suite that could have held my entire apartment and still had room left over. And did I mention the view of Central Park? There was a view of Central Park, slowly sinking into a pool of shadow as one light after another blinked on in the surrounding city. New York was waking up for the evening.

In response to being enveloped in unprecedented luxury after a day of being held hostage to the city's law enforcement establishment, my stomach growled. Loudly. I blushed. It didn't care.

"I'll call room service," said Brendan.

I was ready to fall down and eat the carpet, but some reflexes will not be stilled. "Oh, no, don't. We'll get better . . ."

But Brendan held up his hand, picked up the room phone and punched a button. "Brendan Maddox in 2018. Can I speak with Chef Martinelli? Yes, I'll hold." And he did, but not for long. "Hey, Pete. How's it going? . . . Saw the review in the *Times*. They said the duck with five-spice marmalade was unbelievable. Was that meant to be a good thing? . . . Nah, I was just going to go get a burger. Okay, okay, I'm not going anywhere. But I do have company, and I need to make a good impression . . . I'm sure I will be amazed, but you know, again, is that meant to be a g—" From where I stood, I heard the phone slam down.

"That's supposed to be my trick," I told him.

Brendan shrugged. "We were at school together before he quit the MBA program for culinary school."

I looked at him and he looked at me. I wondered if this would feel less awkward if he hadn't just bailed me out of jail. Probably, but not by much.

"If you want a shower, go ahead."

I did want a shower. I could smell myself and there was nothing good about it. With Brendan's reassurance that Chet hadn't been taken up by the Bad Guys, I felt like I might have some space to get over my very long, very, very bad day. But I hesitated. There were more things I had to say; apologies he deserved, explanations I needed him to hear, things I desperately needed to understand, but I didn't know where to begin.

Brendan crossed the room and touched my hand. "It's okay," he said gently. "Just get your shower. We can talk more when you're done."

Tears threatened. I was so tired. Everything was so messed up, and everything new I learned just piled that mess higher and deeper. But for this moment I was safe, high up above the darkening city, secure in a plush jewel box of a room.

"You keep rescuing me," I whispered. "Why do you keep on rescuing me?"

"Because I want to."

It was too much. I couldn't take it. I'd never had backup like this. Nobody could take what I had to throw at them. Even my own parents had left me alone to deal with the mess I'd made out of my brother's existence. But Brendan kept coming back, and he not only took it, he made it better. Really better. Not because of the money or the magic, but because he saw me at a level of bad I wouldn't have been able to imagine a few days ago, and he still came back.

I started to cry.

These were not decorous Elizabeth Taylor tears. These were great, loud sobs that shook my exhausted body and made my throat instantly raw. No pride, no dignity, no strength, just a river of guilt, regret and confusion I couldn't hold back anymore.

Brendan folded me tightly in his arms. He didn't worry

about hurting me. He seemed to know I needed to feel his strength. I rested my cheek against his chest, wrapped my arms around his waist and bawled. He said nothing. He didn't move. He just held me close, one arm around my shoulders, one hand cupping the back of my head, and let me cry.

Slowly, the storm dissipated, and extraneous sensation began to shine through. I could feel Brendan's heartbeat beneath the hard plane of his chest. He smelled of warmth and Ivory soap. I lifted my head and I looked into his amazing blue eyes.

I kissed him. There was nothing soft or subtle about the gesture. It was as raw as my crying jag and born of a pent-up desire to know what his mouth would feel like against mine.

I can report that Brendan Maddox was an absolutely topflight kisser. Direct, open, thorough, and filled with all kinds of promises. He slid his hands around my shoulders and pulled me onto my toes as I clung to his solid waist and kissed him back with everything I had. A hot, sweet ache filled me to overflowing. I wanted to pull up his shirt and run my hands over his skin. I wanted to drag him down onto the plush carpet, or let him drag me down. It didn't matter. I needed the tumult, the tenderness and heat that would make all the rest of this mess go away. Just for now. Just this once.

Except it would matter, and that realization laid a cold finger on my heated brain. It mattered because I didn't know what the hell was really happening now, or what would be happening ten minutes or two days from now. I did know, though, that Brendan wasn't the kind to walk away. If we became lovers tonight and I changed my mind, he would not leave me with nothing but the memory of one night of poor judgment. He'd stay. I'd have to turn on him and force him away to get him to go, and as badly as I wanted him now, that was not a possibility I was ready to live with.

My libido fought me every inch of the way, but I pulled back. Brendan let me go. But then, I'd known he would.

We stood there, both panting, with a good six inches between us. Brendan's cheeks were flushed and he had an adorable, kissable smile on his face that he was trying to get under control.

"Sorry?" I said.

He shook his head. "You?"

I considered the possibility. "No."

"Good."

"It was just stress?" I tried.

He thought about that. "We'll find out, won't we?"

"I guess we will." And if I stood here another second, I was going to throw myself at him again. He'd catch me too.

"I'm going to get that shower," I said.

Once in the bedroom, which could have comfortably slept half my line crew, I shut the door firmly. I'm pretty sure I had a goofy smile on my face as I stripped down and sauntered into the bathroom. The water was instantly hot and a twist of the showerhead had it coming down in a pummeling rain to rinse off the stink from cells and cop cars. The towels were gloriously fluffy. So was the complimentary bathrobe. The toiletry kit included a heavy brush. A hair dryer hung in its holder on the wall. I spent a solid twenty minutes on my hair, teasing out the tangles and blowing it dry until finally I recognized the woman who stood before the mirror.

The combination of being physically clean and working with my hands, even if it was just to tidy my hair, settled my thoughts. This left me with enough room in my brain to stack the information I'd gotten hold of in some kind of order. Fact One: There was a human-blood-running underground in New York City. Fact Two: Chet was looking for a legal way to deliver a better product than the runners could supply. This could very easily have made somebody nervous. Fact Three: Bert Shelby had a history of dealing with criminals. A tourist goth bar would make a great place for dealing actual human blood. You'd be hiding in plain sight.

Taylor could have told Shelby about Chet's spa. Shelby, or his employers, could have gotten nervous and decided to try to warn Chet that he'd better get out of the business. Or maybe, they wanted to take over the spa and Chet wouldn't sell.

All of which left Burning Question Number One: Had Taylor Watts turned in his keys when he left? Because if he had kept a key to the walk-in, he could have dumped both the body and the blood in Nightlife.

But where did the Maddoxes fit in? Starting with Pam and Dylan but moving on to Margot and, as much as I hated to admit it, Brendan. Brendan said Chet was trying to set Pam up. He was gathering information on her and from her. Had Pam gotten herself involved with Shelby's operation? She was a security expert and a vampire hunter. That'd be a very handy skill set for a gang of blood runners.

Could I be sure that it was Shelby who was in charge, though? What if it was Ilona St. Claire? What if I had things backward, and Ilona, Chet and Marcus the Nebbish Vamp—or some combination of those three—were trying to muscle in on Shelby's operation rather than Shelby and Pam trying to muscle in on theirs?

Or . . . or what if Pam was still working for her family and was acting as a mole in Shelby's operation, and Dylan had been killed as a warning to her? No, that couldn't be right. If they knew Pam was a mole, why not just kill her?

And why dump the body at Nightlife? Pam must really be in Shelby's operation, and poor, dumb, lovesick Dylan was trying to pull her out before the fact of her criminal involvement could jeopardize the Maddox family's chance at a city contract.

Or maybe . . . I scrunched my eyes closed. I was dangerously close to giving myself a headache from going around in so many circles. I was also missing something. I could feel it.

I set down the hairbrush. This much I was sure of. My world had collapsed and my brother was on the run in Connecticut, but for just a minute I needed to set that aside. I was physically clean and dinner was on its way to my hotel room. Everything else could wait, just for an hour. Just one hour more.

That I had no clean clothing was a problem. Well, this was the Ritz. There would be a laundry service. But when I walked back into the bedroom, I got my next surprise. The filthy T-shirt and slacks I'd tossed onto the bed were gone. In their place I saw a long black skirt and a soft sapphire-colored top made of what looked suspiciously like watered silk. With loose sleeves. And silver spangles.

I knew I shouldn't. I had already taken too much from Brendan. Besides, if I was absolutely honest with myself, there were still questions about exactly how much of this mess was just family and how much was really him. I didn't want to owe Brendan, for that reason, but there was more to it. I didn't want him to think that when we—I mean *if* we—got physical, it was because I owed him. I didn't want to have to wonder if he was going to expect something because I owed him so much.

I didn't want to have to wonder what Anatole would think about my being with Brendan.

That was another one of those ice-cold thoughts that opens the door wide to reality. Because I knew that if it had been Anatole holding me when I broke, I might have acted exactly the same, and felt the same sweet ache as a result.

I looked at the ceiling. "It would have killed you to send them one at a time?"

There was no answer. I sighed and got dressed.

23

When I emerged from the bedroom, Brendan stood up. He'd been at the dining table, which was laden with covered dishes. I smelled duck and ginger, and rice and warm bread. There were candles, and red wine.

I refused to be distracted. I gestured to the clothes.

"Lobby boutique," Brendan said.

"How'd you know my size?"

"I looked at your labels."

"Why didn't you just rummage around in my purse while you were at it?"

"Because I didn't think you kept your measurements in your purse." He smiled and my heart tried to hide behind my ribs. He looked down at my Mary Sue Scarlet toes and I felt myself blush. "Nail polish?"

"My roommate's idea."

"I like it." His eyes traveled back up to mine. "I know now is not a good time for the charm offensive, but you do look wonderful."

"Thank you." I don't get to wear girlie clothes very often. Or twirl around gently on painted toes to let a hem flutter around my ankles while my hair ripples around my shoulders. Brendan responded to this most unusual sight with another one of his bone-melting smiles. Then he pulled out my chair for me and poured the wine.

Unfortunately, my blossoming hopes of holding reality at bay for the length of one intimate, delicious dinner were dashed in short order. First Trish called, demanding to know where the hell I was and what the hell had happened to me. When she responded loudly to my mention of the Ritz, Jessie ripped the phone from her hand and said they *had* to come over right now, so I wouldn't be alone. It took five minutes of wrangling to convince Roomies One and Two that this would be a bad idea, because where they went, the FlashNews mob was sure to follow.

Then it was time for the second tail Brendan had on Margot and Ian to check in. The other Maddoxes were still in their hotel, and should he stay put? The answer was yes.

Then it was Elaine West, demanding to know where I was and what the hell had happened and telling me we had to talk first thing in order to work out how to spin this, and she could come to the Ritz straightaway for a confab, and oh, she was sending me her bill for overtime.

Then it was another of Brendan's people. Then it was Suchai. Then it was Marie.

But by the time we got to the chocolate-hazelnut gâteau with candied citrus peel, raspberry sauce and bittersweet chocolate curls, I found myself thinking about one of the people we hadn't heard from. A new knot of worry tightened in the back of my neck.

"Maybe I should call Anatole," I said carefully. I still wasn't entirely sure how Brendan and Anatole felt about each other, especially after the huge mess at Ilona's theater. Especially now that Brendan and I had kissed. "He was with me when I found out Chet had taken off." I said this to the dessert plate. "I should let him know what's going on."

"I called him from the courthouse." This was another surprise and it jerked my gaze back up to see Brendan checking his phone again. "No message yet."

"Is this the part where you say, 'He's a big vampire, I'm sure he's fine'?" I asked, one hand already on my phone.

"No. You should try calling."

I thumbed my way through my contact list until I found Anatole's number and put the phone on speaker. It rang only once before the voice mail answered. "This is Anatole Sevarin. I regret that I cannot speak with you at this moment. If you would be so kind as to leave your message and contact information, I will return your call as soon as it becomes possible."

"The man's physiologically incapable of constructing a short sentence," I muttered. "Anatole, it's Charlotte. Call as soon as you get this."

I hung up and bit my lower lip. That the call went straight to voice mail didn't mean anything. Anatole could be on the other line, or maybe his battery had died, or he was in a dead zone. He'd call back in a minute.

My excellent meal sat heavily in my stomach.

"I'm overreacting, right?"

"Maybe. Maybe not." Brendan thumbed his own phone again. "Keith? I need a confirmation on your targets."

"You don't think . . ."

"I don't know. That's why I'm checking. Yeah, Keith, I'm still here. . . . Yeah? . . . Did you check the trip wire? Okay. Stay sharp." Brendan hung up, but he didn't meet my eyes. Instead, he stared out across the black pool of Central Park. I looked at the crumbs and the bones on our plates, the half-empty wineglasses and the disarray of the rolls and crispy breadsticks. I felt the silk sliding against my skin and my scarlet-tipped toes digging into the thick carpet. Chet was not the only idiot in the family. I was an idiot too. A completely selfish idiot. While I'd been wasting time getting the star treatment, the rest of my life was still headed on the fast track to the drain.

I shoved my chair back. "I can't stay here. We've got to find Chet and find out what he's got on Pam and whoever she's running around with." How many spas could there be in the Connecticut phone book? We had the number. We should be able to backtrack—unless of course that was Marcus the Nebbish's number. . . .

Brendan sighed and looked at the remains of dinner, and I could tell he was missing all the things we hadn't had a chance to get around to. "I think I can help you narrow down where he is," he said.

"You've got a tail on him too?"

"I wish, but no. We're going to have to try magic." The prospect of showing off that aspect of his abilities did not seem to please him, which surprised me a little. Who wouldn't want to whammy their way through life?

"Let me see what I can MacGyver up here." Brendan glanced around the room. "And we're going to need Chet's cell phone."

"Because I would not believe the kinds of paranormal things that can be done with a cell phone."

His quick smile did not reach his eyes. "We used to do this kind of thing with mirrors, but if you can get the person's cell it works a lot better. It's the phone's nature to reach other people. In fact, with you here, that sympathy will be reinforced, because your brother calls you a lot. I should be able to get a good connection."

"Well, there's a first time for everything." I gave him the phone.

While Brendan rummaged around the room, I stayed quiet and focused my energies on not obsessively checking my own phone to see if Anatole or Chet had sent a text. Brendan, in the meantime, got the sash off the complimentary bathrobe and pulled a pen and notepad from the desk drawer. He unscrewed the top on the salt shaker and poured a neat white circle on the floor around the dining room table. Housekeeping was going to love that. Finally, he cleared a space on the tablecloth and set both candles in it.

"I need your hand."

I extended my hand between the candlesticks. Brendan laid Chet's cell in my palm. He wrapped the sash around my wrist, then looped it around the top and bottom of the phone and tied the cell to my hand in a loose but complex knot. And yes, being tied up by Brendan did make my brain go all sorts of new and inappropriate places.

"You can find Chet with a cell phone, but you can't find Cousin Pamela?" I said, mostly to distract myself.

"Pamela's a witch. Not a very powerful one now that she's separated from the family, but she is still a witch."

Brendan laid his palm over the phone and my hand. "No matter what you see next, Charlotte, I need you to keep quiet until we've got the connection, okay?"

I nodded. Brendan gazed into the candle flame and began to whisper. I couldn't make out any of the words, but I could feel a new warmth rising between us that had nothing to do with intimacy or candles. It was good he gave me warning to keep quiet, because what he did next was wrap his hand around the candle flame.

I heard the sizzle. I smelled the smoke. Brendan didn't even flinch, and he never stopped whispering. His eyes became unfocused and he stared into the distance, holding the fire, holding the cell phone, and me. But whatever he saw, it wasn't me, or anything else in that room. Slowly, he uncurled his fist from the candle flame. Hot prickles ran across my skin like a spatter of warm oil. That hand drifted slowly down to pick up the pen and hold it poised over the pad. I felt something pushing, and then something pulling, and then something snapped into place. Brendan did not glance down, or even blink. He did scribble something, in big, loopy cursive letters.

"Got it." Brendan lifted his hand off mine and pushed the paper toward me. The address was in Hartford.

"What time is it? I'm going out there." I tried to picture the Metro North train schedule. Unfortunately, I never went to Connecticut. Unlike Chet, I never found the time. I reached for the knot tying me to the cell phone, but Brendan touched my hand.

"It's almost ten."

"There's got to be another train." I had totally screwed this up. I'd let myself be lulled by the prospect of being a guest for once. I'd thought for a second someone else could take care of me.

"Charlotte, you've had no sleep and you've just gotten out on bail."

"Your point?" I picked the knot on the sash loose and yanked off the sash. The phone went cold and the candle winked out. Brendan winced. Probably I'd just broken some sympathetic bond or something. I'd apologize later.

Brendan grabbed my hand. "Wait until tomorrow."

"We don't have until tomorrow. By tomorrow whoever killed Dylan Maddox could have caught up with him." If we'd found this spa, they could. If they didn't already know about it. I mean, it didn't seem to be a secret from anybody else, did it? Ilona knew, and their partner, and a whole bunch of investors and guests. . . .

Brendan said nothing, but I heard his question anyway. "I'm not calling O'Grady. Chet'll just run again."

"Yeah, but you won't be blamed for anything when he does."

I had no answer to that. I just needed my purse, my clothes—my real clothes—and my shoes. I had to get out there and drag my stupid, thoughtless brother home before he did anything else to bring himself closer to getting killed.

"Charlotte, when are you going to stop protecting Chet?"

"I'm responsible for him." The room phone had about a billion specialty buttons and I couldn't find which one was for the laundry.

"Why?"

"He's my brother."

"Not good enough," said Brendan. "He's lying to you, he's run out on you, he's gotten you arrested, and you're still covering for him. This is way beyond 'He's my brother.'"

Coming from the man who had people following his sister around to make sure she didn't go ninja on the nightblood population again, that was just too much.

"It's also none of your business."

"Still not good enough."

Who the hell did this guy think he was? What did he think he knew about me and Chet? He didn't know jack. He had no business asking. I drew myself up, fury building to Saturday night dinner rush levels. My line cooks would have all been backing up by now. Brendan just stood where he was, arms folded, radiating patience. In that instant I knew that even if I yelled myself hoarse, he'd just keep standing there. I couldn't frighten him, and he clearly didn't think I could shock him.

What if I did tell him what really happened? What would he think of me then? Maybe I should do it. Maybe after he knew the whole story, he'd give up this insane idea that he could take care of me. That'd be good. He could just walk away before one of us really did something stupid.

The problem was, even though I opened my mouth, I had no idea where to begin. I'd never told this story. There had never been anybody I could even consider telling.

"My parents live in Arizona," I said.

"You told me that."

"They moved there after Chet was . . . turned. It was my father's idea. And you were right. He wanted to go someplace really sunny. And Mom wouldn't leave Dad, so she went too. I see them at Christmas. Chet e-mails Mom." At least, I thought he did. "Anyway, before they left, Mom said to me, 'You have to look after him now.'"

"Why you?"

"There's no one else." That wasn't what I wanted to say. That had nothing to do with it. Well, a little to do with it. But this wasn't the important part, the part I hadn't been able to tell Anatole, or anyone else.

"Why can't Chet take care of himself?"

I scrubbed my hands across my face. The words had all jammed together inside my brain, and I couldn't move any of them.

"Charlotte . . . how was Chet turned?"

A few words fell out of the brain jam. They weren't the right ones yet, but they were a start.

"We grew up in Buffalo. I was the strange one. Chet was the athletic one."

"Football or hockey?"

I almost smiled. Those were the only two sports that meant anything on that side of the state. "Football. High school champion and Hollywood-level handsome. By the time he was seventeen, he was king of the world. Colleges were lining up to recruit him." Memories tumbled over each other; of misty autumn drizzle cold against my cheeks; the smells of charcoal and roasting peppers from my king-sized hibachi; the harsh glare of the fluorescents next to the open side of the rust-bucket Vanagon I'd bought for five hundred bucks. I sold sandwiches, bratwursts and pocket pies out of that van during the games, and listened to the crowd shouting my brother's name.

"Have you ever . . . have you ever seen what happens to a topflight athlete when it's time to go to college?"

"I've heard stories."

"They're all true. I was living at home then, saving my money for culinary school. When the recruiters came . . . it was crazy." All those bluff, hardy men sitting in the living room, with their beefy hands and their ties in the school colors, talking about the excellence of their universities' academics, all the while checking out Chet like they'd check out some chick in a bar, wondering how he'd perform once they got their hands on him. "The money was just the start of it. They'd take us to campus and keep me and my parents busy with the tours and shopping and stuff, while they took him over to 'take a look at the facilities,' and 'meet the players.' "

"Parties?" asked Brendan.

I nodded. "And girls. And booze, and pot. I smelled it on him." My hands shook like they didn't want to let go of all this truth. "I tried to say something. I swear to God, I tried. But my parents wouldn't *listen*. They thought I was jealous because my brother was actually going to be successful instead of working in a diner. I tried to talk to Chet, but what could I say? Everything he'd ever wanted was being handed to him, and he knew he was king of the world, so of course he could handle it."

"And he met his nightblood sire at one of the parties?"

"Melody Linkowski." Tall enough to look down on me, she had that flat, willowy build that looked good in spaghetti-strap dresses with swishy ruffled skirts. Her chestnut hair curled into long ringlets around her skinny white shoulders, and her coffee brown eyes hadn't had time to grow old yet.

"She was all of sixteen when she turned. She cruised the campus parties, looking for meals. There were so many girls at the football parties, who'd notice one more? Chet charmed her. He could always charm anybody, even

Dad. And she . . . He told me she'd decided they were soul mates. He *laughed* about it." My words faltered. "She was a sixteen-year-old vampire girl. She thought she'd find a human to be her true love, just like . . ." *Just like in that stupid,* stupid *movie.*

"When did you find out Chet was feeding her?"

We were getting closer.

"I saw the bite marks. Chet decided to go to SUNY Buffalo, and she came up from Alabama to be with him. She started sharing blood with him during his freshman year, and of course he got stronger, didn't need sleep, healed faster. . . ." My whole body trembled now. We were almost there. "I was at school by then, and I'd gotten a part-time gig in the city with a caterer. I was home only some of the time. I tried to get him to give her up. I begged. I threatened. He told me he could handle it. He had it all under control. She loved him. She'd do anything he said. She was just a kid, it was no big deal."

"And then he didn't make it back to the dorm one night and your parents got a phone call."

"She said she loved him. She said they were soul mates, like in *Midnight Moon*, and now they'd be together always . . . and I couldn't . . . I couldn't . . ." I couldn't let her get away with it. She'd taken his life. She'd made him into one of her kind because he was too stupid to see what she really was, and I hadn't stopped her. Chet thought he'd be king of the world forever because Melody Baby had put the bite on him. I was so angry, I could have staked them both. Maybe that would have been better.

"Charlotte, what did you do?"

Chet had thrown his whole life away because instead of *listening*, he'd let himself be snowed by a vampire named *Melody*, for God's sake.

I sat down, hoping that would still some of my tremors. Wrong again.

"You ever hear of Be Positive?" I asked.

"That's the network for friends and relatives of vampires?"

"They were having this big fund-raising banquet. I was on the catering team. This was five years ago."

I watched reality slowly rearranging itself in Brendan's head. Five years ago. He was putting it together with the billboards and posters all over town. With the endless replays of the last interviews and video clips on Flash-News. It was one of those things you couldn't miss, even if you wanted to. "Five years ago Joshua Blake disappeared after an appearance at a Be Positive banquet. . . ."

"Dinner dance. Seven-course meal, with eight kinds of hors d'oeuvres and a plated dessert."

Brendan's mouth opened, and closed, and opened. "You got Chet's sire into the banquet," he breathed. "You got a teenaged fan-girl vampire into a party with the reigning angst-actor of his day."

"Chet told me she'd seen *Midnight Moon* a million times. She'd gone on and *on* about how she and Chet were going to be just like Trent and Clarinda in the movie. She was too stupid, too permanently sixteen, to know she was deluding herself." So I was going to prove that too. In the face of all Chet's denials and protestations through his brand-new fangs, I was going to prove to him that *I* was right.

"I told her about the party, and where to meet me." The back alley, her eager, hungry eyes, the wad of bills. "We slipped the guy on the door fifty to take a smoke break while I walked her through the kitchen in a borrowed uniform."

"Joshua Blake vanished." It had been all the media could talk about for months. The rumors were nonstop. His body had been found in Chicago. Richard Gere had smuggled him out to a monastery in Tibet. He'd been spotted with Elvis at that Burger King in Kalamazoo.

"Melody Linkowski vanished too." Not that anybody else cared. But Chet never heard from her again. So much for the eternal bond between sire and vamp. "They set up house on a ranch outside Duluth."

"How do you know?"

"They sent me a thank-you card." Which included a gush about how Joshua was happy to retire. Now that he was the star of Melody's life he didn't need to be any other kind. Which just goes to show Chet wasn't the only king of the world taken in by a declaration of eternal love from the undead waif. I had been right, totally and completely right. Chet should have listened to me, and now he knew it.

The problem was, it hadn't made anything better.

"I didn't know how much he'd miss her. I didn't know he'd never grow up . . . never grow out of being that stupid football-hero kid. I didn't know it was going to be forever." Those last words came out as a whisper. "He's got nobody left but me, Brendan, and it's my fault."

Brendan sat next to me. I thought—I hoped—he'd put his arm around me. But he didn't. He just rubbed his hands together.

So I was right again. Now that he knew what I'd really done, it was too much for him to handle. I was way too far gone to be worth taking care of.

Batting a thousand was supposed to feel better than this.

"You can't go up to Connecticut on your own," Brendan said without looking at me.

"You've got to get to Margot and Ian," I reminded him. "Keep your family from hurting themselves worse." *Don't screw up, like me.*

"At least let me get you on the train."

I didn't have the strength to protest. We could have ourselves a decent good-bye scene. "Okay."

And that was that. A call to housekeeping produced

my dry-cleaned clothes. While I climbed back into T-shirt, jacket and black slacks, Brendan Googled departures from Grand Central Station and found out there was an 11:22 train we just had time to make.

His car drove us to the station. We didn't talk on the way. I was back to my real life now, and he had no place in it. No need to remind either one of us of that. We crossed the great hall of Grand Central under the dome with its sparkling constellations. I kept having these visions of Linus O'Grady and his P-Squad charging past the information booth and announcing that I was under arrest for . . . something.

But Little Linus didn't appear. I bought my ticket and Brendan walked me down to the platform to stand beside the battered red-and-blue-striped Amtrak train.

"You'll call and let me know you got in okay?"

"Yes." He was too tall for Humphrey Bogart and I was too short for Ingrid Bergman, but our problems still managed not to amount to a hill of beans in this crazy world.

"This isn't over, Charlotte."

Yes it is. "We'll talk when I get back with Chet."

He leaned in and I closed my eyes. The second kiss surprised me, and it was every bit as good as the first. If it had gone on a second longer I would have started crying all over again.

Brendan finished the kiss, and I stood there for a moment, seeing my hand on his chest but not remembering when I put it there.

"Be careful," he said.

"You too." I turned away, because I knew I wasn't going to be able to force "good-bye" out of my mouth.

I climbed aboard the train and made my way forward, where I wouldn't have to watch him getting smaller when the train pulled out. The car wasn't even half full. People settled down to sleep, or worked on their laptops or thumbed their BlackBerries. I passed rows of empty seats, but none of them looked right. I crossed into the next car, and the one after that, all the way to the front, until there was nowhere else to go.

"Hello, Chef C."

My head jerked up. There in the very front quartet of seats waited Taylor Watts, with Tommy Jones the alley vamp beside him.

I whirled around in time to see Julie loom up behind me and grin.

"Now, you just hold still, Charlotte Caine."

Then the world went black.

24

Charlotte.

Now you just hold still, Charlotte Cain. That laughing command blocked out every other thought. There was nothing in my head but her eyes and that laugh. *Just hold still.*

Charlotte, look at me. There was another voice. Another scary voice right inside my head with the laughter. This was bad. Really bad. I wanted to squeeze my eyes shut. I wanted to scream, but I couldn't even do that.

Hold still. Hold still.

You can move, Charlotte, said that other voice. It was familiar. I could almost recognize it. I wanted to recognize it. *It's all right. Just look at me.*

But he couldn't hear the laughter. He couldn't see the eyes. *I can't.*

You can. Look at me.

No, please. Don't make me. She'd be angry. She'd hurt me. She was right inside my head and she'd split me open if I so much as . . .

She will not harm you, Charlotte. I will not permit it. Look at me.

I looked. He had green eyes. I knew them. I knew him. I'd think of his name in a minute. It was in my mind, way back behind the orders and the fear.

"You are free, Charlotte Caine. You need obey no one. You are free."

Something snapped, and the fear and the laughter fell away.

Then everything went black again.

"Charlotte."

My head hurt. Migraine-level hurt. My throat was dry and my tongue felt like old leather as I cursed. Then I realized my eyes had opened, but I was still completely in the dark. I was also cold. Cold enough that my finger joints ached. Refrigerator cold.

"Charlotte?" a man's voice said from somewhere to my right.

I shivered and groaned, cursed some more, and sat up. "Who the hell . . . ?" I croaked, but consciousness settled in before I finished the question. "Anatole?"

"Unfortunately. Are you all right?"

"Mostly. I think." I rubbed my hands together and tried to think how I'd gotten into this cold, dark place. I remembered the train, Taylor Watts, and Julie and Tommy the hench vamps. (Or would they be minions? Did henches and minions have separate unions?) Then . . . nothing except Julie's eyes and I couldn't move and . . . and . . .

I'd been whammied. She'd ordered me not to move, and I hadn't, until Anatole freed me. His was the other voice. Anatole Sevarin had followed Julie Vamplette inside my head.

I sat there in the dark and decided I wasn't going to think about that right now.

"Can you see where we are?" I asked instead.

"I believe we may be in a restaurant walk-in."

"How . . . ironic."

"Our captors showing their sense of humor. The front door is directly behind you. I regret I cannot stand up."

"Oh. Okay. Hang on." I turned and pushed myself onto my knees. The floor was ice cold underneath me. I rubbed my hands together and blew on them, and groped out around me. My left hand found splintering wood and brushed something ruffled. I rubbed the ruffled something and my fingertips identified lettuce leaves. Bibb lettuce if I had to guess. Behind that was a wire shelf. I grabbed the upright support and pulled myself to my feet. Dizziness washed over me. Pins and needles danced up my shins, but I stayed standing. With my left hand resting on the shelves, I shuffled forward.

"I promise you, Charlotte, the next time you and I are alone in the dark, I will arrange for the circumstances to be far more pleasant."

I ignored this, as much as you could ignore a vampire metaphorically whistling past the graveyard. My searching fingers brushed a thick plastic flap. Bingo. Those flaps hang over the entrance to a walk-in to help keep the temperature inside stable even while people are going in and out through the course of a dinner shift. I had just found either the walk-in's front door or a door to the freezer at the back. I rattled the handle. Locked. No surprise there. It also meant this was probably the front door, which was good news. Walk-ins are not like your fridge at home. The door does not control the light. There would be a switch. I skimmed my hands up and down the wall until I felt it, squeezed my eyes shut and flipped it on. My eyelids turned dark red. I counted ten and slowly opened my eyes.

Yep, walk-in. The wire shelves were crowded with plastic bins of various sizes. White five-gallon buckets were stacked on the floor along with wooden crates and cardboard boxes of fresh produce, and blue Rubbermaid tubs of onions and potatoes. Oh, and Anatole Sevarin lying on his side with his hands cuffed behind him. The tattered remains of what had been a black sack hung around his neck.

"Oh. Shit."

Anatole clearly had not fed before he was caught. His skin was sallow and loose and his eyes were sunken. I couldn't help noticing he was very carefully not looking at me, especially not my neck.

I crouched down beside him, pushed him into a sitting position against the shelves. I also pulled the torn bag off. I tried not to think about how it looked like it had been chewed open.

"Thank you," Anatole said.

"Can you break these?" I touched the cold handcuffs. They didn't look quite like the ones I'd been treated to by the NYPD. The locks seemed . . . different.

He shook his head. "They are made of silver, and very uncomfortable, may I add." Silver doesn't produce the same level of toxic shock in vampires that it does in were-wolves, but it doesn't do them any good.

"Swell." I collapsed beside him and leaned my head back against the shelf support.

"So, tell me, how did you come to be here?" asked Anatole. He still wasn't looking at me. I returned the favor.

I told him about Connecticut and the spa and my latest attempt to chase my brother down. To my surprise, Sevarin threw back his head and let out a loud laugh. "Brilliant! This may be the ultimate triumph of the capitalist system! Ilona and your brother have found a way to make money from both the diners and the dinner!"

"I'll be sure to let him know you're impressed. So how'd you get in here?"

Sevarin grimaced. "I don't know. I had gone back to my apartment to get ready for sunrise. When I woke again,

I was here. I admit I was thinking some very unkind things about your Brendan the security expert until Julie arrived with you." He frowned. "Perhaps I should hire Mr. Maddox. Clearly my personal security is not what I had believed it to be."

"Julie and Tommy have got to be working for Shelby or Pam Maddox." I rubbed my forehead. "But which one?"

"What rules out your brother or Ilona?"

I shook my head and wished I hadn't. "This whole thing is about controlling access to human blood outlets for profit. It's like Prohibition, or crack cocaine in the eighties; people are fighting over the control of territory and distribution networks. Chet's working his own angle on that, and since he and Ilona are working together . . ."

"Unless she has a side gambit of her own."

"No." I'd had a lot of time to think, in the cells and on the way to the train as I sat silently next to Brendan and avoided thinking about him. A lot of things were beginning to make sense "Dylan Maddox was dumped in Nightlife as a warning to Chet, something to do with his particular blood-running scam. Ilona wouldn't have needed to give Chet that kind of warning. She's his girlfriend; she could just talk to him. Besides, Dylan was dumped around sunrise, maybe even after dawn."

"Which means his body was dropped by daybloods. Given her worldview, it is unlikely Ilona would have trusted such an important job to those not of her own kind. Of course."

"She's one of yours, isn't she?"

"Yes."

I didn't press any further. The truth was, I didn't really want to know, not yet anyway. The fact that we were discussing my brother's girlfriend did not make things any better. "Somebody drained Dylan's blood to sell. I mean, he was dead, why let valuable product go to waste? They had some left and they planted it at Nightlife and then tipped off the P-Squad so I'd be arrested and out of the way. That could have been Margot Maddox. She's offered me a very big bribe to shut down Nightlife for good. Or it could have been Pam or Bert Shelby trying to get me out of the way so they could use Nightlife as a blood outlet."

"You're certain Pamela Maddox is involved with the blood runners?"

"She's doing something that's got Chet trying to set up an amateur sting operation on her, Margot trying to cover for her, and Dylan getting killed over her. What else could it be?"

Anatole thought about this. "If you are correct, then it becomes a question of whether it's a Maddox or Bertram Shelby who's in charge of the actual operation."

I bit my lip and recalled what Robert had said, and all the assumptions I'd made back when this looked just like a little hissy-fit power play.

And I knew. I knew who'd killed Dylan Maddox.

"We've got to get out of here," I said.

"I agree." Anatole shifted his weight—and winced.

"What's the matter?" I asked.

"You mean what else is the matter? You will notice it's only my wrists that have been shackled."

"Yes?"

"Because they took the precaution of breaking my leg before they handcuffed me."

"Oh. Shit."

"I see we are once again in agreement."

I tried the door handle again for form's sake. It didn't budge. Wires dangled from an open panel above the light switch. Somebody'd taken out the panic button. I peered out the window and saw a dormant kitchen that I didn't recognize.

Think. Think. I ordered myself as I turned around, rubbing my hands together and blowing on them. *Whether Shelby or a Maddox is in charge, the next person through that door is not going to be your friend.*

I rummaged in my pockets, but turned up nothing useful. My keys and change were all gone. So was my phone, of course.

I turned back to Sevarin and after a minute was able to make my mouth ask, "If you had . . . if you fed, would you be able to heal the break?"

Sevarin was silent for a long, nerve-racking moment. "Thank you, Charlotte," he said softly. "But unfortunately, no. I would feel better, but I would still have the broken leg, and you would be much weakened."

"Yeah. Okay." I tried not to sound relieved. Anatole had already . . . saved me. Again. I should trust him. Why didn't I trust him?

I decided not to think about that either. I looked at the door. We still had to get out of here. I looked at the shelves behind me, loaded with produce, *mise en place*, and bins and buckets of everything from ground beef to salad dressing. I looked at the door again.

"Fine," I said. "We'll do this the hard way."

I rolled up my sleeves and set to work.

By the time someone came through the walk-in door, I was gritting my teeth to keep them from chattering. I'd switched the light off again and held a rock-hard butternut squash up to my shoulder like I thought I was about to hit a home run. Anatole was back on his side, with the black bag draped loosely across his face.

"Okay, Chef C, time to go," said a familiar voice.

Taylor Watts parted the plastic flaps. Perfect. I held myself very still.

My ex-bartender took one step into the cooler, hit the Italian salad dressing I'd smeared across the floor and did a perfect Three Stooges pratfall—legs flying, arms flapping, eyes bugged out, loud "whagh!" and best of all, the sharp crack of his skull against the floor. He struggled, but I brought the squash down hard on his forehead. His eyes rolled back in his head, and he went as limp as a vamp at high noon.

I dropped my vegetable, kicked Taylor on the shoulder to slide him out of the way and turned to Anatole.

"Get out of here, Charlotte. Call the police."

"Sorry. It's payback time."

Anatole was a big guy, but he didn't weigh more than a full sack of flour. That was good, because otherwise I never would have been able to haul him out of there, especially since I had to walk across my own booby trap to do it.

"Can you hear anybody?" I murmured.

"No, but that doesn't mean we are alone. Charlotte, you have to get out of here."

"Working on it."

The kitchen was dark and silent. So far, so good. "We'll call the cops on the house phone and then . . ."

"Put the vampire down, Chef Caine."

Pamela Maddox, not one perfectly styled blond hair out of place, walked through the swinging door and smiled.

There are days it truly sucks to be right.

25

Pamela Maddox wore a Hillary Clinton pantsuit with only a push-up bra underneath it. Given her level of endowment, she looked like she had a baby butt mooning the world from out of her perfectly tailored jacket.

I considered bolting, but with my arms full of vampire there was no way I would make it to the exit before Pamela caught up with me, even though she was wearing platform pumps. And that was before I saw Julie and Tommy the Hench Vamps come sauntering in behind her.

"Sorry," I murmured to Anatole as I set him on the floor near an empty counter.

"It was an excellent attempt."

Pamela sighed and shook her head at us. "I told Taylor to be careful."

"Yeah, well, he always was pretty useless." I put my hands in my empty pockets and tried not to seem like I was looking around. If she would just come a little closer . . . There was a tenderizing mallet in easy reach, just waiting to make contact with her perfectly made-up face.

"You don't seem surprised to see me, Charlotte."

"It wasn't that hard to figure out." Eventually. Once I

realized it had to be either Shelby or a Maddox. Robert had pointed out that Shelby was never in charge of the actual crimes he'd been involved with. He liked to be able to skedaddle and leave other people to take the blame when things went bad. So it had to be a Maddox. It couldn't have been Margot or Ian, because Brendan had been watching them, and he would have checked on when they'd actually arrived in the city, because he was much less into denial than I was and would want to eliminate Margot right away. That left Cousin Pam.

"So, now what?" I said out loud.

"Now you listen to me very carefully," Pamela said. "Because you've only had a small taste of how miserable I can make things for you and your little nightblood brother."

"Not as miserable as you made them for Cousin Dylan," I said.

"Silly-dilly," she murmured, like someone remembering the good old days of tweaking pigtails and dropping cats down wells. "He thought he was being so clever."

"He did find you when none of your other family could."

"And we have Chet Caine to thank for that." She smiled at me and Julie smirked. "If I were you, Charlotte, I'd have a talk with your brother."

"Not that she's going to have a chance," murmured Tommy, gliding past his boss. "Dibs on the neck."

"Touch her and I will come back from hell itself to destroy you," said Anatole, and I think that frightened me way more than it did Tommy.

"Now, now, boys." Pammy smiled indulgently. "There's no reason to be rude. We can discuss our business in a civilized fashion. Especially since as dense as she is, Chef Caine knows I can have her and her boyfriend here killed in a New York minute if she steps out of line."

Which unfortunately was true. "What do you want from me?"

"Nothing at all." Pamela drifted around the edge of the prep counter, trailing her long, perfect fingernails across the stainless steel. "After this little matter of the contraband on your premises is cleared up, you and Chet will be opening Nightlife again. You will find yourself in need of a new bartender." She stopped just out of reach. "I will give you a name. You will hire that person and go back to your kitchen."

A new bartender. A new bartender and a bucket of human blood among all the other containers of blood at my restaurant, which served vampires. . . . "You want to turn Nightlife into a blood dive."

She shrugged. "It's going to happen, Charlotte. It's just a question of whether you live through the process or not. At least with me, you know you get to keep your management position."

Before I could think of anything to say, a loud, muffled thud sounded behind me.

"Bitch!" I could barely hear the bellow of outrage through the glass. "I'm gonna kill you!"

Pam rolled her baby blues. "Tommy, go let Taylor out of the walk-in."

Grinning wide enough to show both fangs, Tommy went and released the lock on the walk-in. A very green around the gills Taylor Watts staggered two steps forward, choked and reeled to the hand-washing sink. Pam winced and started to say something.

I scooped up Anatole and ran, making my best guess at the direction of the back door. Lousy time to be wrong. I came up in the employee locker room. Abrupt reversals aren't easy when carrying a full-grown vampire, but I managed. Pamela was bearing down, so I took the only other out offered and ducked into the office. I dumped Anatole in the desk chair, slammed the door, locked it,

and snatched up the phone. A stack of invoices on the
desk told me I was in the kitchen of Post Mortem.

Oh, why am I not surprised?

"You'll be dead before anyone can get here, Charlotte," called Pam through the window. "Both of you."

My hand froze over the phone keypad.

"Dead and drained." The flirtatious little-girl lilt had
entirely left her voice. "And then since I won't have you
around to keep your brother in line, I'll have to alert the
boys I sent down to Arizona to pick up your parents."

"You're bluffing!"

"Maybe, but you're the one behind a highly breakable
glass window with no exit except through me. Maybe you
could get past me on your own, but hauling poor Anatole?
Of course, you could just leave him, but I don't need him
for anything and when the sun comes up, I'll just toss him
out into the alley."

"If I am so very superfluous, why did you bother
bringing me here?" inquired Anatole.

She shrugged. "You were making a nuisance of yourself."

"Son of a bitch," added Taylor. He'd propped himself
up against the wall and looked about as healthy as Anatole. The lovely bruise blossoming across his temple was
a very small triumph.

"What about Chet's spa?" I asked, stalling for time.

"Oh, he'll get to keep right on running that little operation. There will be a few changes, of course, to reflect
new executive thinking." Pammy's eyes gleamed. "Such
a nice, isolated location and all those woods. Absolutely
nobody to hear the screams."

I wanted to scream myself, right now. I wanted to
punch her in her lying face. She was a liar and a murderer
and a witch from a screwed-up family, and she was the

reason my life was in shreds. And there was nothing I could do but stand there beside Anatole and take it.

"You drained your own cousin and used the blood in a frame-up to take over one restaurant and one spa," I pursed my lips like I was considering all the implications. "How'd Post Mortem come into it?"

"Bert decided he didn't like going straight after all. Ilona and Chet had been using PM for private shareholder . . . parties where they distributed the legal blood, but he thought there might be more profit in moving a higher volume to a wider clientele. He contacted me."

And they talked. They talked a lot. They talked about expanding distribution, and weak links, like Chet and the Nebbish.

"You should know Shelby has a history of running out on his employers," I said.

Pamela shrugged again. "You work with what you have. I thought you'd appreciate that."

"Brendan's going to be looking for us."

This statement did not have anything like its intended effect. Pamela gave a bubbly little laugh that would have done Lolita proud. "In case you hadn't noticed, Brendan couldn't find his ass with a flashlight and a GPS. Or did he fool you with that high-powered office on Fifty-fourth?" I didn't answer and she shook her head. "God, doesn't anybody do their homework? Listen, Charlotte, my dear cousin's in debt up to his charmingly shaggy hairline, right along with the rest of the family. He needs the city contract at least as much as they do. I would have tried to bring him into my business because—you should excuse the expression—blood's thicker. But no. He's also fastidious and prefers his white-collar graft."

"Brendan's out to cheat the city?" I didn't believe it. Okay, I didn't want to believe it. But with the rest of his family in debt, and so much money at stake . . . people fudged their CVs for less.

"Whereas I am an entrepreneur with a product which is in great demand." Modesty practically oozed out the ends of her immaculately styled hair. "I just needed an outlet."

"Bitch, please."

"Manners, Charlotte. You don't want me to wash your mouth out with soap, now do you?"

I almost said, "Try it," but I remembered just in time what Brendan said: whatever else she was, Pamela Maddox was still a witch.

"So, Dylan Maddox tracked you down," said Anatole. *With some help from Chet and Marcus the Nebbish, who were looking for a way to get her off their case,* I added silently. "And not appreciating your entrepreneurial spirit, he threatened to get the family to shut you down. Blood being thicker and, incidentally, more lucrative, you killed him for it."

I bit my lip and glanced at Anatole. I couldn't tell anything about what he was thinking, but we had to keep playing for time.

"What about the other bodies?" I asked. "There were four other syringe drainings."

"Trial runs," said Pam with a calm that tied my stomach into fresh knots. "We needed to be sure we could continue to supply quality merchandise. And, of course, we needed the right people to know that our network should not be interfered with."

Which made sense in a horror-movie kind of way. I bit my lip. What next? What now? If I could keep her talking long enough, maybe a way out would materialize. I had to focus on that. Pam Maddox needed me to deal with Chet and to hang on to Nightlife, which would double the human blood outlets she controlled. There'd be another chance to get us out of this, if I could just get the time. Maybe I'd get to clock Taylor again in the process.

I hesitated too long. "I'm so glad we've had this little chat," said Pam brightly. "But you do realize, Charlotte, that if I have to come in there and get you, I'm going to be feeling much less charitable."

I felt something nudging at my mind. A memory, of Taylor and Anatole. The last time I'd seen Taylor it'd been in a kitchen too . . .

I saw our chance, and I knew it was Anatole who put the idea in my head. That was something we'd talk about later. Right now I had to try to deal with these . . . these things holding us. They'd made a mistake. A big one. They didn't know they had not one weak link but two.

And they were trying to hold a chef in a kitchen.

"Okay," I whispered, to myself and to Anatole. He nodded, just barely.

"Okay?" Pammy cocked her head.

"You win."

"I'm sorry. I didn't hear that."

"You win. It's yours." I spread my arms, and then let them fall so they flapped against my thighs. "Take it. Nightlife, the spa, the whole thing. Just . . . just leave Chet alone, okay? He's no threat to your operation."

"Oh, no, I don't think you quite understand yet, Charlotte. I am dictating the terms here. You're mine too."

"Charlotte, don't do this," said Anatole, but his eyes narrowed and I felt that tiny little push again. Pushing me away. Out the door, in fact.

"Okay, whatever. It's over, anyhow." I touched his shoulder like I was saying good-bye, left him where he was and walked out into the main kitchen. I did shut the door behind me. I wasn't much of a barrier between him and Pam, but it was better than nothing. I hoped and prayed.

I shoved my hands in my pockets and glanced around the kitchen. I'd lost track of days. It had to be Sunday or Monday night for this place to be so dead. Those were the most common nights for clubs to be closed. "You want something to eat?" I asked.

"What?" Now it was Pam's turn to narrow her baby blues.

"Eat. I'm starved."

"She's stalling." Julie snapped her fangs.

"So? I also didn't get dinner." I pulled open the mini-fridge by the pastry station and everybody jumped. There was a kind of grim satisfaction in that.

There was a carton of eggs in there, just as I'd known there would be. In a professional kitchen, some things are predictable. "Omelette?" I asked.

Come on, come on, Pammy. You're in charge. I'm sur-rendering. You want me to serve you. Here I am doing it. I'm showing you my chef-white belly. Come on.

I watched all of this and a little bit more light up the world for Pamela Maddox. "Sure," she said. "Why not."

I set the eggs on the counter by the cooktop and grabbed a hotel pan. "I'll need some stuff out of the walk-in."

"She's gonna try something," groaned Taylor. "Don't let her in there."

"Tommy"—Pam tossed him the keys—"keep an eye on her. Julie, you go and bring our friend Anatole out of the office. No need for him to be in time-out."

Tommy clearly didn't think much of this, but he unlocked the door and pulled it open. I walked past him, remembered the salad dressing I'd smeared on the floor just in time to avoid my own Three Stooges moment. There was plenty of what I needed in here and I started loading up the pan—shallots, flat-leaf parsley, a chunk of Parme-san, a brick of butter.

"Hey, Tommy," I said without looking around. "There

should be some ox blood in the freezer." Shelby was making his version of my house sangria out of something and I hadn't found any thawed blood in the walk-in buckets when I'd been locked in here with Anatole. "Bring me out a brick."

I put my groceries on the counter. "There should be some Chardonnay somewhere too. Probably the cooler behind the bar," I said. "I'll need a bottle."

Taylor looked at Pam, and Pam nodded. The vampire's glower was venomous, and hungry, but she went.

It's amazing how much people will do if you just tell them.

Julie had pushed the wheeled desk chair holding Anatole out of the office and stationed him by the rack of chef's coats. I didn't bother looking at Pam. I just reached for pans and pots. Despite the witch at my back, and the hostile vampires roaming free, my body instantly relaxed as I concentrated on thoughts of cooking. I didn't glance at Anatole more than once. I couldn't risk any of these three thinking I might have some backup there.

Tommy came out of the freezer and dumped a plastic-wrapped brick of frozen blood onto the counter.

"Thanks." I pulled a chef's knife out of a drawer and checked the edge against my thumb. Tommy stiffened. "Relax, genius. This is for the food." I sliced the ends off four shallots.

Pam strolled around the end of the counter, keeping a healthy distance from Anatole, I noticed. Maybe she wasn't as much of an idiot as I thought.

"So, what brought about this change of heart?" she asked, leaning her elbows on the counter.

"I like living." I got a fire going under a saucier, sliced open the plastic wrap on the frozen blood brick. A wisp of steam rose up, carrying the scent of fresh meat. "And, despite everything, I don't want Chet ending up in ashes either."

"What are you going to tell Cousin Brendan?" prompted Pam. "You two were looking awfully cozy there in the Ritz."

Note to self: tell Brendan his manager friend had a mole in the organization. "It didn't work out."

Pam sighed. "I could have warned you."

"Yeah, well, shit happens."

For a long moment the only sound was my knife thudding against the board as I treated the shallots to a fine dice. The sweet-pungent scent woke my dulled senses and focused both hands and brain. Details matter. Size of the chop affects texture and cooking time. Even in a rough chop, you want to get each piece close to the same size; otherwise it won't cook evenly.

The shallots went into a *mise en place*—aka "ready in place"—container. I wiped and flipped the board and started prepping the parsley. This was nine-tenths of the work in a kitchen, getting everything chopped, peeled, and otherwise prepared for the night's work. I pulled out the grater and set to work on the cheese.

Taylor thumped the bottle of Chardonnay down on the counter. Judging from the flush in his cheeks, he'd been out there helping himself to some of the booze. He was going to regret that later.

"Want a drink?" I said to Pam.

"Sure. Why not?"

"I saw some glasses over by the dishwasher," I said to whichever of the hench vamps was nearest.

"Boss . . ." whined Tommy, half to Pam, half to Julie.

"Just get the glass," said Pam.

It occurred to me that she was interested, maybe even fascinated. As an aspiring mobster, she'd surely seen people scared. Probably she'd seen them in various shades of desperate. But seeing someone just flat out giving up without a fight—that could be something new. That was okay.

Let her take a good look at how Charlotte Caine threw in the towel.

Tommy sloshed some white wine into a glass, shoved the glass toward his boss and slammed the bottle back down. I pulled it over next to my *mise en place*. Then I opened the utensil drawer to fish out a wooden spoon so I could give the blood a quick stir. Another minute and it would be body temperature. I spared a thought for Anatole and hoped the smell wasn't getting to him too badly.

I pulled down a fourteen-inch skillet from overhead and lit a burner on the cooktop. My skin flushed in the familiar heat. I dropped in a chunk of butter to bubble and steam. Its fragrance joined the smell of white wine and warming blood. The surrounding quiet pressed in from every side, and I was still being watched by the living and the dead and they were just standing around, waiting for me to try something. Waiting for me to give myself away, or to decide I might want to live after all.

I swirled the butter to coat the bottom of the pan. Just as it started to get that nutty smell, I dropped the shallots in, tossed them a couple times to coat, and turned the heat up. Normally, I'd just do a quick sauté to soften them and bring out the sweetness, but I wanted these good and brown.

I sniffed at the blood and pulled a couple soup mugs from the waiting stacks of plates and ladled them both full.

"Bon appétit." I slid the mugs across the counter to the vamps. From the suspicious way the two nightbloods eyed them, you'd've thought I had just gone out and drained the pigeons in Central Park.

"Fine, be hungry." I tossed the shallots again and turned the heat up just a little more.

Pam swirled her wine meditatively. "You'd better mean what you're saying about letting me have Nightlife, Charlotte. You do not get to go back on your word after this."

"Believe me, I am long past the point of no return." I

gave the shallots another toss. Heat wafted across my hands and face. The color was good, the aroma was good. I reached for the wine.

"You might want to back away—there could be some flame-up," I said.

The vampires backed up. Pam, predictably, stayed where she was, leaning her elbows on the counter and her chin on her hands.

The fine stream of white wine hit the pan with a hard sizzle, and *whump!* I had a curtain of deep orange flame blazing in the pan.

"Told you," I said to Pam.

"You did, but I trust your professionalism."

"Nice to hear somebody does." I picked up the pan and gave it a good swirl, watching the alcohol burn.

"Help me."

Anatole. We all turned. From where I stood, I could see him lolling in the desk chair as if he lacked the strength to even lift his head.

"Help me," he rasped. "I thirst. Please."

"Well, well." Julie took a healthy swallow of blood. "Poor little Anatole. Doesn't seem to have been taking very good care of himself, does he?"

I looked right past her to Pammy, the Woman in Charge. "Can I take him something? There's plenty." I nodded toward the pot of blood. Pam tipped her head so she was looking at me sideways. The alcohol flames flickered blue and orange between us.

"No, I don't think so," Pam said slowly. "But there's no need for the poor thing to go hungry."

"What . . ." I began. My skin was starting to crawl from the gleam in Pammy's stare.

"Taylor, bring me our friend Anatole."

Taylor's grin split his face as he got behind Anatole's chair and shoved it forward. The chair's cheap wheels squeaked badly. Anatole didn't look up as Taylor positioned him in front of Pamela. He didn't so much as twitch. In fact, he looked truly dead.

"Give him your neck, Charlotte."

"What!" I said again.

"You say you're ready to work for me now." She grinned. "Prove it."

Anatole raised his head. His eyes met mine and I saw the hunger. It had almost swallowed him whole.

Almost.

"Give him your neck, Charlotte. I'm sure he'll stop before he kills you. Or you could take your chances with Julie."

"Okay," I whispered. "Just one thing."

"What could that possibly be?"

"Dracula!"

26

"Baaaa-daaaa, da-da-da-da-dump! Baaaa-daaa, da-da-da-dump!" Clap, clap, clap!

Taylor didn't even blink, just started flapping his elbows and shaking his tail feathers in a vigorous version of the chicken dance that would have been a hit at any wedding reception—just as Anatole had whammied him to do.

"Baaaa-daaaa, da-da-da-da-dump! Baaaa-daaa, da-da-da-da-dump!" Clap, clap, clap!

"I knew she'd try something!" Julie shrieked. "Lie down and bare your neck, Charlotte Caine!"

So that was what she'd left in my head. Hopefully I'd be able to thank Anatole later. Julie lunged toward me and I snatched up the hot skillet and tossed the entire flaming mass straight in her face.

All at once, the air was filled with smoke and steam, a woman screaming and the horrendous smell of burning hair. Alarms blared. The heat and roar and rush of fire bowled over me as Julie toppled to the floor. Fear hit hard and sent me reeling backward.

Taylor flapped and shook and sang. Tommy grabbed

me and hauled me into the air, his fingers digging into my flesh. Anatole kicked off the counter with his one good leg and sent the desk chair crashing into Tommy's side. The vampire staggered and I went sprawling on the floor, way too close to the screams and flames and the slick burnt-meat smoke.

Choking white fire-suppressant foam rained down. Julie's thrashing arm clobbered my thigh and I screamed and rolled as my pants sprouted half a dozen pilot lights.

Anatole tried to shove his chair around Taylor but mistimed it and Taylor swung his backside, sending the chair bouncing against the wall.

"Stupid bitch!" Pamela snatched up the wine bottle and screamed something I couldn't understand, as she slammed it down on the edge of the counter. Glass and Chardonnay sprayed everywhere. In the same instant, something snapped in my ankle. Fresh pain shot up my spine and I shrieked and spasmed on the floor.

"Help her!" screamed Tommy to Pam. Julie lay in a heap on the floor, speckled with flame suppressant. She lifted her head and even through the haze of pain blurring my vision, I saw too clearly how ashy flesh hung from the ruined half of her pretty immortal face.

Pam stalked over to the vampires. I scooted backward, groping for purchase on the counter above me and instead finding my long-handled spoon. My whole leg was on fire with pain.

Pam loomed over Julie. "I'm sorry."

I heard words. I saw her snap her fingers.

Julie's head dropped off her neck.

I lost it and screamed, scrambling backward, clutching the spoon I'd grabbed off the counter to my chest. Tommy also lost it. He swung around and launched himself at me, like I was the one who'd just made Julie do the Marie Antoinette.

Anatole hollered and I got the wooden spoon up just in time to smack Tommy right upside the head. Tommy fell back, shuddering and screaming. Pam dove for him. Anatole kicked backward again, shoving himself between us. But Pam had trained for such occasions and she dodged, tucking into a shoulder roll, and came up on her feet in a Catwoman crouch. Tommy coughed once and lay still. Pam ignored him and stared straight at me.

In the distance we could hear the sirens wailing. Fire department on the way, alerted by the automatic systems when the alarms went off. They'd be bringing the police with them, and I was absolutely 100 percent positive, the ever-efficient Linus O'Grady, who would have been called by the regular cops as soon as they knew it was a vampire bar on fire.

"It's over, Pammy," I croaked.

"You think so?"

The witch staggered to her feet. She thrust her hand onto the still-lit stove burner and came up with her palm cupped around a ball of flame the size of an apple. These Maddoxes liked to play with fire, and Pam was nothing if not game. I struggled to grab hold of Anatole's chair, to get him behind me, for all the good it would do. Pam grinned at me, whispered another word and dropped the fireball onto Tommy Jones.

Tommy burst into flame, burning blue, like brandy at Christmas. His flailing arm caught the rack of chef's coats. The fire jumped to the fabric and set it alight, scorching the ceiling tiles and sending black smoke pouring through the kitchen. The roar of the flame almost drowned out the vampire's last scream as he collapsed into a heap of stinking ash. They'd disappointed Pam and she had no more use for them, except as fuel. Burning shards of Tommy and clean laundry fell into the puddles of wine left when Pam shattered the bottle and my leg. Fire leapt up across the floor.

The nonskid rubber mats in front of the line stations caught a heartbeat later, filling the air with fresh stink and black smoke. This time the sprinklers stayed quiet.

"What the hell!" hollered Taylor. Fire evidently trumped post-vampiric suggesting and he was running for the door.

"Bye-bye, Charlotte Caine." Pam Maddox smiled down at me and then sauntered away after Taylor.

"No!" howled Anatole, but she didn't even look back. He tried to shove himself after her, but this time he over-balanced and toppled onto the floor, and the fire kept right on burning, edging across the rubber floor mats, looking for more vampire.

It was going to be the last thing I ever did. The counter was hot already, but my hands were tough. The air seared my skin, but I'd reached into plenty of ovens. I could take it. I could take it. I swore and retched and hauled myself upright.

"Pammy!"

She turned, and my thrown egg caught her right between the eyes.

"Gotcha!"

Pam screamed and as I knew she would, she charged me. This is why vanity is a deadly sin. It can make you stay in a burning building to attack some smart-ass who was dead anyway for the crime of ruining your makeup.

I threw another egg, and another. Pam howled in outrage and rubbed frantically at her eyes. But the yolk was too thick and the heat was already cooking it into a mask over her eyes. She stumbled blind around the burning kitchen. She hit the stove, screamed and bounced and fell. I was choking and laughing one second, and just choking the next because I got a lungful of hot smoke. I fell beside her; onto my knees, onto my side, right beside Anatole.

That was okay, because it was over. I'd done it. I was coughing my lungs out and fire crawled down my throat and into my eyes, but I'd stopped her and all her plans to control my brother, to threaten my parents, to destroy my life. I'd done it without my cavalry and my sneaky little brother.

"I'm sorry," I whispered and I coughed again. It was too hot too close, I couldn't breathe. I was going to die. Anatole was going to die. Here and now and nobody would ever know I was really, truly sorry.

Charlotte! cried a voice in my head.

Cold hands grabbed me, jerked me up. Arms like stone held me tight and there was a sense of motion and blazing air grated hard over my seared skin.

Air. Air. My lungs rasped and burned. Cold air flowed down my throat and somehow that hurt worse than the burning air had. I gasped again. I cried and breathed and choked.

And my little brother—my soot-streaked brother who never knew enough to stay the hell out of my kitchen—laid me down on a gurney and stood back to make room for the bald EMT who slammed an oxygen mask over my face. Beside him, Little Linus was explaining something to a uniformed cop, with Brendan, and Margot, and Ian right behind him. And Anatole. Anatole lay on another gurney sucking hard on a bag of blood.

We were alive. All of us. We'd made it. I smiled and drew the sweet, delicious air into my burning lungs.

Then I passed out cold.

27

There was, in the end, a whole lot of explaining to do.

However, it had to wait for three long, painful weeks until my throat and lungs had healed up enough so I could talk again. By that time, the worst of the bandages had come off my hands, so I could supplement my croaking with text messages.

I had to tell Linus O'Grady everything, of course. After Little Linus, I had to tell everything over again to Rafe Wallace, Trish, Jessie, Elaine West, a district attorney named Colman DuPres, a judge named Dali Singh, twelve of my peers whose names I never found out, and the whole rest of the world via every kind of media known to modern humans.

We were in the headlines way too long. Despite the fact that our bank account was a lot healthier than I had thought, a large chunk of it had to go toward paying an extensive set of fines related to being careless with fire. That Bert Shelby had been letting his premises be used for illegal activities somehow kept us from having to pay for actually burning down Post Mortem, which was good, because what money we had left over had go toward paying Rafe Wallace.

Trish and Jessie decided not to kick me out on my rear, although after all the times they had to duck the paparazzi combined with the fact that I wasn't going to be able to pay my share of the rent for a while, I wouldn't have blamed them. But while I'd been busy with my new career as budding arsonist, Jessie had made her bid for Saleswoman of the Month with Mary Sue Cosmetics and said she'd be glad to put her bonus toward keeping me sheltered. Trish reminded me how they depended on my way with a tuna casserole to keep Georgie changing the lightbulbs regularly.

If there was hugging and crying and other heavy-duty female bonding after that, that was our own damn business.

The only nagging ache was that in all this time, the one person I didn't hear from was Chet. Oh, I saw him in court, and whenever there were papers to sign, but other than that, he kept his distance. He resigned from Nightlife via text message. He paid up his rent for the next six months with Doug, packed his things and moved out, without sending me a forwarding address. I only knew he moved at all because Rafe Wallace mentioned it.

In response, I sat on my hands. I didn't call. I didn't text. We both needed to get used to the fact that I wouldn't be looking after him anymore. I promoted Suchai to front-of-the-house management at Nightlife, hired a new accountant, and added the words *let it go* to my vocabulary.

It wasn't like I had nothing to do myself. As soon as I could croak a coherent sentence into a phone, I got hold of Zoe and Reese and told them we were going ahead with the plan for a soft reopening for Nightlife. We held it on a Friday and filled the house with friends and family, leaving just enough room for a little foot traffic, which we did get. Robert and Suchai worked together like they'd been meant for each other. Zoe's duck tasting was a complete hit, as were Marie's new dessert beverages. My warm pomegranate salad didn't go over too badly either.

But that wasn't what was important. What was important was we had all made it through, and that included Nightlife itself. I was in the kitchen. I was home. I was sure that anything and everything else would follow eventually. Most days, anyway.

This time, it sucked a whole lot less to be right. Early one frigid Monday morning, Inez—one of our dishwashers—and I were locking up when I felt someone familiar watching me. I turned, and there was Chet.

"Hey, C3," he said.

"Hey, C4."

"You're looking good."

"You're a liar." My hair had been badly singed in the fire, and I'd had to hack it off to within an inch of my scalp. I also had a burn scar on the side of my throat that made me look like I'd almost lost a fight with Sweeney Todd.

He shrugged. "Yeah, but you knew that. Walk you to the subway?"

I waved good-bye to Inez and Chet and I started walking side by side. December had settled in properly, and my breath showed silver in the streetlight. I huddled in layers of fleece. Chet didn't even have a hat on.

"So, what's going to happen with your . . . spa?" I asked finally.

He sucked on his cheek. "Well, Ilona wants to keep it going. It funds Final Curtain. Marcus too. He thinks it's the wave of the future. Rafe Wallace says he's got a partner in contract law who can update our client agreements, and they're all just waiting to find out if they're going to need to buy me out."

I said nothing and Chet cocked his head at me.

"Do they need to buy me out?"

"Not my decision," I said without looking at him.

"Cut it out, Charlotte."

There were a hundred things I could have said. I couldn't stand his girlfriend and the feeling was mutual. The spa was still a great big gray zone as far as the law was concerned, and the Maddox family was apparently already pushing legislation in Albany to prevent the importation of human blood across state lines for purposes of consumption. The ones who weren't busy working with Linus O'Grady and the Paranormal Squadron to update the city's magical and paranormal defense strategies, anyway.

Despite all this, I knew the right answer, and for a wonder, I was actually able to say it. "What do you want to do?"

Vampires can't let out long breaths, but all the tension left Chet's shoulders right then. "I'm good at this, Charlotte. I like dealing with the clients and the staff. I like being management. It's something I built. . . ."

"You built Nightlife," I reminded him. It sounded like a last-ditch attempt to hold on to him, and maybe it was.

Chet ducked his head. "You built Nightlife, Charlotte."

And if this wasn't the right answer at that moment, it would be, given time. "Okay then."

"Really?"

"Really." I smiled up at him. "But, Chet?"

"Yeah?"

I grabbed my brother's collar and yanked him down to where I could look in his eyes. "You lie to me again and I will ship your coffin to the nearest solar panel farm. Get me?"

"Got you, C3," said my little brother, and if I hadn't known it would be all right before, I did now.

Not that Chet was my last piece of unfinished business. Another piece was waiting for me when I got back to Queens.

He stood at the door of my building, looking killer hand-some in a dark overcoat, white scarf and black fedora.

Anatole bowed when he saw me come around the cor-ner, and held out a bunch of roses.

"For me?" I let my eyes widen in mock surprise.

"As is this." He pulled a newspaper out of his overcoat pocket.

I unfurled an issue of *Circulation*, which had been folded back to reveal a headline.

A TASTE OF THE NIGHTLIFE

You will have heard a great deal about Night-life, the debut restaurant of Chef Charlotte Caine. The establishment and its owners have been keeping the media gossips hunched over their screens for weeks now. But what's been lost in the headlines and attempts to milk the assorted scandals beyond their useful life span is the fact that Nightlife is a good restau-rant. Chef Caine's passion and attention to detail shine through in the parade of creative, but refreshingly unpretentious food. More than this, however, Nightlife is a convivial gather-ing place, where one can always enjoy a good evening over good food.

There was more, but I couldn't read it, because I would start bawling.

"Anatole."

"Shhhh..." He laid a cool finger against my lips. "Your thanks is shining in your eyes."

I removed his finger. "What are you up to?"

"I am delivering you a good review, and flowers," he said.

"And . . . ?"

"And my thanks," he said, "for not abandoning me at Post Mortem."

The roses were deep red and surprisingly fragrant. I wouldn't put it past him to have thought of that. I hated bland flowers.

"I owe you my life, Charlotte."

I was going to have to text Miss Manners and find out what the polite response was in this particular situation. As it was, I shrugged and turned away so I could rummage one-handed for my keys until the flush left my cheeks.

I knew Anatole was smiling. "I also believe we had discussed the possibility of my seducing you," he said.

"That was not a discussion," I reminded him. "That was you making a pass at me."

"It most certainly was not. *This* is me making a pass at you."

Very gently, Anatole lifted my hand to his mouth. He brushed his lips across my knuckles, and then across the palm. I lost the power of independent movement. Anatole smiled, and moved in close. He lifted the roses from my other hand and laid them on the half wall by the door. He pressed his mouth against my forehead, and then against my cheek while he ran his graceful, sensitive hands up my arms and around my shoulders.

"I am fully aware of the competition," he murmured against my ear. His chest brushed mine. He felt far more solid than I would have expected and that realization made my heart flip oddly. "All I ask is that you consider the possibilities, Charlotte. All of them." The words sent a shiver straight down my spine that had nothing to do with fear.

Anatole stepped back and bowed, stiff-backed, courtly, perfect, and still smiling, he walked away.

I drifted up to the apartment, not forgetting to collect my roses. The living room was dark, and I was careful to be quiet as I found and filled a vase. Trish and Jessie had early mornings. I, on the other hand, could have showered and toppled straight into bed, but I didn't. Instinct kept me awake and puttering quietly in the kitchen. That was how I saw Brendan walking up to our door. It was barely dawn out there, but I recognized his silhouette, even from so far up, and I buzzed him in before he had to ring.

"Sorry," he said as he came in, taking off his new wool trilby. "I should have called. I meant to be at the opening, but my grandfather's in town and I had to get him up to speed on what's happening with the contract bid. I hoped you might be still awake and I . . ." His security consultant's eyes zeroed in on the essential details.

"Roses?" he said.

I shrugged. "Anatole."

"Ah. The competition."

"Funny. That's what he called you."

Brendan tipped his head in acknowledgment. "What did you call me?"

This was another one of those moments when there was a whole lot I could have said. But as I looked at Brendan and remembered how we'd kissed and how he'd stood by me through what I sincerely hoped was the worst time I'd ever know, the only genuine option available to me was honesty.

"I don't know what to call you," I said. "Either one of you."

He puffed out his cheeks. "Well," he said. "We'll have to see if we can change that."

"Brendan . . ." I bit my lip. "My restaurant's in an iron lung. I'm going to have to work around the clock to get it on its feet again. I'm on parole. My brother's about to get heavy into blood politics, and I've got a vampire making cow eyes at me."

"In that case, let's go get some coffee."

I blinked. "Love to."

Side by side, we walked into the daylight between the apartment buildings and sprawling shops. Around us, the city woke itself up, yawned and stretched and looked around with knowing eyes for whatever might think about coming next.

Read on for a special preview of
Sarah Zettel's next Vampire Chef mystery,

LET THEM EAT STAKE

Coming from Obsidian
in April 2012.

"Charlotte! He left me, Charlotte!"

I jerked my gaze up from my cutting board. The kitchen door banged open and a blur of color hurtled past the hot line.

"Ten days before the wedding!" The intruder—whose name, incidentally, was Felicity Garnett—clamped her hands on my shoulders. "He walked out on me! Ten days and he left me alone!"

Being suddenly grabbed and shaken by a hysterical woman in a designer pants suit is never good, but just then it was particularly bad. For one thing, I had a boning knife in my hand and a lovely fillet of sushi-grade tuna that needed attention on my board. For another, at five o'clock on Thursday afternoon, I was heading up the dinner prep for my restaurant, Nightlife. My crew was busy at their stations: chopping *mise en place*, simmering sauces, seasoning soups, checking the temperature of the ovens and making sure the containers of fresh ingredients and garnishes were in place for when we opened at eight. They filled the kitchen with steam, spices and the hyperactive drumbeat of thudding knives. Over all this fragrant, noisy chaos boomed the bass voice of Reese, my ex–drill sergeant of a second sous-chef, abusing some of the newer members of the line.

"I said 'fine dice.' Fine. Does that look fine to you? Your answer is 'No, Chef.'"

"No, Chef."

"He can be taught. Do it right this time. Your answer is 'Yes, Chef.'"

"Yes, Chef."

The door banged open again. This time it let in Robert Kemp, my white-haired English maitre d', looking as mortified as I've ever seen him. "I'm so sorry, Chef Caine . . . ," he began, but pulled up short when he saw our intruder had me in a death grip.

"You're going to say no, aren't you?" Felicity gasped and reeled backward. "You can't. If you say no, it's over!"

A minute before, I had had great plans to do some creative swearing, but they never panned out. I had to stop this, immediately. It's one thing when random passersby have hysterics on the street. I mean, that's just New York City for you. It's quite another when those hysterics happen in a confined space full of knives, fire and massive pots of simmering stock.

Knotting my fingers into her gray jacket collar, I forced Felicity to face the door.

"No!" she wailed. "You can't! He left. . . ."

I ignored this. "Zoe, Reese, keep it moving in here. I'll be in the dining room."

"Yes, Chef," Zoe replied calmly from the dessert station.

"Hear that, slackers?" called Reese down the line. "You're mine!" His manic SpongeBob laugh would have given Alfred Hitchcock goose bumps.

"It's . . . !" Felicity began again.

Robert held the door, allowing me to shove Felicity

bodily out of the bright kitchen into the dim, cool and much, much less hazardous dining room.

"But . . . !"

"Felicity!" I spun her back around, put my hand under her pointy chin, pushed her jaw closed and held on. "Cut it out!"

Felicity's tears shut off like she'd thrown a switch somewhere, and her wide, wild amber eyes narrowed in raccoon-masked fury.

"Cut. It. Out," I said again, to make sure she fully understood the nuances of the phrase. "Are you going to cut it out?"

Felicity's chin trembled against my palm, but she nodded.

"Okay." I let her go, and she drew in a deep, shuddering breath. I held up my hand again, just in case. She held up her palm in answer. I nodded and waved back Robert, who was hovering just out of her field of vision. My maitre d' nodded warily and retreated to his station by the door, but not without a whole lot of backward glances.

The truth was, I was feeling more than a little rattled myself just then. Of all the professional acquaintances who I might have suspected, capable of total disintegration during dinner prep, Felicity Garnett was not one of them.

Felicity, in case you don't read the society pages, was not a bride being left at the altar. She is, however, one of the highest of the high-end event coordinators in Manhattan. Under normal circumstances, she was not only willow thin and knife sharp, but completely poised. I had personally seen her face down a bride who had been slipped an extra caffeine dose in her triple-mocha latte, gotten hold of the cake knife and threatened to carve up the room unless the flowers were switched from peonies to delphiniums *right now*. Felicity and I had been drifting apart a bit since she shot up the ladder in her chosen

profession, and I . . . stalled. Well, maybe not stalled, but
there had been some setbacks, particularly last fall, when
Nightlife had experienced a murder on the premises, a
takeover attempt that could charitably be described as hostile, and the departure of my vampire brother, who had been
part owner of the restaurant. All little things, of course, but
they did raise eyebrows in certain circles. I guess Felicity
felt she needed to be careful whom she was seen with.
She regularly stage-manages the Big Day for the discern-
ing daughters of Fortune 100 families. That's a business
that hangs heavily on reputation and appearance. Felicity
was very good at both.

"I'm sorry, Charlotte." Felicity brushed at her jacket
and tried to adjust the collar of the plum silk blouse
underneath. I actually don't think she owned any kind of
clothing except professional pants suits and brightly colored blouses. "But he—"

"He walked out on you," I cut her off because her chin
was starting to wobble dangerously. "Got that. You want
to tell me who 'he' is?"

"Oscar Simmons."

The name hit me with a dull thud. Celebrity chef Oscar
Simmons and I had what gets called "history." Unfortunately, it was the kind of history that tends to involve bar-
barian hordes and burning cities. "Felicity, tell me you
didn't hire Oscar for a high-pressure event."

"I know, I know. But he's one of the most talked-about
chefs in Manhattan. . . ."

"There's a reason for that."

"And he just won the Epicures Award. . . ."

"He was sleeping with a judge."

Felicity's eyes glimmered as anger finally worked its
way through the desperation and self-recrimination. "Sau-
cer of cream with that attitude, Charlotte Caine?"

"That attitude is why I'm not the one running around

Excerpt from LET THEM EAT STAKE   305

like the proverbial chicken with its head cut off on a Thursday afternoon."

"And maybe we should just go back in the kitchen so you can have one of your cooks rub extra salt in the wounds." Felicity pushed a lock of copper-highlighted hair off her cheek and her fragile confidence wavered again. "Oh, God. It's all over."

Now it was my turn for the deep breath. Starting round the bend of another weepy conversational circle was not going to get the story out of Felicity, especially not before it was time to open. Intervention was clearly necessary.

"Want a drink?"

Felicity looked at me like I was an angel descending from on high. "Please. Coffee. Black."

If I hadn't known things were serious before, I did now. Felicity was strictly a skinny-half-caf-cappuccino kind of woman. I pulled two mugs of coffee from the industrial-sized urn we keep hot for the staff and gestured Felicity over to table nineteen. Around us, Nightlife's long, narrow dining room held the kind of hushed anticipation that fills a stage before the curtain goes up. Warm golden track lighting was turned down low, bringing out the highlights in the antique oak bar, which ran along one wall. Our tables were perfectly laid out with gold undercloth, white overcloth and settings of pristine white dishes. The clatter and bustle drifted nonstop out from the kitchen, but it now sounded thin and far away.

"What kind of wedding has got you this wound up?" I asked Felicity as I handed across the coffee.

"Vampires versus witches, to the tune of five hundred thousand dollars."

I allowed a moment of respectful silence for the dollar figure. That alone was worth getting a little dramatic over. But coordinating a wedding between vampires and witches? That took guts, even with this level of promised payoff. Despite all the fuss made about the supposed rivalry between vampires and werewolves, the deepest hatreds run between vampires and witches. In fact, truth be told, witches just don't like other paranormals, and other paranormals don't like them. And, for heaven's sake, don't get either side started on how this came about. It's worse than a bar fight between Red Sox and Yankees fans. Some feuds go back centuries, and if they involve one of the big witch clans, like the Maddoxes or the Coreys, they can rack up serious body counts and gallons of—excuse the expression—bad blood.

Felicity tipped her mug back and gulped down hot coffee like it was ice water. I watched, eyebrows raised.

"You'll get a stomachache."

She gasped and lowered the mug. "Too late. Give me a Tums and I can tell you what vintage it is. God, why don't *sane* people get married?"

"Sane people do get married. Sane people just don't spend ten years' salary on the party," I replied. "And I hate to say this, Felicity, but if you want my help for something, you need to get a move on." My front-of-house staff would be arriving soon. We had family meal to serve, prep to finish, and, based on the reservations list, a decent-sized incoming dinner crowd to keep happy.

"Okay, okay. You see, back in November I got a call from Adrienne Alden." Felicity paused and looked at me.

"Adrienne Alden!" I exclaimed.

The corners of Felicity's mouth flickered upward. "You've got no idea who she is, do you?"

"Robert," I called over to my maitre d', who was busy with the computer at the host station, "who's Adrienne Alden?"

"Mrs. Adrienne Alden, married to Scott Alden," replied Robert without hesitation or even looking back at me. "Scott Alden, CEO of North Island Holdings and oldest son of the very prominent Alden family. Mrs. Alden is on the board of several important charities and galleries, and she lunches with a highly exclusive group of similarly connected ladies." Robert has a social register in his brain that is the envy of restaurateurs throughout Manhattan.

I turned back to Felicity and translated this into my own terms. "Adrienne Alden gets a good table on Saturday night and possibly a complimentary appetizer."

"She's also got a daughter named Deanna," said Felicity. "Last year, Deanna Alden got engaged to Gabriel Renault, a nightblood most recently from Paris, or so he says." "Nightblood" is the polite term for vampire, and some of them get a little cagey about where they are actually from. It's much more dramatic to be Nightblood Victore from "Gay Paree" than plain old Vampire Vic from Hoboken.

"So, groom's the vamp, and the bride's the witch?"

Felicity frowned. "Well, the mother's a witch. I'm not entirely clear on the daughter."

There were a whole lot of things I could have said about this, but I decided discretion was the better part. It was clear Felicity already had plenty on her plate.

"Anyway, Mrs. Alden decided Deanna and Gabriel were going to have the wedding of the decade, and she's got the budget to pull it off." Felicity paused and lifted her eyes from her coffee mug. "I would have called you to do the catering right away, you know." She seasoned her earnestness with that special blend of tense desperation you get when you realize you may have already screwed up. "But back in November, things . . . still weren't going so well for you."

"You mean because back in November I was standing in front of a jury while recovering from smoke inhalation, trying to explain that I shouldn't be sent to jail for burning down a vampire bar." A situation that was, in fact, a direct result of a clash between the aforementioned

Maddox witch clan and some vampires, one of whom happened to be my brother, Chet.

"I think that qualifies as things not going so well."

"Agreed. But they did get better." Sort of. Kind of. Mostly. Except for some small problems like keeping ahead of the growing stack of invoices on my desk. And side problems, like how the fact that I had been seeing Brendan Maddox on a semiregular basis since last fall had not endeared me to some of the more hard-line members of that particular old, powerful, magically oriented family.

My life, in case you haven't noticed by now, is a little more complicated than your average chef's.

Focus, Charlotte. "So, you called Oscar Simmons, even though you know he's the restaurant world's biggest prima donna. A title for which there is hefty competition. What were you thinking?"

"The society page of the *New York Times*," said Felicity to what was left of her coffee. "And did I mention five hundred thousand dollars?"

"You've seen both before."

"I know, I know." Felicity wilted down until her chin was in danger of dipping into her mug.

A very unpleasant idea settled into my brain. "You weren't sleeping with Oscar, were you?"

"What do you take me for? I don't sleep with chefs. No offense."

"You're not my type. So, if it wasn't personal, what pushed him over the edge?"

"That's the problem. I don't *know*. Yesterday, Oscar calls me and says he's canceling. But he won't say why. I spent hours on the phone with him. I went over to Perception and camped out on his doorstep. All he'll say is he's pulling out, and he's stopped returning my calls."

"Sounds like he's trying to up his fee."

"He returned his fee."

If I'd had another sarcastic comment ready, it died an early death. Oscar Simmons had given back money? Not possible. Part of the reason Oscar was so successful was that he was an Olympic-level penny-pincher. "Oh." I took another swallow of coffee while the gears in my head ground hard to keep up with this new conversational turn. "What about his staff? He must have a sous who—"

"He told them he'd fire them all if they took over the job."

Which was hardly reasonable, but at least it sounded like the Oscar Simmons I knew. "And you've got no idea why?"

"I swear, Charlotte. I've tried to find out, but no one will tell me anything." Felicity leaned toward me, and I realized that at some point in our conversation, she'd stopped blinking. "The client's talking about postponing. The bride's talking about eloping. . . . Charlotte, this was supposed to be the biggest paranormal event since the vampires came out of the coffin, and I've got no caterer and only ten days until the zero hour. You've got to help me."

"Felicity, I don't know. Nightlife's on shaky ground, and I haven't got a full staff. . . ."

"Did I mention the hundred thousand dollars?"

"That's the food budget?"

"That's your fee."

It was a long moment before I could answer, because I had to concentrate all my energies on not leaping to my feet or starting to drool. Felicity clearly found hope in my hesitation. She was blinking again, and the color was starting to return to her ravaged face. She was also jumping to conclusions, probably assisted by her rapid caffeine intake. I freely admit the price tag she'd just mentioned was way more than enough to turn both head and attitude around. But something was missing in her story. I could feel it poking at me like a pinbone under my fingertips.

"Felicity, tell me what this job entails. Exactly."

"Wedding day catering includes breakfast and lunch buffets, hors d'oeuvres, sit-down five-course dinner, plated dessert, plus the cake. Besides that, you come out to the house and act as personal chef for the family and guests until the wedding."

I let all this sink in and settle next to the internal spreadsheet that all executive chefs carry deep within them.

"One hundred thousand," said Felicity again. "Pure profit after taxes. You can plow it all straight into Nightlife."

I took a deep breath. "Felicity?"

She leaned forward. "Yes?"

"Two hundred thousand."

"One fifty," Felicity shot back.

"One eighty."

I waited for her answer, and waited some more. Felicity was used to drama brides and imperious mothers-in-law. I, however, regularly dealt with egos holding knives. As such, we were close to evenly matched when it came to negotiation. My only real edge was that I knew she needed me to say yes to this.

Given that, I also should have known she still had an ace up her sleeve. "One seventy-five," said Felicity. "But you come with me right now to meet the family so I can show them everything is under control."

"What? Are you crazy? I've got a dinner shift." This is the cardinal rule of kitchen work. You show up for your shift, no matter what. If your aged grandmother and all her cats are being held hostage by rabid zombie terrorists, you send her a condolence card, and you show up for your shift.

"You come with me now, or it's all off." She had that look in her eyes that comes when you've got nothing left to lose.

Slowly, I got to my feet. "'Scuse me one sec."

I went back into the kitchen. Ignoring the quizzical glances, I walked over to my battered desk and stood there, fingertips resting on the scarred surface, staring at one particular pile of colored papers with crumpled edges. This pile represented every expense that was not a staff paycheck. Meat. Blood. Flour. Milk. Eggs. Linens. Cleaning supplies. Liquor. Electricity. Gas. All the things without which I was not in a restaurant—I was in an empty room. These invoices were all coming due. Some of them were past due and heading into emergency territory.

Felicity was offering me a solution to the problems represented by these pieces of paper. One hundred seventy-five thousand dollars was more than enough to take care of this stack. It could, in fact, be properly called a whole hell of a lot of money. Surely it was worth taking off for one shift. But my chefly sense of impending trouble had been left very sensitive by recent circumstances, and it was tingling now. Because that one seventy-five was in fact a whole, heaping, incredible, suspicious lot of money, even for an emergency. Even for an emergency involving very rich people, both living and undead.

"Zoe! Reese!"

"Yes, Chef?"

To their credit, neither sous betrayed any hint of exasperation as they came over to my desk, even though they were the ones left dealing with the million rampaging details of the impending dinner shift while their executive chef was sipping tea in the nice, cool dining room. Well, okay, I was gulping coffee, but you get the point.

My sous are a study in contrasts. Reese has a linebacker's build, rich brown skin, cornrowed hair and the words EAT THIS tattooed on his knuckles. He swears the ink is the result of losing a bar bet, but he won't tell me what that bet actually was. I throw him the hard cases who come into the kitchen—the ones who think they know more than they actually do, or who might once in a while consider it beneath their dignity to take orders from a woman.

Zoe Vamadev, on the other hand, is a petite young woman who has a critical eye on the level of Simon Cowell with a toothache. Her parents are from Bengal and Bali, and she came to the U.S. by way of Bangkok, Amsterdam, Edinburgh and London. She speaks more languages than a career diplomat, and she has made no secret of the fact that she wants to be my competition, and she's good enough to give me a serious run for my money, even in my own kitchen.

I stared at the bills. Zoe and Reese stared at me staring at the bills. The bills stared back and, I swear, they snickered.

"I've got to go see about a catering job with Ms. Garnett. Can you two handle the dinner shift?"

That was what I said. Having been in similar situations back when I was still a sous, I can tell you what they heard: *I'm taking off suddenly, removing a pair of skilled hands you were counting on and taking with them a large chunk of institutional knowledge and kitchen authority, which will put you to a test you had no idea was coming.*

There was only one answer they could give: "Yes, Chef."